HIDDEN HEROES

HIDDEN HEROES

ANTHOLOGY OF NORTH KOREAN FICTION

Translated by

IMMANUEL KIM AND BENOIT BERTHELIER

 FIRST HILL BOOKS

FIRST HILL BOOKS
An imprint of Wimbledon Publishing Company Limited (WPC)

This edition first published in UK and USA 2025
by FIRST HILL BOOKS
75–76 Blackfriars Road, London SE1 8HA, UK
or PO Box 9779, London SW19 7ZG, UK
and
244 Madison Ave #116, New York, NY 10016, USA

British Library Cataloguing-in-Publication Data
A catalogue record for this book is available from the British Library.

Library of Congress Cataloging-in-Publication Data: 2022932348
A catalog record for this book has been requested.

ISBN-13: 978-1-83999-465-4 (Hbk)
ISBN-10: 1-83999-465-7 (Hbk)
ISBN-13: 978-1-83999-466-1 (Pbk)
ISBN-10: 1-83999-466-5 (Pbk)

Credit: Kim In Sok, Rain Shower at the Bus Stop, 2018, Chosonhwa, 217x433cm

This title is also available as an e-book.

CONTENTS

TRANSLATION SOURCE

INTRODUCTION: (RE)PRESENTING
NORTH KOREAN FICTION

In "The Key," one of the short stories included in this volume, the heroine compares her failed marriage to an abusive, criminal man with the love stories from the "romantic novels and movies" she enjoyed as a young girl. "Fantasies are not reality," she concludes. And yet her reality, the grim reality to which she compares the love stories of her teenage readings, is likewise a fiction.

Fiction is not real and yet we still often expect it to tell us something about reality. This is all the more true in the case of North Korean literature. As translators, we are well aware that a majority of our readers will be driven toward this volume by ethnographic curiosity, a desire to learn about North Korean society. It may indeed be tempting to take the narrator's realistic accounts of domestic violence and peer pressure in "The Key" as representative of a North Korean reality. Yet this short story also ends with a happy ending worthy of a romance novel and a pledge of loyalty to the Party. The question is not whether the heroine's tribulations or the cliché ending and its propaganda are a more accurate representation of reality, but rather how both come to be part of the same mimetic regime.

The question of (re)presentation is germane not only to the content of the short stories we selected (How accurate are their presentations or depictions of life in North Korea?) but also to this volume as a whole (Are the pieces selected representative of contemporary North Korean literary production?). Anthologies necessarily raise the issue of their own representativeness. As one of the few collections of North Korean literary texts in English, the volume poses the question of what image of North Korean literary production it will present to its readers. In particular, with a country like North Korea, so often

1

depicted as alien, the two common pitfalls of anthologies highlighted by David Damrosch – choosing works either "just like ours" or "curiosities whose foreignness [...] can only reinforce our sense of separate identity"[1] loom over the task of selecting texts. Should we, as editors of this volume, have included hagiographies of the leaders and dithyrambs to the Party at the risk of reinforcing the representation of a society entirely defined by its ruling family? Or should we have sought out rare, propaganda-free pieces most palatable to a foreign reader? We chose neither as both options do not (re)present the state of the literary writing in North Korea. Most fiction does convey a political message (support for the military, necessity to implement current agricultural policy, etc.), but works praising the Leaders are only a very specific subset.

Instead, we selected works of fiction that implement a narrative trope that has become dominant since the late 1970s, that of the *hidden hero*: seemingly average citizens who perform their duty with extraordinary dedication and little regard for recognition or compensation. While this approach largely excludes genres such as detective fiction, science fiction or historical novels, the ubiquity of the theme nonetheless allowed us to select work among the most common genres of North Korean literary fiction. These texts will also offer the reader a diverse array of protagonists and settings: middle class families in Pyongyang, industrial and rural workers on their work site, starving artists in Japan, and white-collar, urban professionals.

North Korean Realism and Reality

In order to better understand how the stories presented in this volume relate to the representation of reality in North Korea, let us first look at the country's literary history and culture. From the proclamation of socialist realism as the favored artistic style of "national democratic culture" in 1947 to its replacement by the current official method of Juche realism a few decades later, North Korean literature has always been defined as "realist" by the state-sponsored union of writers in charge of its production.[2] Yet the term was never used to

---

1 David Damrosch, *What is world literature?* (Princeton: Princeton University Press, 2003), 133.
2 The first mentions of "Juche realism" (*chuch'e sasiljuŭi*) as a new creative method followed the establishment of the Juche ideology (often translated as "self-reliance") as the North Korean Workers Party monolithic ideology in 1967. Juche realism maintains the principles of Soviet socialist realism but aspires to adapt them to North Korean characteristics.

mean the faithful description of objective reality – something criticized by North Korean critics as bourgeois "naturalism" (*chayŏnjuŭi*). Realism, instead, is the task of "extracting fundamental and meaningful elements from the complex continuity of reality" and using them to generalize the particular.[3] Characters are meant to be (stereo)typical (*chŏnhyŏnjŏk*), embodiments of the characteristics of their social class in a certain historical context. Their actions and the plot are driven by conventions and tropes rather than personal idiosyncrasies.

Far from claiming transparency, socialist realism aims at modeling reality, even if the models are more normative than positive. Indeed, the original Soviet socialist realist doctrine upon which North Korean literature was built was about portraying reality in "its revolutionary development," *i.e.* as it could be if the precepts of the Party were followed by all.[4] Writers could, and even should, incorporate into their narratives extraordinary feats of production and discovery, the myths and legends of folklore, or the imaginary technical breakthroughs of science-fiction.[5] For all of these served to "promote the consolidation of revolutionary achievement in the present" and gave "a clearer view of the lofty objectives of the socialist future."[6]

Cf. Kim Jong Il, *Chuch'e munhangnon* [Theory of Juche literature] (Pyongyang: Chosŏn rodongdang ch'ulp'ansa, 1992), 86-110.

3 "Chayŏnjuŭi" [Naturalism], in. *Munhak Taesajŏn* [Great Dictionary of Literature] (Pyongyang: Sahoe kwahak ch'ulp'ansa, 1999), 233.

4 Andrei Zhdanov, "Soviet Literature – The Richest in Ideas, the Most Advanced Literature," in *Problems of Soviet Literature: Reports and Speeches at the First Soviet Writers' Congress*, ed. H.G. Scott (London: M. Lawrence, 1973), 15-24. While North Korean writers' faithfulness to the socialist realist doctrine has been debated, it is hard to deny the inclusion of North Korean literature in the socialist realist tradition given the influence that the doctrine had – and continues to have – on literary theory up until today in the DPRK and the fuzzy nature of the original doctrine which never constituted a formalized, homogenous set of criteria. Cf. Brian Myers, *Han Sŏrya and North Korean Literature: The Failure of Socialist Realism in the DPRK* (Ithaca, NY: Cornell East Asia Series, 1994); Tatiana Gabroussenko, *Soldiers on the Cultural Front: Developments in the Early History of North Korean Literature and Literary Policy* (Honolulu: University of Hawai'i Press, 2010); Evgeny Dobrenko, *Political Economy of Socialist Realism* (New Haven, CT: Yale University Press, 2007).

5 Maxim Gorky, "Soviet Literature," *Marxists Internet Archive* (2004). https://www.marxists.org/archive/gorky-maxim/1934/soviet-literature.htm (Accessed August 15, 2021). For a North Korean example, cf. Cho Kich'ŏn, *Paektusan* (Jilin: Inmin munhwasa, 1949).

6 Maxim Gorky, "Comments on Socialist Realism," in *Documents of Modern Literary Realism*, ed. George Joseph Becker (Princeton: Princeton University Press, 2015), 487.

The early trajectory of North Korean fiction can be described as an increasing shift towards the normative in the way reality was represented. By the late 1960s writers were rewriting the history of colonization and national liberation as it should have been – the sole product of a long struggle of the entire Korean nation led by Kim Il Sung without foreign help – and depicting society according to "Juche anthropology," as a body of model citizens living according to the teachings of the Leader.[7]

Kim Jong Il, who started his political career in 1964 in the Party's Propaganda and Agitation Department, was instrumental in orchestrating this change. He institutionalized the production of his father's cult of personality with the April 15th Literary Production Unit (LPU), a group of select writers responsible for producing hagiographical writings about the Leader. A new canon of North Korean literature was produced, with the creation of the *Immortal History* series of novels about the life and revolutionary exploits of Kim Il Sung and transmedia narratives of anti-colonial resistance such as *Sea of Blood* and *The Flower Selling Girl*.[8] These works were heralded as the epitome of ideological orthodoxy and literary masterpieces (the boundary between the two being blurry). Writers were then expected to emulate this modality of writing for the next two decades.[9]

However, the grand deeds of anti-Japanese fighters and exemplary socialist citizens eventually gave way to a different type of heroism. In 1980, the 6th Congress of the Workers' Party launched the "Hidden Hero" campaign aimed at defining a new model of socialist behavior. The example to emulate was not the revolutionary guerrillas of the colonial period but people who "work in silence, without wishing for any honor or reward, always loyal to their motherland and the Leader."[10] While past heroes basked in fame and

---

7 Sin Hyŏnggi and Oh Sŏngho, *Pukhan Munhaksa* [North Korean Literary History], (Seoul: P'yŏngminsa, 2000), 266-267.
8 These works were allegedly created by Kim Il Sung as operas during the anti-Japanese resistance period in the 1930s, and then adapted into films in the late 1960s and early 1970s. Later, they were published as novels in the 1970s, and finally remade into theatrical productions that are still performed today.
9 The Immortal History (*Pulmyŏlŭi ryŏksa*) series is about the life of Kim Il Sung, the Immortal Leadership (*Pulmyŏlŭi hyangdo*) series is about the life of Kim Jong Il, and the Immortal Journey (*Pulmyŏlŭi ryŏjŏng*) series is about the life of Kim Jong Un. Writers of the April 15th LPU are the only ones who can write novels for these series.
10 Anonymous, "Widaehan suryŏngnimkkesŏ chesi hasin ungdaehan kangnyŏngŭl nop'i pattŭlgo hyŏngmyŏngjŏk munhak chakp'um ch'angjakesŏ saeroun angyangŭl irŭk'ija"

glory proportional to their extraordinary deeds, the new hidden heroes humbly worked their mundane jobs and diligently carried out their political duties. They assisted the collective without anyone knowing and yet were presented as essential to the functioning of the country's socialist system. "Without anyone knowing" was the operative phrase that defined the hidden hero's characterization in literature, delivering a heightened sense of sentimentality and romanticism when other characters in the story eventually realize the extent of the hidden hero's devotion and sacrifice.

In the context of the 1980s, with the dissolution of the communist block and a stagnating domestic economy in which promises of improving living standards and growing material wealth appeared increasingly hard to fulfill, the Hidden Hero movement was a strategic attempt at mobilizing labor by calling upon absolute loyalty to the nation rather than monetary compensation. The campaign also allowed writers to explore broader topics and themes in their fiction. While literature had focused on a limited selection of character "types" – infallible workers, class-conscious peasants, and patriotic soldiers/ guerrilla during the 1960s and 1970s – it now depicted average office workers, teachers, scientists, provincial Party officials and managers with greater attention to psychological interiority and the private sphere, such as family and romantic relationships.[11]

The questions and challenges that these characters faced also evolved to become more complex. Where dramatic tension used to arise solely from innocent misunderstandings, foreign threats, or differences between the older and younger generations, experienced and inexperienced farmers or educated and uneducated factory workers, one could now find conflicts inspired by the social and economic transformations of North Korean society such as tensions over status between members of different social classes, financial disputes between

[Let's uphold the magnificent principles of the Great Leader and enhance the production of revolutionary works] *Chosŏn Munhak,* 11 (1980), 7-13.

11 In a survey of North Korean short stories published in the literary magazine between 1959 and 1973, Marshall Pihl underlines the predominance of agrarian (54 percent) and industrial fiction (32 percent) and notes that "the family structure is never involved." (Marshall R. Pihl, "Engineers of the Human Soul: North Korean Literature Today," *Korean Studies* 1 (1977), 91). By contrast, a survey of the same magazine between 1977 and 2013 finds the family to be almost as common a topic as the industry (8 vs 12 percent), with the bulk of literary production concerned with science and education. (Benoit Berthelier, "Quantifying Quality: A Computational Approach to Literary Value in North Korea", *Journal of Asian Studies* 81, no. 2 (2022): 267-288).

married couples, company corruption and embezzlement or dissipating faith in the socialist ideology.

This new way of writing has persisted until today and has allowed for the literary treatment of difficult subjects such as the famine of the 1990s – the "Arduous March" that claimed the lives of between 600,000 and 1,000,000 North Koreans – and its dire economic consequences. To the reader interested in learning more about North Korea, these narratives may appear to have a documentary value, in their depictions of quotidian life and social ills. Literature might even seem a privileged source. For few other state-censored sources in the country would offer the candid descriptions of starving street children and black-market activities of, for instance, Ri Sinhyŏn's 2002 novel *Kanggye Spirit* or depict the banality of corruption the way Han Ungbin's *Hoping for Luck to Strike* (included in this volume) does.[12]

It might therefore be tempting to read between the lines. To try to abstract the optimism of every literary denouement and the political didacticism of the stories in order to focus on the dysfunctions and issues that reveal the "real" North Korea. But these elements are used to propel the plot and are just as fictitious as other scenes featuring dramatized displays of loyalty to the Party and the leaders. There is no assurance that the former constitutes a more accurate representation of reality than the other. That depictions of social dysfunction appear more realistic has more to do with outsiders' perception of North Korea and an aesthetic tradition that, unlike socialist realism, sees flaws and shortcomings as the most reliable signs of the real.[13]

Following the hidden heroes of our stories also let us see more trivial aspects of North Korean life: what people do for fun, how work meetings and business trips are done, how families are structured. These glimpses of the everyday offer a refreshing, humanizing perspective on a country usually only approached through the lens of human rights and national security policies. Yet the same mimetic issue remains. Neither the good-humored keeping-up-with-the-Joneses type of competition between the protagonists of Ch'oe Sŏngjin's "Neighbors" nor the impromptu concert of Kim Chŏng's "Seventeen People's

---

12 Kanggye is a city in the northern Hamgyŏng province that was hit particularly hard by the famine. The eponymous "Kanggye spirit" refers to its inhabitants resilience in the face of adversity. Ri Sinhyŏn, *Kanggye Spirit* (Pyongyang: Munhak yesul ch'ulp'ansa, 2001).
13 Chris Vials, *Realism for the Masses: Aesthetics, Popular Front Pluralism, and U.S. Culture, 1935–1947* (Jackson: University Press of Mississippi, 2010), 204.

Laughter" actually happened. The scenes are constructed, imagined and may be nothing more than propaganda.

If the "realist vision" [14] of North Korean fiction is not to be taken at face value, perhaps, then, the inward turn taken by novels in the 1980s can open a window into the sentimentality, the mentality, or the psychology of North Korean citizens. After all, cultural historians have, since long, warned against putting trust in the representations of realist fictions and the figurative arts in general.[15] Realism is rooted in deception. It is a technique of illusion to make the fragmentary look like the whole. On the other hand, as Alain Corbin notes, "when a poet evokes an emotion, there is a good chance that they actually felt it."[16] Sentimentality may paradoxically have a higher truth value than factual narration.

One might consider, for instance, the conflicted sentimentality of the heroine of "The Key" or the complaints of the lonely young woman in "Spring Evening" about her absent fiancé, to offer a window into what love and desire might mean to North Korean women. The existentialist angst of the protagonist of the "The Actor's Last Class" as he searches for his authentic self and criticizes a capitalist society that has "turned the world into a stage," forcing people into merely acting or performing their identities, could be read as a mirror of the author's diasporic experience, or as an expression of a more general discomfort towards what social life entails in capitalist nations – and perhaps also in North Korea.

Accepting the veracity of these emotions then implies that one may not so easily discount the descriptions of joy at being accepted into the Party or the internal monologues about the love felt by a character for the Leader. We know that the North Korean Workers' Party is actively involved in literary production, through censorship as well as the prescription of certain literary themes and the setting of production targets.[17] These literary displays of emotions are more than fabricated affects merely serving a rhetorical purpose. Literary

---

14 Defined as a visual "inventory of the world" that claims to represent reality as it is. Peter Brookes, *Realist Vision*. (New Haven: Yale University Press, 2005), 17.

15 Allan H. Pasco, "Literature as Historical Archive." *New Literary History* 35, no. 3 (2004): 373-94.

16 Alain Corbin & Georges Vigarello, "Entretien avec Alain Corbin, " *Perspective*, 1 (2018). https://doi.org/10.4000/perspective.9187

17 Immanuel Kim & Paek Namnyong, "The Interview: Life of North Korean Author Paek Namnyong," *Journal of Korean Studies* (2016), 21, no. 1: 245–257. Meredith Shaw, "Inside North Korea's literary fiction factory," *The Conversation*, January 26, 2018. https://

narratives, like all cultural products, contribute to shaping their consumers' sentimentality. Considering the privileges enjoyed by its members, there are few reasons to doubt that acceptance into the Party would be cause for elation.

Ultimately, reading North Korean literature for insights into the country's reality assumes the possibility of matching literary representations to an objective immutable reality. Yet as pragmatists remind us, there is no ready-made reality against which to compare representations, no single true correspondence between word and things, for what we experience and understand as reality is always itself mediated by a linguistic description.[18] What we compare realist literature against is not reality, not things-in-themselves, but rather "a fairly widespread consensus about the character of reality" achieved through language.[19]

This does not mean that questioning the reality of what is depicted in North Korean short stories is a futile exercise. When depictions of the country's difficulties – electricity and commodity shortages, corruption, or adverse labor conditions – appear more realistic than collective expressions of love for the Leaders or the behavior of a model socialist worker, perhaps the most interesting insights may not come from trying to disentangle truth from propaganda, but rather from analyzing how differences in consensuses over reality between different readers (the North Korean author's model reader and the foreign reader of this volume) may lead to this feeling of discrepancy. Such reflexive prompts are one of the appeals of reading North Korean literature, allowing the reader to pause, question their biases and reflect on how they assess what is realistic and what is real.

For example, the dualistic structure of Kang Kwimi's "The Actor's Last Class," opposing the poverty-stricken existence of its Korean protagonists in Japan with their successful and happy lives after their return to North Korea, will surely strike the reader as a crude exercise in propaganda. We "know," through our representations of Japan and North Korea, that the former is one of the wealthiest nations in the world while the latter, in the words of former

theconversation.com/inside-north-koreas-literary-fiction-factory-89901   (Accessed August 24, 2021.)

18 Richard Rorty, *Philosophy and Social Hope* (London: Penguin Books Limited, 1999), 48. Hilary Putnam, *The Threefold Cord* (New York: Columbia University Press, 2002), 100-101. 19 Salman Rushdie, "Truth, lies and literature," *The New Yorker* (May 13, 2018), https://www.newyorker.com/culture/cultural-comment/truth-lies-and-literature   (Accessed August 12, 2021).

U.S. president Obama, "can't really even feed its own people."[20] We also have defector testimonies documenting the discrimination of citizens repatriating from Japan by the North Korean state.[21] But to a North Korean reader, "The Actor's Last Class" is written by an author who left Kobe at age sixteen — at a time when most of the Koreans in Japan were racially discriminated against and deprived of civic rights — and moved to North Korea where she became one of the country's most celebrated writers. The real-life figure of the author and her successful career mirror that of the protagonist who becomes a nationally renowned actor upon his return to North Korea, giving an aura of authenticity to the trajectory of the story's characters.[22]

This example may be dismissed as mere rhetorical artifice or tokenism, but in order to do so one still needs to acknowledge the North Korean position. To accept that there exists a difference in vocabularies – in commonly shared representations of, for instance, Japan, Korea, writers, literature – in and outside of North Korea, and that this difference may be discussed, criticized, and perhaps one day reduced. In other words, uncovering the truth happens not by trying to match a narrative with what we think we know is real, but by accepting that North Korean descriptions of reality, while different, can be confronted with our own to achieve a better understanding of the country. As Rorty puts it, when attempting to uncover truth, it is much more efficient to "see human beings as generators of new descriptions rather than beings one hopes to be able to describe accurately."[23] Here lies one of the ambitions of this volume. To present North Koreans not as objects of knowledge but as a diverse group of individuals whose voices can enrich and challenge our representations of reality.

Picking our Heroes

The texts present in this volume are short stories published in the last thirty years in the country's main literary journals, *Chosŏn Munhak* and *Munhak Sinmun.*

---

20 "Obama says North Korea is bound to collapse," *The Korea Herald.*

21 Kang Chol-hwan and Pierre Rigoulot, *The Aquariums of Pyongyang* (New York: Perseus Press, 2001).

22 Sonia Ryang, "The Denationalized Have No Class: The Banishment of Japan's Korean Minority—A Polemic," *The New Centennial Review*, 12, no. 1 (2012): 159-187.

23 Richard Rorty, *Philosophy and the Mirror of Nature* (Princeton: Princeton University Press, 1979), 378.

They therefore represent a genre-specific and historically limited subset of the country's entire literary production. Short stories are an important genre in the North Korean literary landscape. Virtually every writer starts their career writing short stories, as full-length novels are usually reserved for senior writers. But even the most established writers will continue to publish short stories regularly in addition to full-length novels. The North Korean literary scene is divided between professional writers who are members of the Writers Union and receive a regular salary, and amateurs who have another occupation but produce art in their free time. The Writers Union offers a pathway for amateur writers who wish to become full time writers, and several of the writers selected for this anthology, such as Han Ungbin and Paek Namnyong, started their professional literary career after attending one of the Union's training programs.

The two journals that the stories in this anthology were sourced from are considered to be prestigious and reserved for the best output of established writers and professionally trained newcomers. Lesser works by professionals are published in less prestigious national or provincial journals, while the country's large crowd of amateur writers will usually publish in outlets reserved for them.

Our selected stories cannot be considered canonical, in the sense of belonging to a limited corpus of literary writings held to be of higher aesthetic value and representative of a national literary tradition. In North Korea, the literary canon was established in the late 1960s to include narratives of anti-colonial resistance such as *Sea of Blood* and *The Flower Selling Girl*, often attributed to Kim Il Sung himself, and the series of historical novels about the life and revolutionary exploits of the Leaders produced by the April 15th Literary Production Unit.[24] Despite the importance of these texts in the North Korean literary field – they are part of every school's curriculum, bundled as e-books on every digital device sold in the country and written only by the most renowned writers – we made a conscious decision to exclude them from this volume. Texts starting with the depiction of "the Dear Leader Kim Jong Il bathed in the bluish glow of a car's headlight" or "Dear General Kim Jong Il waiting for the Great Leader to return from his on-the-spot guidance trip" would have further reinforced and entrenched preconceptions of North Korean literature as mere hagiographical propaganda when, due to its canonic status, the cult-of-personality

---

24 Kim Jong Il, "Chuch'e munhangnon" [Theory of Juche literature], Speech on January 20th, 1992. In. *Kim Jong Il chŏjakjip* [Selected works of Kim Jong Il] (Pyongyang: Chosŏn rodongdang ch'ulp'ansa, 1992), 11: 237.

genre is only practiced by a few chosen authors and does not constitute the majority of literary production.[25]

We also wanted to avoid selecting texts primarily based on their appeal to foreign readers more used to the literary standards of the Western world than to those of the socialist "People's Republic of Letters".[26] Going through North Korean literary history, one can find occasional instances of writing where direct references to the leaders and the current political system are absent, such as the lyrical poetry of Kim Sunsŏk and the historical novels of Pak T'aewŏn or Hong Sŏkjung.[27] Judging from the reception of these works in South Korea, they also exhibit the sort of literary qualities that appeal to a non-North Korean readership. Yet compiling an anthology of such texts would have required us to justify a collection of historically and stylistically unrelated works compiled based on the aesthetic criteria of a foreign readership. We also opted to exclude works written by defectors who relocated to the South and dissident texts alleg-edly written in secret by North Korean writers.[28] These texts circulate outside of the realm of the DPRK's literary institutions and are not addressed to the country's audience. Unlike the Soviet *samizdat*, for instance, which were widely, albeit clandestinely, circulated domestically, there is no evidence to date that such dissident texts are actually produced or read within North Korea.

We chose to forego a purely historical and chronological approach, as we hoped more recent publications would find a larger audience beyond those with an interest in the country's literary history. All of the works selected were published after the start of the Hidden Hero movement in the 1980s. Some, like Paek Namnyong's "Life," became textbook examples of the movement in

---

25 An Tongch'un, *P'yŏngyangŭi ponghwa* [The fire signal of Pyongyang] (Pyongyang: Munhak Yesul Ch'ulp'ansa, 1999), 1. Paek Namnyong, *Kyesŭngja* [The Successor] (Pyongyang: Munhak Yesul Ch'ulp'ansa, 2002), 1.

26 Rossen Djagalov opposes the Western literary system based on the centers of Paris, New York, London and Berlin and a view of literature based on autonomy to the "highly policed" space of the socialist literary world. Rossen Djagalov, "The Zone of Freedom? Differential Censorship in the Post-Stalin-Era People's Republic of Letters," *The Slavonic and East European Review*, 98 no. 4 (2020): 601-631.

27 Note that while historical novels may avoid explicit references to contemporary politi-cal matters, they are not devoid of political discourse on themes such as the nation or class struggle.

28 Bandi, *The Accusation: Forbidden Stories from Inside North Korea* (New York: Grove Press, 2017). The authenticity of these texts and whether they were indeed written in North Korea is disputed.

literature for undergraduate students at Kim Il Sung University. Others only retain some of the literary features that it enabled, such as the introspective narration on family matters in "The Key" or "Hoping for Luck to Strike." But all of the stories in this collection focus on the daily life of a variety of people: factory managers, truck drivers, actors, university deans, architects and rural villagers.

Each story unfolds as an attempt to solve a problem such as an inadequate housing situation, a workplace conflict, or the difficulty of obtaining conspicuous consumption goods. Aware that the volume's most common usage will be as part of syllabi for courses on North Korea, we selected stories whose core problems could be used to illustrate the themes typically explored in such a pedagogical context. Instructors looking for materials on gender, the urban/rural dichotomy, education, corruption, class structure, labor relations or diaspora will therefore certainly find relevant stories among this volume's selection, with the caveats highlighted above about the reality of representations. As the reader will notice, the texts present problems but also solutions. These take the form of optimistic, didactic, *deus ex machina*-like conclusions that often feel forced, prescriptive, and anything but realist. We deliberately looked for texts where that gap was stronger because, beyond the sole depiction of social issues germane to global academic curricula, we wanted texts that could prompt the reader to think about their own position as consumers of realist literary representations.

We grouped the stories into three categories: Identities, Communities, and Power. Each of these serves to give a better understanding of the interplay between individuals, collectives and the multiple and complex power relations that bind them. As an Asian and socialist country, North Korea is often reduced to a single collective where no individuality, except for that of the Leader, is possible. Our categories work to challenge this representation by highlighting the way individual identities are constructed by taking on diverse roles and negotiating the contradictions between them. Far from being a single monolithic collective, North Korea is a complex assemblage of diverse individuals and social groups with diverging interests.

The first category "Identities" explores how individuals present themselves and perform intersecting social and gender roles. The first story is set in the aftermath of the North Korean famine. "The Key" reflects the inner struggles of a woman who attempts to reconcile the imperatives of the roles she takes on as a mother to a young child, a wife to an estranged, criminal husband, a daughter, a worker, and an aspiring Party member. "A Day in a Life of a Female Manager" depicts the struggle of a North Korean woman who juggles between her roles as a mother and a factory manager and has to reconcile the contradictory expectations of both identities. The introspective narrative of "Face" contrasts the life trajectories of two childhood friends – a gentle, sensitive boy nicknamed the "bride" and his assertive, handsome companion, nicknamed the "groom" – as they attempt to find their authentic selves.

The second thematic category is "Communities," highlighting not only the importance of the collective in North Korea but also its diversity. Through the story of a friendly outing among residents of the same apartment floor, "Neighbors" offers a look at the life of the urban middle-class and how they perceive themselves in relation to the larger North Korean society. The next story, "Hoping for Luck to Strike" offers an interesting counterpoint to this idealized urban communality, by contrasting the highly individualized lifestyle of the city-dwelling protagonist with the strong communal ties of his in-laws' rural village. This story also hints at the tension that exists between urban and rural regions, and the difficulty of moving from the latter to the former. "Seventeen People's Laughter" focuses on a workplace community and the sacrifice of an individual who overlooks his personal difficulties for the happiness of others. We end this section with "Last Actor's Class" that expands the notion of community to the imagined community of national identity, depicting the transnational and diasporic identities of North Koreans in Japan.

Finally, the last category is "Power," with "Life," "Spring Evening," and "Life Expectancy Chart." These stories challenge the representation of the DPRK as a place where dissent is nonexistent by depicting individual acts of disobedience. "Life" presents the case of a university dean who refuses to admit the children of local elites despite being pressured to do so. In "Spring Evening," a young driver disregards his supervisor's orders to attend to his marital duties. "Life Expectancy Chart" focuses on an avid worker who refuses to perform unproductive administrative tasks and eventually publicly criticizes the manager who requests them.

Notes on translation

The dilemma between familiarity and foreignness that we encountered as we selected the texts that make up this anthology resurfaced during the process of translation. More than the distinct linguistic structures of Korean and English, it was the different stylistic assumptions and imperatives of the literary systems we engaged with that proved problematic. North Korean literary style

proscribes neither cliché nor repetition. Style guides for writers[29] encourage
the use of well-established expressions and offer lists of clichéd expressions and
epithets that best describe the different elements of typical narratives. Thus,
scenic descriptions are often repetitive with numerous adjectival modifications;
character delineations are quite prototypical; and dialogues can also often
sound stilted and didactic.

Alleviating these differences, making the text sound more natural to the
anglophone reader might seem here a necessity, to avoid alienating the reader
and further othering North Korean literature. But we'll argue with Meschonnic
that a translation that "strives to avoid sounding like a translation" merely falls
for the "illusion of transparency," the belief that a target language is expressive enough to be able to accommodate the differences inherent to a foreign
language text without itself having to sound different.[30] Yet that confidence
is not universally shared. Rather, cultural preferences for literalism over free
translation tend to map to relations of power and subjection, with sense-for-
sense translation being the prerogative of imperial languages. In the USSR, for
instance, translation policies frowned upon literalism when translating from
foreign languages as "the Russian language can defeat any difficulty."[31] For
English language translation, Lawrence Venuti likewise notes that the predominance of the expectation of fluency and easy readability in translation
is "symptomatic of a complacency in Anglo-American relations with cultural
others, a complacency that can be described—without too much exaggera-
tion—as imperialistic abroad and xenophobic at home."[32]

---

29 Ri Hoyun, *Hyŏngsang-ŭi pŏt* [Creative writing helpbook] (Pyongyang: Munhak Yesul
Ch'ulp'ansa, 2012).

30 Henri Meschonnic, *Poétique et politique du traduire*, (Paris: Equivalences, 1994), 11-24.

31 Yet literalism was concomitantly encouraged when Russian works were translated
into other, minor languages of the union. Nikolai Liubimov, "Translation – An Art"
cited in Brian James Baer, "Translation and the Making of Modern Russian Literature"
(London: Bloomsbury Publishing, 2015), 130. See also, Susanna Witt, "Between the Lines
: Totalitarianism and Translation in the USSR" in *Contexts, Subtexts and Pretexts: Literary
translation in Eastern Europe and Russia,* ed. Brian James Bear, (Amsterdam, John Benjamins,
2011), 149-170.

32 Lawrence Venuti, *The Translator's Invisibility* (London & New York: Routledge, 1995),
20-22.

Applying the domesticating regime of free translation, or what Berman called "ethnocentric translations,"[33] to texts from a culture anchored in the denunciation of American imperialism seemed like an inappropriate course of action. While we attempted, in the translation and in the subsequent revisions among ourselves and with our editors, to stay close to the source text, our intention was not to overtly foreignize the texts either.[34] Rather, we chose to signal difference rather than pretend to transparently render it. To do so, we left the marks of translation apparent. Several parts of the narration and dialogues might sound like translations, because they are. They signal a characteristic of the source text while shifting the responsibility for the unnatural language introduced to our work as translators. One might argue that such a method will introduce a strangeness that would not exist for a North Korean reader consuming the source text. That is certainly true, but we are not trying to deliver the original. We do not want to erase the subjectivity of the translation process. Much to the contrary, we are offering a translation, the product of a work of intermediation, *as such*. The transparency we are seeking lies not in the belief that the reading experience of the source text by a native speaker could be rendered as such, but in refusing to conceal the nature of this volume as nothing else but a translation.[35]

The expectation that original North Korean texts would read "fluently" as the literary texts typically marketed in capitalist societies must also be relativized. Contemporary literary works are consumable goods, that have gone through an editing process to ensure fluency –ease of consumption – for the final reader.[36] But North Korea's socialist aesthetic regime is characterized by

33 Antoine Berman, *The Experience of the Foreign: Culture and Translation in Romantic Germany*, trans. Stefan Heyvaert (New York: State University of New York Press 1992), 5-6.

34 We did not, for instance, keep some of the original North Korean units such as *ri* (0.4km) or *kŭn* (roughly 600g or 1 pound). We also often chose to use pronouns where the original text would have repeated a character's name or title.

35 Jean Boase-Beier, "Who needs theory?" in *Translation: Theory and Practice in Dialogue*, ed. A. Fawcett, K. Guadarrama García and R. Hyde Parker (London: Continuum, 2010), 25-38.

36 Lawrence Venuti, "The Translator's Invisibility," *Criticism*, 28, no. 2 (1986): 179-212.

supply-side, rather than demand-side, literature. That is not to say that editing is nonexistent. Reviews by colleagues, editors and censors are ubiquitous parts of the writing process. Yet they aim to improve the work according to ideological and aesthetic standards that may be orthogonal to concerns of readability and consumability.[37]

---

37 For instance, while the USSR relied, for a short period of time, on library surveys in an attempt to model popular taste and increase demand for socialist realist novels, the North Korean Writers Union, following earlier debates among proletarian intellectuals on the meaning of popular literature, never sought to emulate the practice. Elizabeth A. Papazian, "Literacy or Legibility: The Trace of Subjectivity in Soviet Socialist Realism," in *The Oxford Handbook of Propaganda Studies*, eds. Jonathan Auerbach, Russ Castronovo eds. (Oxford University Press, 2014), 67-90. Kim Yŏngmin, *Han'guk kŭndae munhak pip'yŏngsa* [History of modern Korean literary criticism] (Seoul: Somyŏng Ch'ulp'an, 2012), 175-220.

IDENTITIES

CHAPTER 1

THE KEY[1]

Kim Hyesŏng was born in Pyongyang in 1973 and graduated from the Department of Language and Literature at Kim Il Sung University. She made her literary debut with the short story "The Key" (*Yŏlsoe*), translated here, which was featured in the 2004 April edition of *Chosŏn Munhak*. Her historical novel *Kunbaba* (2005), set in pre-colonial Seoul and depicting the increasing encroachment of the Japanese military over the Korean peninsula, received critical acclaim in North Korea. In 2007, it became the second North Korean novel to be published in South Korea after Hong Sŏkjung's *Hwang Chini* (2002). Kim is currently the Chairwoman of the North Korean Central Writers Union in Pyongyang.

"The Key" stands as one of the first literary texts to be written about the consequences of the Arduous March – a period of several years of natural disasters and famine during the 1990s. Despite claiming hundreds of thousands of lives and marking the total collapse of the country's agriculture and industry, the period was conspicuously absent in contemporary literary production. However, as the North Korean economy began showing signs of recovery in the 2000s, the first literary representations of the famine started to appear. A notable turning point was Ri Shin-hyŏn's 2002 novel *Kanggye Spirit*, a fictional account of Kim Jong-Il's travels through flooded fields, abandoned factories

---

1 Kim Hyesŏng
    2004
    Translated by Benoit Berthelier.

and starving villages filled with homeless orphans. As if the integration of the famine within the personality cult of the Kim dynasty had signaled that discussion of the Arduous March was now permissible for writers and artists.

The famine is the starting point of "The Key", as Pŏmsik, husband to the protagonist Yŏngmi, is caught misappropriating factory property and stealing to support his drinking habit amid the anomic climate of the Arduous March. Following Pŏmsik's release from a "legal re-education camp", Yŏngmi is faced with equally impossible choices: rekindling her marriage with her violent, now-estranged husband or enduring the social stigma of being a divorced, single mother. The introspective narrative of "The Key" projects the inner struggles of a woman who attempts to reconcile the imperatives of the multifaceted roles she takes on – as a mother to a young child, a wife to an ex-convict, a daughter to a disapproving father, a factory worker, and an aspiring Party member. In so doing, it provides a nuanced exploration of Arduous March's lingering trauma, changing social norms and the aspirations of young working-class families.

<1>

There must not be any married woman on this earth who does not love and respect her husband. Yet, there was a time when I lost all feelings of love and respect for mine. If anyone heard me talking like this, they would surely blame me.

But I am more than happy to be blamed. People might ask what kind of woman could hate her own husband when love and kindness are the very things that make us human.

I will never forget the day my husband came back from legal re-education camp. I was uneasy. I was on my way home like every other day, after finishing work, when a familiar voice greeted me. I stopped, stupefied. The voice had risen like the distant echoes of a forgotten past and my heart started pounding fiercely. I stood perfectly still—paralyzed, empty. But I recognized that voice; I could feel it with my whole body. It was him. It was my husband, Pŏmsik, the one who had made me and my son objects of pity and public humiliation; the one who had made our lives wretched; and, as if that was not enough, the one who haunted me in my dreams. I bit my lip and turned to face him. But I could hardly raise my eyes. No, I was afraid to raise my eyes, afraid that my resolve to live without him, the resolve I'd focused on so many times, would be weakened.

We stood motionless in the middle of the road like two tombstones. People passed by, glancing at us. Thinking that someone who knew us might see us, I rushed to a more secluded place. He followed me.

Does he still have feelings for me? I felt a surge of resentment and repulsion as the thought crossed my mind. But as soon as I saw how emaciated and dejected he looked, my anger dissipated, and my heart filled with pity. *Ah, this is what people mean when they speak of marital love.*

I pulled myself back together. We were not a couple anymore.

He did not come closer to me, nor did he utter the first word, as if he had been trying to read my heart.

I suddenly felt my vision become dim and turned my head. The unseasonably dark clouds in this late autumn caught my attention. There were two large dark clouds floating in the sky. *If the wind pushes those clouds together, they will collide, causing lightning to strike and rain to pour. Then the sky will clear up again. How wonderful would it be if our relationship could clear up like the sky after an outpour of regretful tears? No. I have a feeling it won't be like that. It must never be like that.*

I wanted to end this encounter as quickly as possible, so I broke the silence first.

"You're back."

"Yes, I am," Pŏmsik replied, his voice lifeless.

I didn't know what to say next. As the painful memories raced through my mind, my eyes filled with tears.

"I..." I opened my mouth to speak, eager to say something, but the words caught in my throat.

"I know," Pŏmsik said, "I don't blame you, comrade. I deserve it, I'm a worthless chump. I completely understand." He'd called me "comrade" instead of "honey."

Hearing the regret in his voice, I couldn't hold back my feelings any longer. I fell to the ground and sobbed convulsively. Tears streamed down his face too, falling onto the dry ground. But his tears were coming too late. He didn't even have to cry a lot, he just had to cry at the right time, and that time had now passed.

It didn't rain, but the sky was still overcast and gloomy. Even after we had shed tears, our broken relationship remained as gray as the sky.

I felt much better and calmer after letting myself cry. From my bag I pulled out the key to our house, which had remained empty for so long. I had kept the key with me just in case a moment like this ever came.

"Take it," I said.

His lips quivered like they always did whenever he was indignant. I gently closed my eyes, anticipating his reaction—the curses, the violence, the kicks and punches…

Instead, he took the key without a word. He sighed deeply. His hands shook like someone having a seizure.

"When I left for my parents' house," I told him, "I only took Ch'ungguk's clothes and left everything else in the house. I thought this was the right thing to do for Ch'ungguk. So, from now on…"

I didn't have the heart to finish my sentence. I had imagined this moment more than a hundred times; I had practiced my words repeatedly, but in real life, it was too painful to say. He must have realized what I'd been about to say, and so he closed his eyes.

We had nothing more to say. Silence fell upon us along with the dusk.

"What do you intend to do?" I asked him.

"I'll do my best to make things right, with all the strength I have left."

"I have to go now," I replied.

He nodded but showed no desire to part ways. I hesitated for a moment, then went my way.

"Wait," he called.

I stopped and turned my head to him.

"Honey, let me see Ch'ungguk just one last time. I won't take him away from you, so don't worry. Please, let me see him just one time."

He begged and called me "honey" as he used to. Suddenly I recalled Ch'ungguk, shaking his head, saying, "I don't have a dad," just the way his grandfather had taught him.

I shook my head gently. I thought, *No, please don't confuse Ch'ungguk. He's an innocent child.*

I staggered back to my parents' house. The road was neatly paved with cement, but I stumbled as if I were walking on a rugged, rocky trail. I was so lost in my thoughts that I didn't notice him following me. Only after I'd reached the main gate did I realize that he was there with me.

I passed through the main gate alone while he remained outside. In the past, he had always been respectful towards my parents when he had visited, but he was no longer welcome here.

My mother and father were furious. "Are you insane? How can you let this dirty bastard follow you here? I will end this with him!" my father yelled. It was the first time he had ever raised his fist at me.

As I stared at the floor, my father lowered his fist and ran out the door. I could hear him curse at Pŏmsik. Then, I heard the heavy metal bar being lowered to lock the main gate. It felt as if it the metal bar was being driven through my own heart.

At the dinner table, I had to sit facing my parents and their gaze, but I could hardly eat anything. *Has he had dinner yet? He probably has other things on his mind. Well, why do I care?* I couldn't even find the strength to hold my spoon.

That evening I lay down holding Ch'ungguk in my arms, but I couldn't fall to sleep. Ch'ungguk had fallen asleep right away after I softly patted his back. His face was bright and smiling. *How wonderful would it be if you could always remain this happy?* I felt like I was going crazy. I held him even tighter. The past that I had worked so hard to forget was rushing back, haunting my present and future.

An hour passed, and then another. I still could not sleep. Then, I heard a rustling sound from outside.

It must be Pŏmsik!

Suddenly, I recalled the days before we got married. The memories of our early romance, of our past lives, soothed me for a moment.

Whenever I was sick and unable to go to work, I would hear that same rustling sound. Everyone had warned me against dating Pŏmsik, so I tried to avoid him, but he courted me tirelessly. He'd say he couldn't live a day without seeing me, and, on days when I wasn't able to go to work, he would linger in front of my house until late at night. I was worried that people would begin gossiping about us, so I had no choice but to stick my head out the window. Only then would he grin at me and disappear into the night whistling. I am feeble and often fall ill, so whenever I lay on my sickbed, I secretly hoped I'd hear him outside my window. Even when I thought he wouldn't come by because he was busy, he'd still manage to drop by deep in the night.

I heard the sound again. Impulsively, I got up and went to the door. But as I gripped the handle, all of my strength vanished. *What is wrong with me?* I chided myself for my behavior, but something beyond my control was forcing me to open the door. I forgot about my fear and crossed the gate.

Sure enough, it was Pŏmsik. The evening was dark, like someone had painted it with black ink, but his face appeared intermittently between the pulsing light of his cigarette. It was as if his heart itself was burning like embers.

I grabbed his hand and led him into the house.

"Don't you dare turn on the lights when you come in," I spat those words without even realizing it. I hadn't meant to speak so harshly, and I felt guilty for being so cold toward a father who desperately wanted to see his son for the last time.

He seemed content with the chance that I had given him. He put his face on Ch'ungguk's cheek and then embraced him, crying and trembling.

"Now, don't ever come back. I told him that he doesn't have a father."

He jolted back as if he'd received an electric shock. His face was still obscured by darkness, but I could tell he was deeply hurt.

He left the room, gone from this house and this family forever. I didn't bother closing the door behind him. I fell to the floor and sobbed. The fact that I could not even cry as loudly as I wanted only added to my sorrow. The door squeaked in the lonely autumn wind as if it were scolding me for not closing it now that everything was over.

After that night, Pŏmsik never came by to see Ch'ungguk again. He never came by to see me either. But because we both worked at the same factory, our paths inevitably crossed, either by chance or by necessity. When we did run into each other, I was cold and he was awkward, both of us trying our best to ignore one another.

<2>

"Yŏngmi, with ruthless people, you've got to be ruthless. I know life and I can tell you that it is during hard times that people show their true colors. Think about it. You've seen what he has done when the country was going through difficulties, so just think about what he could do if really hard times were to come? I'm telling you this because I care about you, so please take my advice and divorce him."

I remember my father telling me this after Pŏmsik had received his sentence. While I was slowly falling apart, my father became the voice of reason.

Adversity is the touchstone of a person. We truly suffered during the Arduous March, but we endured those difficulties with smiles on our faces. Following the slogan of our Party "Let's not live for today but for tomorrow!" we overcame hardship with hope and faith. But it was a different story for my husband. He became corrupted. When everyone else kept their faith and tried to protect the nation, Pŏmsik could not even protect himself.

Even though he was not very good at it, the factory had granted his wish to be a driver and entrusted him with the task of operating a bulldozer. But he broke that trust. When the chief operator was not around, Pŏmsik frequently stole gasoline from the bulldozer and traded it for alcohol. He was sentenced to re-education camp after he had offered to use the bulldozer to plow a field for one of his drinking buddies. Instead, he'd ended up driving the vehicle into a ditch at full speed. He blamed the accident on the liquor. But was alcohol the real reason, or was it the "Arduous March" that had corrupted him? No, it was neither. He'd brought the misfortune upon himself.

The truth was that Pŏmsik was nothing more than a thug. After his father got sick and died, his mother pampered him with love. She raised him with great care and made sure there was never a speck of dust on his fingers. Blinded by her love for him, she praised him when he did well and needlessly defended him when he did wrong. This blind love had spoiled him, and he grew up as a self-centered, reckless child.

Fearing that growing up without a father would make him weak, his mother had pushed him to take boxing lessons at an academy, which only turned him into an untamed fighter. He was like a wild beast. His real name was P'yo Pŏmsik but he had removed the last syllable, "Sik" and only went by "P'yobŏm," meaning "leopard."

The world had to revolve around him. He went to work only if he was in the mood to go, but otherwise wasted his time drinking and gambling. Whenever people tried to admonish him for being absent from work too often, he would get angry and raise his fists. Eventually, people started avoiding him. Even his mother, who had once loved and treasured him. Tears, heartache, and regret were all she had now.

Given these circumstances, no one believed that the accident he had caused could have been a mistake. It was clear that reeducation camp was the only justified form of punishment.

People say that a women's fate is determined by the man she marries. I truly believe this. For any woman, a husband is something essential.

There is also a saying that no mother would scold a foolish child. But mothers do sometimes vent their frustration to others about their offspring's flaws. Wives, on the other hand, try their best to hide their husbands' issues, even if it deeply distresses them. Perhaps it stems from the idea that a husband and wife are one body and soul, that a husband's honor is also his wife's. Yet I had criticized my husband, not just with my words but also with my deeds. I spat in his face and turned my back on him, publicly, in front of everyone. Had I done the right thing? As a woman? As a wife?

I'm a woman, too. I want to live like other women. I just want to live simply, happily, harmoniously. But Pŏmsik crushed even those simplest of dreams. He shattered my hopes, my expectations, my desires. And yet, must I live with him?

Why can't I make a firm decision? Am I afraid of being humiliated? That's not it. No one would blame me; On the contrary, people would sympathize with me. Then, is it because I don't want my son to grow up without his father? But he is better off without such a father. No. I am ready for everything and my resolve is strong. All I have to do now is act.

<3>

But taking action wasn't easy. Many times, I'd planned to go see him to end our relationship, but every time I saw him, I couldn't bring myself to say anything. Just seeing him with his slouched shoulders and work clothes drenched in sweat made me unable to face him, yet alone talk to him.

It would have been better if he were seeing another woman …

But he didn't seem to be thinking about such things; all he cared about was his job.

One day, I left work later than usual because we'd been struggling to collect enough scrap metal to solve our machine factory's shortage of raw materials caused by steel industry problems. Staying idle and giving the excuse that we lacked materials wasn't an option when we had farmers left and right asking for machinery parts. "Even if the road is hard, let's walk with a smile!" Just like this slogan posted on the front gate of the factory, all the workers were brimming with energy and working hard to collect scrap metal. There were even competitions between teams to see who could collect the most. The collection campaign had lasted one month, and this was the last day.

I had diligently collected metal pieces like everyone else, but I still fell short of the target amount. I felt that I should have done more, but I reassured myself that I would do better next month and I changed out of my uniform. At that moment, the secretary of the Party's local cell approached me quietly. He stared at my outfit for a while – I was now dressed up nicely as I had put my regular clothes back on – then he spoke hesitantly:

"Comrade Yŏngmi, make sure to fill your quota before you leave."

I was taken aback.

"You looked like you had something else on your mind so I wasn't going to say anything. But one comrade who was still missing a hundred grams said that he wasn't going leave without filling his quota. He too, was about to leave, but decided against it, put his work clothes back on and went out to collect the rest…"

I was embarrassed. Of course, gathering the scrap metal was not part of the factory's production plan. But I couldn't leave after hearing those words, especially when, given my position, I should have worked harder than anyone else. I completed the work and left late, feeling quite hungry and exhausted, but I was happy to have filled this part of my heart that would otherwise have remained empty.

As I was about to walk through the factory's main gate, I noticed someone coming toward me, hauling a wheelbarrow full of scrap metal. He seemed to be struggling. It was late in the evening and well past the shift, but I was curious to see who was working so diligently. To my surprise, it was Pŏmsik.

I quickly turned away. My heart raced, and my face got red. I couldn't help but steal a glance at him, as though irresistibly drawn to him like a magnet. His sweaty back, his heavy shoulders...

How did I not recognize him? I thought, as I stared blankly at him. *Is it because I tried so hard to forget him? No, that's not it. I've tried so hard to forget him, but have I really forgotten him?* I have been thinking about him more than I had before. *Then why hadn't I recognized him immediately?* This pathetic figure that I had just seen dragging its feet across the street. That was it. It was because of his miserable demeanor and his emaciated face. But I knew I was not being honest with myself. It is always possible to recognize the people one is close to, no matter how much their appearance had changed. Yet, Pŏmsik was unrecognizable, like a different person. *A different person? Has he changed from the person I used to know? No, it can't be.* Even so, he seemed like a completely different person.

When I arrived at my parents' place, I found the door locked. I went through my bag to find the key, but then it hit me. *Where am I right now?* I was so caught up in my thoughts that I did not realize I was standing in front of "our house," the one Pŏmsik and I used to live in together. I lowered my head, my face red as sorghum, and left.

I hadn't gone far before I heard someone calling me. I turned around, but there was no one. I took another step, and someone called me again. I turned around again, but there was still no one. Or rather, there was. The white chimney of our house pierced my gaze like a nail and tore at my eyes. Unlike the chimneys of the other houses which were all spouting the white smoke of dinner, it alone was smokeless. This was what made me turn around.

I kept thinking in silence. I passed this place twice a day on my way to work but I couldn't recall seeing any smoke rise from the chimney. I'd never seen any. *Is he eating well?* Suddenly, the image of Pŏmsik's bright face as he enjoyed my dishes came to my mind. At the same time, the image of his gaunt face lately, and his unkempt clothes, flashed before me.

The next morning, I was surprised when I learned that he had achieved the highest result in the scrap metal collection contest. The man that the cell secretary had given as an example was actually Pŏmsik. He had gone to collect the hundred grams he was missing, and he'd found a whole pile of metal junk. He'd gathered everything diligently and ended up exceeding the monthly quota. The factory workers cheered for Pŏmsik, but his head crawled into his shoulders like a turtle's. But that wasn't the true reason for my surprise. What really surprised me was that I too was complimented at the monthly meeting. Compliments don't always please me, and this one definitely didn't. I'd done nothing extraordinary, just fulfilled my quota like the others. Yet people were praising me for being a responsible, diligent worker. I felt uneasy about these compliments on their own, but what really disgusted me most was when they said "Comrade Yŏngmi is like Comrade Pŏmsik." *Why are they comparing me to him? Do they think it's funny?*

I glared at the cell secretary, who was acting as if he had no part in this. He responded to my expression with a warm smile. As the old saying goes, "Would you spit on a smiling face?" I bit my lips in frustration.

From that point on, Pŏmsik kept receiving praise from everyone. It must have been the influence of the Party cell secretary, who followed him everywhere he went.

At first, people began talking behind Pŏmsik's back, saying that he been educated properly thanks to the positive example of Party members, but that bad habits die hard and that soon enough, he would become the same person he'd been before. Of course, I agreed silently every time I heard such talk. But now, all such chatter ceased, almost instantly, like a flame plunged into water.

The cell secretary had even scolded some people: "Don't always assume the worst in people. If you can't help a man who is trying to begin a new life, at the very least don't discourage him." After that, everyone at the factory treated Pŏmsik kindly. I almost felt ashamed…

But then, everything played out as I had expected. They say that a resolute heart does not last longer than four days. Soon, he was getting severely reprimanded during each of our work review meetings for being frequently late to his shift after his lunch break. Each time, he would pretend to fix his behavior for a couple of days but soon returned to his old habits. I tried to convince myself that he no longer had anything to do with me, but I still felt ashamed when he was criticized.

One day, the secretary came to talk to me during lunch.

"Comrade, Yŏngmi, do you stop by the kindergarten after work?"

"Yes, I go to pick up my son," I replied.

"He's a big boy now. Why don't you just let him walk home by himself?"

I was dumbfounded at his unexpected mention of my son.

"That will make him more independent," he said, smiling to clear the air of awkwardness. *Why would the secretary suddenly be so interested in my child?* It was puzzling. Later, I found out that Pŏmsik had been secretly going to the kindergarten during lunch to see Ch'ungguk. That was why he was always late for work in the afternoon. I also understood then why the secretary had come to see me on that day. He was truly interfering in my problems, or rather in our family's problems.

<4>

Why in the world did I choose Pŏmsik as my life companion? I asked myself countless times with tears and regret.

When I was single, I, too, had dreams, ideals, and ambitions just like any other girl my age. When I read romantic novels or watched movies, I dreamed of experiencing exhilarating passion. In my fantasies, I often pictured the ideal image of a happy family. Of course, fantasies are not reality. But the reality that I was now living in could not have been further from my fantasies.

I first met Pŏmsik in our factory's Youth League. He stood out from the crowd not only because his name was unique but also because he broke every single rule. What surprised me even more was that he didn't even show up to the meetings. I couldn't believe that there really were such people out there! Not only did he never attend the Youth League's events, he also skipped the factory employee assemblies and other important meetings. When I realized this, my interest in him faded, and my perception of him started to align with everyone else's. For somebody like me, who always strived to be on the factory's honor roll, he was of absolutely no interest.

But he somehow entered my life. He followed me everywhere I went and tried to win me over. He was confident that persistence would succeed, adhering to the saying that a tree will eventually fall if you keep hitting it with an axe. There were times he harassed men I spent time with, out of jealousy. I tried my best to avoid him, even to the point of rejecting him. But his passion for me only escalated. This tug of war lasted for two whole years, and with time, he eventually found a place in my heart.

Our hearts finally met on what started as an ordinary day. The factory had tasked us with building a warehouse for spare parts, which required the workers to prepare some aggregate to make concrete. Our Youth League unit volunteered to do the job. Regardless of rank, every member went out to the streets to collect materials for the aggregate. We put up tents by the river and ate and slept there. Everyone was excited to show what the youth could achieve. To maximize efficiency, we had divided up into teams of two with one man and one woman and organized a contest between all the groups.

Of all people, I was partnered with Pŏmsik. *Was it fate?* Of course not. It turned out that he had pulled some strings to be on the same team with me. He told me that he was determined to win the contest. He was working harder and with more enthusiasm than I had ever seen him work, maybe because he didn't want to lose to other men in front of the woman he loved. In any case, I did my share of work diligently.

One day, I caught a cold after being out in the rain.

He forced me to stay in the tent and as he left by himself for the worksite, told me, "I'll do your share of work, so just focus on getting better." I will not mention anything else about the way he nursed me, but my illness did not get any better. I felt guilty seeing him exhaust himself in order to fulfill the objectives of our group all by himself. So, I asked the Youth League secretary if he could reduce our workload.

That day Pŏmsik got angry with me for the first time.

"Do you think I'm worthless even after all I've done?" he shouted.

I didn't understand what was going on, so I just looked at him in confusion.

"You think I'm not man enough?"

"What…?"

"A man has his pride. Just as it's bad manners to ask a woman her age or weight, you don't hurt a man's pride."

"What in the world did I do to you?"

"I know what you think of me. But you should know this. If I set my mind to something, I do it. I will do whatever it takes to win first place."

"I was looking out for you, comrade…but why are you…"

"What? You're still going to look down on me?"

Suddenly, his eyes turned violent. I was scared. I had heard about his uncontrollable temper. That night, I had trouble falling asleep. If he'd always been a model worker, I would have understood his anger. But wasn't the reason he became partners with me just to prevent other men from approaching me?

What does this have anything to do with pride? I pity the woman who ends up marrying him. Although he is quite…

In the end, however, he succeeded in winning first place for our team. I couldn't believe it, but I learned from my colleagues that he had worked overtime several nights by himself. I never imagined that he had such determination in him.

After the contest's final results were announced, there was a dinner reception for the workers. I noticed Pŏmsik's bruised hands and chapped lips. The need to apologize, along with other feelings I could not explain, pushed me to go see him and tell him I was sorry. He stared at me, then sighed and said, "If I set my mind to something, I do it. Remember that."

"Right." I thought the best way to escape this awkward situation was to agree with everything he said. What more was there to say? I knew the discussion would continue if I argued with him, and I didn't want people to find us together so late in the evening still talking.

"So, I guess you've figured out what kind of relationship we're in," he added.

"Right." I replied without much thought. But then when I realized what he'd meant, I was taken aback. Flushed with fury, I glared at him. But the look on his face at that moment belied his stern voice. His smile was at once mischievous and innocent, a mesmerizing contradiction in the moonlight. I still cannot forget the way he looked that night. A man's face can be beautiful. And at that very moment, Pŏmsik looked beautiful. I felt the walls I had erected around my heart tremble.

We talked deep into the night, of this and that, but his stories made me more and more curious about men. Afterwards, we had many night talks, even after we'd returned to the factory.

But it was still nothing more than friendship. I don't know how he felt, but at least for me, it was friendship. Of course, looking back at it now, that friendship was the beginning of our love.

We had only been close for a few months when his mother passed away unexpectedly from a heart attack. I attended the funeral with the other workers. He was supposed to be in charge of the funeral service, but he was absent. People were outraged.

"What kind of a son is he?" they murmured.

How could he behave this way? He said that he needed to do something, but what in the world could be more important than his own mother's funeral?

He didn't return until very late that night. I couldn't believe my eyes when I saw him rush in, drenched in sweat as if he'd been caught in the rain. In his hands, he held a few unripe persimmons. When she was alive, his mother had always loved persimmons.

He fell to his knees and placed the persimmons on the funeral table. Heavy tears fell from his eyes to the rhythm of his shaky hands.

"Mother, don't leave me!"

He cried inconsolably, beating his chest and grabbing at his shirt as if try-ing to rip out his heart. My eyes filled with tears, as well. It was the first time I'd ever seen him, or any man, cry.

"Comrade Pŏmsik, please calm down," I said. But even I choked up.

"I killed my mother! It was me! Mother, how am I supposed to live without you? Mother!"

He buried his head in his hands and banged the floor with his forehead. Each time he banged the floor, the walls shook and the persimmons on the table rolled around.

"Comrade Pŏmsik, look on the bright side. Why do you think you're alone? You have your comrades and the league."

He shook his head, unable to control himself. His dejected spirit made me lose control of myself. I grabbed his arms and cried, "Comrade Pŏmsik, please calm down! Look on the bright side. You have…you have me now."

I couldn't believe what had just come out of my mouth. But what I had just said resonated in my heart. *You have me. You have me by your side.*

I kept my word. Did I say those things out of pity or because I was caught up in the moment? I wouldn't deny it. But there was something more than that— all the times we shared under the moonlight, the image of the green persimmons he brought for his deceased mother. That was it: pity, the heat of the moment, but also, in the bottom of my heart, I loved him. I didn't know what love was, but I loved him. I loved him without even realizing it. He had his problems, but I loved his passion and his manliness. He was not afraid to cry.

Everyone told me that we were not a good match, but I ignored them. I was attracted to his passion, his manly passion, and I loved the burning heat of that passion.

<5>

Our relationship was not without problems. Workers at the factory were sur-prised when they heard that we were going to get married. Not only my family, but my relatives and everyone in town were shocked. *Does Yŏngmi really want to get married to the "leopard?"* Many came to see me, asking if the rumor was true, and they all advised against me marrying him.

It was the first time in my life that I had been criticized by so many people. Even my close comrades who had usually understood me well did not take my side on this matter. Even Ch'unsil, my best friend since we had met on our first day at the factory, had warned me:

"Are you out of your mind? You're beautiful, so why would you go for someone like him? Don't let your feelings rule you…"

Since other people felt this way, you can imagine how my parents reacted. My father exploded and the whole house was filled with the thunder of his rage while my mother and I poured the rain of our tears. My mother was crying out of anger, and I out of despair.

Would I really be able to spend my life with him?

I asked myself this question whenever people admonished me, and each time, I reminded myself to defend our love. *Don't think this way, there can be no doubts in love, why are you hesitating? Some people might get the chance to experience love like in the movies or novels, but not everyone. Love has to be nurtured, then that love will blossom like a flower. I will nurture my love better than others. Besides, there are many men who become more responsible after they get married.*

Since his mother had passed away, there was no one in his family to bless our union. And with every day that passed, my expectations, hopes, and dreams of a happy marriage slowly dimmed. There were sweet moments at the beginning, but Pŏmsik quickly returned to his old habits—skipping work to hang out with his friends, spending his time drinking, gambling, and getting into fights.

Every time Pŏmsik caused trouble, I thought about the fathers of other households. All the men his age were becoming Party members and living honorably. He didn't have to be a Party member, but I would already have been happy if he'd stopped causing trouble.

People often refer to a wife as the *minister of the interior*, probably because the role and position of the wife is important in a family, but I never became a *minister of the interior*. Whenever I would "nag," as he called it, he would verbally attack me and shake his fist at me. I strategized all possible solutions and tried all possible tactics in the hopes of changing him.

Even now, it's painful to think about it. I cannot repeat this pattern again and again. Even if he is the father of my child, I must be firm.

On my way back from work one day, I saw Ch'ungguk flying a kite.

"Mom, look! Isn't it cool?" he shouted, running towards me with the kite string in his hands.

"Yes, it's really pretty." My son's laughter brightened my gloomy heart.

Ch'ungguk grabbed my hand, and we both ran. The kite soared in the sky.

"Mom, look how high it is!"

"Yes, it's really high."

It had been a long time since I ran like this. I was out of breath but thrilled.

"Who made you this kite?"

"That man over there."

Ch'ungguk pointed with his free hand towards the east side of the town. I followed his finger and froze. The joy that I'd felt a moment ago vanished.

It was Pŏmsik.

"Mom, let's run again," Ch'ungguk said, tugging at my arm. But I was nailed to the ground. The kite descended from the sky like a dead leaf and landed in front of Ch'ungguk.

"Mom, let's run again," Ch'ungguk begged, jumping.

"Enough! We have to go home now." I dragged Ch'ungguk by the hand.

"No! I'm going to stay and play alone with the kite!"

He begged again, pulling away from me as if he were playing tug-of-war, and looked helplessly at where Pŏmsik was standing.

Suddenly, I felt like my son had more affection towards Pŏmsik than me.

"Ch'ungguk, you shouldn't play with things like this!"

I snatched the kite from Ch'ungguk, ripped it, and threw it at Pŏmsik.

"My kite…My kite…"

Ch'ungguk cried as he reached for the kite. I dragged him home and spanked him. Ch'ungguk was the one getting spanked, but I was the one feeling the pain.

I've got to end this once and for all. How dare he use Ch'ungguk to get to me. He's got this all wrong.

I could see his sneering at me, which made me furious. He had never truly loved Ch'ungguk. He was more interested in drinking and gambling than loving and educating our son. The interest he was showing in Ch'ungguk was just a hypocritical ploy to get my attention. People who do not realize this might think I am a heartless woman. *Let's settle this once and for all! I will not wait any longer.*

The next day, I went looking for Pŏmsik during my lunch break. I looked everywhere, but couldn't find him. I wanted to ask the other workers if they had seen Pŏmsik, but I didn't have the courage. But without help, I wouldn't be able to track him down. Suddenly, I remembered Ch'unsil, who was the best person to ask.

"Hey, Ch'unsil…have you seen *him*?"

Although we were good friends, I felt a bit embarrassed to ask. Ch'unsil looked puzzled for a moment before my meaning dawned on her. "You mean Pŏmsik?"

I was very grateful that she knew me so well. But she didn't know where he was either. Defeated, I turned and walked away.

"Yŏngmi, wait!" Ch'unsil called out. "How about the kindergarten?"

Not knowing how to respond to that, I just widened my eyes at her.

"You still haven't figured out why he's late for work every afternoon?" Ch'unsil asked me in a rebuking tone.

I recalled, then, what the cell secretary had said. I rushed to the kindergarten, where I found Pŏmsik squatting by the swing-set in the kindergarten playground. Ch'unsil was right.

I walked toward him with determination. Part of me was hurting, but the need to get it over with was stronger than my pain. I walked up to him, but he was concentrating on something so intently that he didn't notice me. My curiosity propelled me still closer, until I froze and gasped. I couldn't believe my eyes. He was lubricating the hinges of the swing. *No, that heartless man would never do such a thing!* But reality outweighed my doubt. He worked on the swing-set as if it was the most important task of his life, applying oil here and there and testing to see if it moved smoothly. I remembered hearing the swing squeaking, but I had not given it much thought. Even though I, a mother, had failed to notice it, the noise must have weighed on him.

Of course, it could also have been hypocrisy. Isn't that the very definition of hypocrisy, to portray yourself as caring and thoughtful when you are not?

A moment later, he wiped the sweat off of his forehead, stretched his waist and smiled with satisfaction. That smile, that face. It was the same face I had seen under the moonlight many years ago on the construction site. Suddenly, I felt something burning inside me and tears came to my eyes. My body felt weak, and the sense of determination that had driven me just moments before now escaped me all at once. A small wailing noise flew out between my teeth. I covered my mouth with my hands. *Why do you keep playing with my feelings? You were never like this before. Or is this truly who you are?*

<6>

Finally, people began advising me to have a fresh start with him, even Ch'unsil, who had so adamantly discouraged me from marrying him. The more people witnessed changes in Pŏmsik, the more they encouraged me to work things out with him.

Start over? It was easy to say, but would they say the same if they knew what I'd gone through? I knew that in their place, I would have said the same thing. But words are cheaper than deeds.

I'd considered getting back together with him before, for instance after Ch'ungguk was born and I saw the joy on his face while holding our newborn. That had given me a little bit of hope that he might take responsibility as a father and that we could start over. I still remember the day we named our son.

"Honey, I want to name our child Ch'ungguk," I said, looking with affection at my husband who was struggling to come up with a decent name.

"Ch'ungguk, huh?" he replied, contemplating the name.

"Yes, Ch'ungguk. Honestly, you and I are here thanks to our country's generosity, but what have we ever done for our country? When he grows up one day and asks what we have done for our motherland, how will we respond? I don't want him to live a meaningless life like us, so I think the name is fitting. It's a good reminder to us and his future."

My husband remained silent, his face filled with self-reproach.

"Ch'ungguk… *Ch'ung*, 'loyal', and *guk*, 'to the country'. 'Loyal to the country.' I like it. Let's go with that."

Whenever Pŏmsik decided on something, he had a habit of flailing his right hand for a cigarette. As he lit his cigarette, we made eye contact. He quietly chuckled, put out the cigarette in the ashtray, and said, "I've nearly forgotten that I'm not allowed to smoke around the 'boss.'" He then gathered up Ch'ungguk in his arms.

"Honey, I don't think our son will cause you any problems. Hey, boss, don't make your mother worry, or else I'll come and get you," Pŏmsik said, squeezing Ch'ungguk and laughing.

My eyes welled up because what he was saying to Ch'ungguk was actually directed at me. It was the first time in our marriage that I shed tears of joy. It seems that everyone wants to become a better person for the sake of their children. But even if Ch'ungguk's birth had given my husband joy, it didn't give him a new start.

Was it possible to celebrate the spring rites in fall? Since he'd never managed to reform in the past, how could he start over now that he was at his lowest? I knew he was trying to start again, but I also know that his determination never lasted long. The rest of his life would be committed to atoning for his past. In that case, shouldn't I be with him to support him? Help him carry the weight of redemption? But should Ch'ungguk also have to carry that weight along with us? Of course not. I would never let that happen.

My stoic rationality pulled me away from Pŏmsik, but my wretched emotions kept me tied to him. People were delighted to see his transformation, but I was overwhelmed by mixed emotions. I sensed that people pitied him but detested me. Even Ch'unsil's eyes gave me this impression. Pŏmsik had been marginalized by the other workers before, but now it felt like it was my turn.

<7>

"Mom...why are you crying so much?"

I had been crying more than ever, casting a shadow on Ch'ungguk. And each time I cried, he would look at me with tears in his eyes, not knowing whether to embrace me or not. It was heart-breaking.

"Don't worry. I just wanted to cry, that's all."

I would hug him and give an evasive answer while holding back my tears. I was terrified at the reflection of myself in his eyes.

Pŏmsik was undoubtedly changing, becoming a better man in all aspects of his life, except for his slouched shoulders and unkempt clothes. It was also evident from the way the Party cell secretary always looked after him. The secretary appeared brighter each day, as if he had accomplished something great. And I felt the same affection in the eyes of all those people who came in contact with Pŏmsik. Even my attitude toward him began to change from a cold anger to a compassionate pity.

Pŏmsik! Why didn't you think of changing sooner? This question echoed from the deepest part of my heart. But, now that I think of it, the question was not directed at him as much as it was simply venting my frustration.

One morning, as I entered the factory, there was an unusually large crowd in front of the bulletin board. I unconsciously drifted towards them to see what had been posted. I could not believe my eyes.

"Congratulations to Comrade Pŏmsik for being the first person to exceed the monthly production target! Let's innovate every day!"

The poster's stark black calligraphy seemed to whip my face painfully. I averted my eyes because the picture of Pŏmsik painted on the poster was so lifelike that I felt I was standing in front of him. The only difference with the real Pŏmsik was that on the picture he was smiling radiantly.

People by the bulletin board said, "My, how much he's changed!"

"This P'yo Pŏmsik really was a leopard after all."

"Here's a real man."

It felt like they were commenting for my benefit. I couldn't bear to stay any longer, so I scurried away, my face completely red.

The thought of Pŏmsik lingered, and for the rest of the day I was unable to focus on my work. Most people, including me, don't read the bulletin board or consider it anything special, especially those who always meet the monthly quota. The bulletin board, after all, is not the same as national recognition. But I was surprised to see Pŏmsik's face there. It's nice to be recognized by your colleagues. The one who used to receive only criticisms was now receiving compliments. This new image of Pŏmsik made me tear up.

That evening, Ch'unsil grabbed my hand and said, "Let's go to celebrate Pŏmsik's success."

My heart was pushing me to go with her immediately, but I couldn't find the courage. I left the factory and walked aimlessly around town. My parent's place was only twenty minutes away from the factory, but it took me over two hours to get home.

The atmosphere at home was different than usual. My father puffed on his cigarette while my mother held Ch'ungguk on her lap and wiped tears off her cheeks. Normally I would have asked them what was wrong, but I was too despondent to ask. Silence filled the room.

Without warning, my mother jumped up and went into the kitchen, returning with a bottle of expensive liquor. It was common for her to set up drinks every time my father was anxious, so I didn't think much of it. Oddly though, she pushed the bottle towards me instead of towards him.

"Your colleagues stopped by and said it was Pŏmsik's birthday. Go see him."

My heart raced like a guilty criminal's, and my eyes got misty. I hung my head to hide my tears. My mother began to sob, "It's all because of that stupid old man. He's lost his mind. Pŏmsik is still our son-in-law, for the better or for the worse…"

My father didn't try to defend himself and kept smoking, blowing the smoke each time he sighed. My mother's words must have hurt him. I was heartbroken and distressed. I could not take it any longer. I ran out of the house.

I wandered the streets, my mind cluttered with thoughts, until I found myself at our house. There was a lively party within—familiar voices, people singing, and among them Ch'unsil singing her favorite song "Nothing to Envy."

I was alone, pathetic. I stood outside without the courage to enter my own house. In the sky, the twinkling light of the stars was dimming as if they felt sad to see me like this.

"Comrade Yŏngmi?"

The unexpected presence of someone startled me at first, but it was the familiar voice of the secretary.

"Let's take a walk," he said, leading me down a path.

I was grateful to him for understanding my situation. He escorted me back to my parents' place, but, looking back now, he was also walking me back to Pŏmsik. He said many things to me that night, but one in particular stuck with me:

"Comrade Yŏngmi, I know how you feel. Comrade Pŏmsik committed a crime. But there were many others who strayed from the right track during the Arduous March. And now they've realized their mistakes through tears and regret and understood that there is a new day under the guidance of the Dear General. Look how much Pŏmsik has changed. Our Party will never abandon someone who repents and changes. Rather, the Party embraces people like that."

I didn't sleep a wink that night, and my pillow was drenched with tears. I recalled the picture of Pŏmsik on the bulletin board that morning. I now realized that his jovial expression, which had at first struck me as contrived, was an accurate depiction. Today, he had smiled. Among the congratulations, with the love of his comrades and the community and society, he had smiled. And oddly enough, I was the one crying. It was time to start over. No, it was too late. Not for him, but for me. This new start was not for him but for me! A new beginning! But how could I dare to claim a new start, after abandoning him when he needed me the most?

<8>

Shortly thereafter, there was a farewell party for those who had volunteered for the Dear General's land reform program in Kangwŏn Province. We cheered and applauded for these volunteers. Pŏmsik was among them. While the other volunteers stood tall and dignified wearing flower garlands around their necks, Pŏmsik lowered his head as if he were counting the number of flowers on his wreath.

I looked at the crowd that was leaving, one question repeating in my mind: "What should I do?" If I followed them to the station, then people would think that I was there for Pŏmsik. But then the image of his standing alone with no one to send him off pained me.

No. I had to go and say goodbye to him. I hadn't been present when he was taken to the labor camp, but this was a different story. Rather than commit a crime, he was doing something admirable for the country. And still, I couldn't find the courage to go. I was embarrassed because I did not know how he would react. At that moment, I felt someone's hand on my back. I turned around and saw the cell secretary.

"Let's hurry to the station," he said.

His eyes looked like they could see straight into my heart, and I didn't have the courage to refuse. I followed him like a calf would his master, but I felt light on my feet.

There was a large crowd at the station, with friends and family huddled around the volunteers. I pulled myself together and looked for Pŏmsik. He was nowhere to be found. Just then, someone tapped me on the shoulder.

"You've made it," Ch'unsil said. She didn't have to say much; I knew exactly what she meant. "Comrade Pŏmsik said that he needed to do something and left me his bag. Take it so that I can go find him."

Ch'unsil handed me Pŏmsik's duffle bag along with a large bundle. My face flushed with embarrassment. But I was not really angry at her for doing this. Much to the contrary, I was almost crying with gratitude. *Ch'unsil, you're such a good friend!*

I looked at his duffle bag and the bundle and realized that the other volunteers also had the same bundle. It was a bundle of supplies that our factory workers had put together, and I felt proud to have taken part in its preparation too.

But then, I realized that while the other volunteers each had a large suitcase, Pŏmsik only had a small, worn-out duffle bag. So small to the eye and so light in the hand. I placed the bundle on the ground and peered into his duffle bag. I felt like people were looking at me, so I quickly closed it. He only had one set of summer clothes and a few toiletries. He also had a family picture encased in a glass frame. These items were not enough to even fill the bag. I held back my tears and opened the bag again. It was a picture of the three of us, and in it I looked happy. And I looked detestable in the picture. No, I was detestable in reality. And still, Pŏmsik had put all the love and affection he had for me and Ch'ungguk in this small bag. I was ashamed of myself for not reciprocating that love and not helping him pack.

No, Pŏmsik. You can't go like this. I won't let you go like this!

I began to sob and ran out of the station in self-reproach. I still don't know how I made it to my parents' home. I opened the closet and drawers to gather his clothes. I rushed to prepare him food, leaving the kitchen a mess. My parents looked at me as if I were insane. I packed the items in a bag and ran back to the train station.

As I was heading to the station, I happened to glance over at the kindergarten, where I saw Pŏmsik in his unkempt clothes leaning against the fence and peering into the school with regret. I dropped the bag in shock and bit my lips as I stared at him. He paced in front of the kindergarten for a bit and then decided to enter the school grounds. But then, at the school gate, he stopped and lowered his head. It looked like he was determined to enter this time, but he was nailed to the ground.

Just go in and see Ch'ungguk.

Pŏmsik shook his head and turned around. But then, his somber eyes regained life. He raced over to the swing-set and noticed how it no longer squeaked. He hugged the swing as though he was embracing Ch'ungguk. Even from afar, I could clearly see the spasms that shook his shoulders. His tears glistened in the sunlight before falling straight on my heart, piercing it like so many sharp knives. He took one last look at the kindergarten and muttered something. I did not hear what he was saying, but I felt it in my heart.

"Son, wait for me!"

He rushed back to the train station, running like a drunk person, losing his balance at times because he was looking back at the kindergarten, which as if he could not tear his eyes away from it.

Sobbing, I went inside the kindergarten and picked up Ch'ungguk, who was sleeping peacefully as if nothing had happened. I had forgotten about the clothes and food I packed for Pŏmsik. When I arrived at the station with Ch'ungguk, the train had already begun to depart. I ran after the train, dragging Ch'ungguk behind me. People were piling up around the train's windows and I could only swerve around them. The train, insensitive to my predicament, kept gradually accelerating.

I put Ch'ungguk down and chased the train. The train's windows soon disappeared from my sight. I could not see him. He had no reason to wave his arm outside the window like the others, so he had remained absentmindedly seated in the cabin. Without even knowing it I shouted:

"Pŏmsik! –"

It was not the sound of my voice. It was the sound of my feelings bursting out of my chest where they had remained buried for so long.

<9>

The train disappeared into the horizon, taking Pŏmsik farther away from me. I could no longer hear the whistling of the train. I didn't realize that Ch'unsil was standing next to me.

"Take this, Yŏngmi."

I stuck my hand out without thinking, but then retracted it as if I had touched something hot. It was the key to our house.

"Pŏmsik asked me to give this to you. He wanted you to keep it until he returned."

Suddenly, I recalled what he had promised me while we were dating.

"Comrade Yŏngmi, I fear that I'm going to make you unhappy at times, but just remember that I will always love you."

"I will always love you, too."

But I had been unable to keep this oath. That was it. It was entirely my fault if our love and our family didn't stay on the same path. If only I had believed in him like I had in the beginning. If only I had been able to rekindle the flame in his heart with such faith, would we have had such hard times? What kind of a woman was I who couldn't even support her husband? This key that I held in my hand was the trust and the hopes that my husband had given us, Ch'ungguk and I, when he left.

As I turned around, I noticed the cell Party secretary and his superior looking at each other and then smiling at me.

Thank you! Thank you so much! In my heart, I bowed deeply in front of these two men and their benevolent smiles.

I've made up my mind!

I returned to our empty house. Inside, I held the key as if it were my husband himself, and I cried tears of atonement.

Pŏmsik, I'm so sorry.

I had given him the key to our house out of spite, to end our relationship. In this flowery garden of brotherly love that is our society, where everyone lives in unity and helps each other, I did not believe that Pŏmsik was capable of changing. But he had found a way to change, returning this key to me out of love. I would never leave this key, and I now sat with tears of regret.

I sent a telegram to Pŏmsik:

"Honey, please be well. Ch'ungguk and I are waiting for you at home – From Yŏngmi."

I finished the telegram, but I felt I was missing something. He didn't need to receive a telegram from the Yŏngmi of the past who knew nothing of love but rather from the Yŏngmi who had discovered true love and companionship. I erased "From" and wrote "Love, your wife" instead.

Even if you reject my love, just know that I will never let you go again!

The young woman at the post office smirked at my letter, but I didn't care. I just hoped that the letter would give him a little bit of strength.

What is needed in love? Everyone will have a different answer to this question. But personally, I would say that to have faith is enough.

<Epilogue>

Six months later, when I came home from work, Ch'ungguk handed me a telegram. As I was reading the letter, I began to cry. *Can this be true?* I could not contain my excitement, so I raced onto the street with the letter in my hand. I wanted to share the news with anyone who would listen.

I stood in the middle of the street and cried like a child. Several passersby gave me strange looks. Intrigued, a few people from the village came up to me, looking worried. One must have called my parents, because they soon came running. They were all looking at me in silence.

Can this be true? I had read the letter just a minute ago, but I still could not believe it. I read and read again, two times, three times, dozens of times. My pupils were still filled with emotion.

"I became a Party member! From Pŏmsik"

Just a few short words, yes, but of tremendous importance. I gripped the letter tightly.

I'm so proud of you, Pŏmsik! Thank you!

I buried my face in the telegram and soaked it with tears.

How hard my husband must have worked! I recalled my visit to him a couple of months earlier, when I took food that my parents had prepared made from an entire pig. I have never traveled so far in my life, and it had taken a toll on my frail body, but it was nothing compared to the way Pŏmsik had looked. I still remember seeing his legs. He was living on his bulldozer day and night, saying he had to make up for not doing anything for his country until now. Every night, when he felt tired, he would put toothpaste under his eyes. If he still felt sleepy, he would pinch his leg and pull on the flesh. And when that wasn't enough to keep him awake, he would pierce his leg with an awl.

I looked at his bruised legs and cried. In the past, he would come home, bruised from getting into fights. This always made me sad, but these bruises were different, like medals that my husband had earned.

As I cried, Ch'ungguk grabbed my dress and crawled into my arms.

"Mom, are you crying again?"

"I'm crying because I'm happy. Your father is a Party member!"

"What's a Party member? Is he as strong as a hero?"

"Yes, indeed! Your father is a hero."

"Hurray for dad!" Ch'ungguk shouted and raced over to his friends. I didn't have a chance to stop him; I did not want to stop him. He'd spent too much time, probably, feeling envious of other children holding their father's hand.

Ch'ungguk, boast of your father. Be proud and cheer with all your might. Cheer for me, as well!

CHAPTER 2

A DAY IN THE LIFE OF A
FEMALE MANAGER[1]

Kang Pongnye was born on July 29, 1932 in Sap'o, Hamhŭng city, South
Hamgyŏng Province. She attended the Pyongyang University of Literature
and graduated in 1960, making her literary debut that same year with her first
short story "Suyŏn."

Kang's writings are characterized by subtle yet persistent explorations
of gender dynamics in North Korean society. Often set in a military setting,
against the backdrop of war, her narratives are led by heroic female figures
whose actions challenge gender roles but also concomitantly seek to illustrate
traditional conceptions of femininity. In *On the Frontline Again* (*Tasi chŏnsŏn esŏ*,
1989), for instance, one of her most famous novels set during the Korean War,
she draws the portrait of a female medical officer unyielding amidst the dev-
astation of war and unafraid to stand up to her male superiors. Yet, through
her self-sacrifice and motherly devotion to the male soldiers she cares for, the
protagonist also comes to embody a number of traditional feminine virtues.
Likewise, novels such as *Female Warriors* (*Nyŏjonsadŭl*, 1982) or the short story
"On the Front Line" (*Chŏnsŏngil esŏ*, 1968) put women at the center of the battlefield, interlacing accounts of their military valor with descriptions of their

---

1 Kang Pongnye
  1992
  Translated by Immanuel Kim.

motherly care for the wounded. Kang nonetheless often ventures outside of the military repertoire, with short stories such as "The Construction Site's New Morning" (*Kŏnsŏljang ŭi sae ach'im*, 1976) about a conflict between conservative, pragmatic construction workers and their idealistic, impetuous younger colleagues or *A Distant Mountain Village* (*Mŏn sanch'onesŏ*, 1992), which depicts the desires of a younger generation of farmers to move to a metropolitan city.

"A Day in the Life of a Female Manager" is also outside of the author's genre of predilection, with its focus on the struggle of a North Korean woman who juggles between the contradictory expectations of her roles as a mother and a factory manager. Through the protagonist's two roles, the short story explores similar themes as Kang's military stories with the revolutionary femininity of a strong, professional woman in a position of leadership in a male-dominated environment on one hand and the traditional virtues of motherhood on the other. By highlighting the normativity inherent in these two different gender roles, Kang attempts to grapple with an issue that has long been central to North Korean society: the status of domestic labor.

Since the inception of the country in the 1940s, women have been mobilized as labor to alleviate the country's chronic labor shortage. Despite this, the extensive time and labor required for domestic responsibilities coupled with societal expectations casting these roles as part of the "social duty" of revolutionary socialist women (but not men) led to women's effective participation in the workforce remaining relatively low. It was not until the 1970s, with the advent of public childcare facilities, the introduction of processed foods, and the proliferation of domestic appliances, that the burden of domestic labor began to ease. This marked shift in domestic responsibilities facilitated a significant increase in women's participation in the labor force. Consequently, by the early 1990s, two-thirds of North Korean women had become engaged in waged work. Published in 1992, "A Day in the Life of a Female Manager" is set against the backdrop of this new large-scale entry of women in the workforce. By emphasizing the importance for women of finding meaning in their work beyond domestic confines, Kang crafts a critique of the traditional relegation of women to the domestic space. Yet the professional success of the story's protagonist did not free her from domestic chores which she still largely sees as a wife's duty. Kang's depiction of the emergence of the "double burden" in 1980s North Korea remains highly relevant today. As the males are legally obliged to work in state-owned factories for ever dwindling wages, more and more households have come to rely on income that "housewives" without an official, state-sanctioned job earn from trade and private sector work.

Full of passion and joy, workers rushed to the textile plant in the morning. At the intersection of Sanŏp district, young and lively men and women greeted each other, told jokes, and laughed.

The early morning sun painted the sky gold. The air was clear and brisk.

Sporting a thin, dark blue one-piece dress, Factory Manager Kim Myŏngok lowered her head and rushed past the group of workers. She was married with two children and the mornings were always the busiest time for her.

Her eldest daughter, Ŭnhŭi, who was in the fourth grade, was capable of getting to school by herself, but her youngest son, Kyŏngsu, had just started first grade in the fall and required constant supervision. He needed someone to help him put on his backpack and help him out the front door. Nagging to get him to school was a daily routine for Myŏngok.

There were also many things for her to do as the wife of a dean at the agriculture college. And so there was hardly a day that was not busy for her. On top of it all, Myŏngok, like other managers at her plant, was in charge of hundreds of textile machines and hundreds of employees. While there were smaller factories that created fibers and threads, every one of those factories existed to provide for the textile plant. This is because the goal of the textile plant was not to produce threads but fabric for the nation.

Myŏngok had worked as a weaver for twelve years at the textile plant. For five of those twelve years, she'd attended college and majored in light industry. In college, she got married and had two children. She continued to work at the textile plant after graduation. There was never a day that wasn't busy, but after she became a manager, she was swamped with work and bore the responsibility on her shoulders.

Her slim white face and rosy cheeks suggested a soft, kind woman, but she was not kind at all. Her thick dark hair and sharp eyes made her appearance more rigid, which was precisely her attitude at work. The head technician, production manager, and shift managers who worked closely with her knew her to be a strict manager, someone who would not forgive errors in systems management or production, someone who would not sympathize with others. Her attitude toward her family, on the other hand, was different from her workplace attitude, but she regretted spending so little time with them.

It was very much the same this morning. As she was cleaning the dishes in the kitchen after breakfast, her husband hollered from the other room.

"Honey, what did you do with my dress shirts?"

"I washed them and put them inside. Why?" Myŏngok called back.

Her husband rummaged through the dresser, and when he couldn't find them, he shouted in anger, "Where did you put them? Come and find them for me."

Myŏngok wiped her hands on her apron and went inside the room, mumbling under her breath.

"Why are you looking for them now?" she asked.

"Because I need them. Why else? There's a thesis presentation by the graduating class," the husband retorted.

Myŏngok found a dress shirt, but it needed to be ironed.

Frustrated, her husband said to her daughter, "Ŭnhŭi, plug in the iron."

As Myŏngok was about to head into the kitchen to get water for the iron, her husband stopped her.

"Honey, I know you're busy with work, but couldn't you have my clothes ready? Is that too much to ask?"

Myŏngok tried to hold her tongue, but she spoke out.

"It's partially my fault, but couldn't you have told me last night?"

Her husband lost his temper, "These things should've been done without my having to remind you!"

He yanked the iron's cord out of the socket, put on a wrinkled light gray dress shirt that he always wore, and then stormed out of the house.

Dumbfounded, Myŏngok sighed.

Should I resign as manager and ask to be transferred to a lower position? I can see why he's upset... He's been ironing his own shirts and cooking for himself. He's not a teacher anymore but a dean...But that doesn't mean that I have to quit.

Unable to sort out her scattered thoughts, Myŏngok rushed to the factory. But the image of her unkempt husband standing before a group of graduating students haunted her. She hated the thought of people pitying him and criticizing her for being a terrible wife.

Myŏngok went into her office to change into her work clothes and then left her office to inspect the factory. Hundreds of weaving machines produced a rhythmic sound, and the hard-working weavers and repairmen reflected the energy of the factory. Upon entering the factory floor, Myŏngok had forgotten about the unpleasant incident with her husband that morning. Her troubled thoughts and guilt for not having tended to her husband's needs were gone. Instead, she focused on her work and made her daily rounds through the large plant. She inspected every machine and kept a close watch over every weaver and repairman.

Mounds of fabric were piled on the carts from the night shift, and bundles of fabric were continuously being produced straight from the machines. The factory was experimenting with a new prototype, but machines 396, 421, and 522 were not running because their new frames had not yet arrived.

Myŏngok raced back to her office where the head technician and production manager were waiting for her. After exchanging their morning greeting, Myŏngok went behind her desk and asked, "Comrade head technician, I see that the new frames aren't here. Have you checked with the machine manufacturers?"

"Yes, they said that the new frames have not been produced yet," Yun Yŏngsŏp replied nervously. Yŏngsŏp had graduated from the light industry college in the fall and been hired by Myŏngok 's factory as a temporary technician. He'd only recently been promoted to the head technician position.

Myŏngok was clearly unsatisfied with Yŏngsŏp's answer.

"So, how long do we have to wait?"

Yŏngsŏp felt responsible for this matter and responded, "I will remind the manufacturers again... and tell them to hurry up."

Unknowingly, Myŏngok raised her voice.

"Do you think the manufacturers will feel any urgency to work faster? All you have are excuses. Comrade head technician, know this: the manufacturers and repairmen work for us. Our first priority is to produce fabric. There's no one else who feels this more urgently than we do. You know the saying, 'The thirsty digs a well.' *We* must be the ones running around and getting things done."

Yŏngsŏp could not respond, embarrassed over the matter.

Myŏngok lowered her voice and said, "Comrade head technician, we need to have the weaving machines operating as soon as possible so that we can get the prototypes out. I will look into the manufacturers, as well."

"I understand," Yŏngsŏp replied and left the office. Myŏngok let out a deep sigh with the expectation that the head technician would henceforth be more shrewd, determined, and diligent. She requested the output of yesterday's day shift from the productions manager and then picked up the phone to call the machine manufacturing company. The manager of the manufacturing company answered.

Myŏngok said, "Hello, I'm the manager of the textile plant. We were supposed to begin our prototype production this morning, but some of the frames have not arrived. That's why I'm calling."

The manager at the machine manufacturing company had been in charge since Myŏngok first began as a weaver. He replied curtly, "We know."

Myŏngok tried her best to remain calm.

"Comrade manager, when can we expect to see the new frames?"

"I'll send them over later in the afternoon."

Myŏngok became anxious. She raised her voice, "Comrade manager, do you have any idea how much we're behind because of one idle weaving machine?"

"I'll take responsibility for that."

Myŏngok snorted at the manager's apathetic response.

"Comrade manager, it's not about taking responsibility. If we're slow to produce, then our consumers will not have fabric," she said.

The manufacturing manager became indignant.

"You don't think I know that? There have been so many changes to the weaving machines that we can't keep up. Try to be more patient and wait."

"I can't, comrade manager, because our job is to produce fabric now. I will send over my head technician."

"Fine! We have five factories working overtime. Come and see for yourself," retorted the manager, letting out a deep sigh.

Myŏngok decided to address this issue to the manufacturing manager at the managers' meeting at ten o'clock and hung up the phone.

Just then, assistant managers came into the office for the daily meeting. Myŏngok received reports from one of her assistant managers, Cho Sŏngman, about the equipment operations, the production patterns, and shift work schedules. She narrowed in on the attendance record of one worker, Han T'ansil, who had been absent for two days.

"Comrade assistant manager, do you know why T'ansil was absent?"

"Her kid was sick, so she had to take him to the hospital," Cho Sŏngman replied stoically.

"What? What's wrong with her child?" Myŏngok asked impatiently.

"I don't know. Kids are often sick."

His response was as apathetic as his personality. Myŏngok wrote down "T'ansil hospitalized" in her daily planner so that she could visit the child. After she jotted the note, she raised her head and realized that Cho Sŏngman was waiting to say something.

"Comrade manager, what do you think about transferring women like T'ansil to the service department? They're absent when their children are sick, and when they do come to work, they leave early to pick up their children from daycare. Nothing gets done with them."

Myŏngok had been aware of how the assistant managers felt frustrated with women weavers, particularly the ones with children, and how productivity decreases with them. Nevertheless, she couldn't accept Cho Sŏngman's suggestion.

"Comrade assistant manager, you've got it all wrong. Many women get married, but if you transfer all these women to the service department just because they're married and have kids, then who will run the weaving machines? We're planning to put in more weaving machines, which means we will need more weavers."

"I've seen other factories do it," Cho Sŏngman retorted.

"I don't care if other factories do it; I will not. I think you should watch what you say about these women."

Myŏngok put her foot down and made sure the assistant managers never brought up this matter again. The morning shift assistant manager, who had recently been promoted, did not dare talk about this. But Cho Sŏngman could not hold it in and made a passing remark.

"Anyway, it looks like T'ansil will quit."

"What? How do you know that?" asked Myŏngok, shocked.

Cho Sŏngman mumbled, "That's what people have been saying."

Once the assistant managers left, Myŏngok fell into deep thought.

T'ansil is going to quit?

She was now even more determined to visit T'ansil in the hospital.

Just then, the phone rang and startled Myŏngok. It was regarding the ten o'clock meeting with the other managers. She hung up the phone and looked at the clock. She grabbed her daily planner and left the office.

The city bus from the Sanŏp district to the Taesŏng district was packed even during lunchtime. Myŏngok went home to have a quick bite and then went out to the Sanŏp district intersection. Though it was early summer, the weather was unbearably hot.

Myŏngok and the others at the intersection were all trying to avoid the sun by finding anywhere with a shade. At that moment, she realized that her dress was too dark and heavy for a hot day like this. The city bus pulled into the stop. Pressed up against others, she thought no more about her dress because she was occupied with thoughts of concern for T'ansil's son...and was it true that she was going to quit because of her son? Myŏngok was curious but also felt uneasy. T'ansil had been one of the best weavers in the factory even before she got married. Myŏngok was proud to have a skilled weaver like her.

Myŏngok walked through the hallway of the hospital, recognizing the unique smell of disinfectants. Returning from the hospital cafeteria, T'ansil, with her son in her arms, saw Myŏngok roaming in the hallway.

"Goodness! Comrade manager, what are you doing here? You must be so busy this time of day."

"Yes, but I had to come see you. Hi, Yŏng-ho, how are you feeling?"

Myŏngok held the infant's hand and spoke as if he understood every word
she was saying. Yŏngho was not quite a year old. He looked pale from being
sick, but he smiled with glee just as a healthy child would. Myŏngok smiled
back.

"You cute little boy, look at you smile," she said in a high-pitched tone. She
then turned to T'ansil and asked, "So, what's wrong with him?"

"He started having indigestion since the day before yesterday. Yesterday,
he had high fever, so I brought him to the hospital. After taking some medication, I think he feels much better now. We're ready to go home."

"You shouldn't rush home yet. You have to stay until the hospital says
you're fine to go."

They entered the warm and sunny patient's room. There were four beds.
Myŏngok held Yŏngho and sat by the T'ansil's bed.

"You scared your mommy, didn't you? Yes, you did, yes you did." Myŏngok
then turned to T'ansil and said, "All parents go through this with their first
child. Parents make a big deal of something so small."

T'ansil laughed and said, "You don't know how scared I was yesterday.
When I was told that Yŏngho had to be hospitalized, I panicked. But after
some medication, his fever went down in the morning, and no more diarrhea."

"It's because he's your first child. Anyway, he needs proper treatment,"
advised Myŏngok. T'ansil appeared relieved, but Myŏngok became solemn.

"Let me ask you something, T'ansil. I heard you wanted to quit."

T'ansil smiled awkwardly and remained silent. It was clear that this was a
difficult matter for her to discuss.

"My husband wants me to quit..."

"Your husband?" asked Myŏngok, surprised. She was hoping that it wasn't
true.

T'ansil turned her eyes away from Myŏngok.

"So, what are you planning to do? Are you going to quit because of what
your husband said?"

T'ansil sighed and mumbled, "I don't know what to do."

"You make over 400 meters of fabric. If you quit now, what are you going
to do at home? A mere housewife who's dependent on her husband? Our factory is excited about making this prototype fabric, but how can our best weaver
think about quitting? I'm going to have a word with your husband."

T'ansil cried, "Comrade manager, it's because I haven't been a good wife.
Because of that, we've been having fights over the smallest things...I feel so
bad."

Suddenly, Myŏngok recalled what had happened this morning with her husband. She, too, had thought of transferring to a lower division so that she could be at home more with her family. If she had had these thoughts, then who could blame T'ansil? Myŏngok lowered her voice, almost as if she were talking to herself rather than to T'ansil.

"T'ansil, I completely understand your situation. I, too, have had thoughts of quitting. But think, how rewarding can our lives be if we always choose to do easy work and look after our husbands? Think it over. I have to go now."

Myŏngok handed Yŏngho over to T'ansil and headed out the door. She felt as though there was more she wanted to say, but right now she couldn't think what. T'ansil did not respond.

T'ansil followed Myŏngok out of the room and said quietly, "Comrade manager, I cannot imagine myself away from the factory. If I quit, I would not be happy. I know that. But..."

T'ansil stopped abruptly and kept her mouth shut.

Myŏngok looked at T'ansil and asked, "Does your husband understand all this?"

"No, he never actually told me to quit altogether...He thought...just until Yŏngho gets a bit older..."

"What are your thoughts on that matter?"

T'ansil could not respond and lowered her head.

Everything became clearer to Myŏngok.

"T'ansil, you're thinking just like how other women in your situation think. It's a problem among women and not their husbands. If wives do a better job at housekeeping and raise their children well, what husband would demand his wife to quit her job and stay at home? As soon as we face the smallest problem, we think of quitting our jobs first. How sad is that? I've always thought of you as a strong woman."

T'ansil looked up and smiled.

"Comrade manager, don't worry too much. I'll think about what you said."

Also smiling now, Myŏngok said, "Please, think about it. I hope your son feels better."

Myŏngok walked to the bus stop, troubled. She knew how difficult it was for women to take care of their families, raise their children, and work at the textile factory. Even highly skilled women like T'ansil, who get married and have children, think about quitting...Women need to be more strong-willed, coupled with the support from their husbands. As revolutionary comrades, who are working alongside men for the nation and the people, women need to be understood and supported so that they can overcome any obstacles.

I have to make time to meet T'ansil's husband at the machine factory, thought Myŏngok.

When she returned to her office, the head technician and the production manager were working across from her desk. She changed into her work clothes and asked the head technician, "Anything new?"

"Machines 396 and 421 are in full operation. The new frame for 522 has just arrived."

"Good."

Myŏngok's response was pithy, but she was relieved at how quickly the head technician brought the frames for the weaving machines. Myŏngok headed out to the plant floor. Just like the head technician had said, machines 396 and 421 were producing the prototype fabric and machine 522 was soon underway.

Myŏngok made her rounds on the plant floor again. The weavers were working hard, and the repairmen were quick. The machines produced bundles of fabric, and the weavers piled them on the cart. She knew that if all the weavers worked this hard, then the projected goal could be met.

As Myŏngok was finishing her rounds, she stopped in front of a machine. The repairman, Kim Chŏngnam, and weaver, Hŏ Sŏnae, were arguing about something. Both were highly skilled workers. The loud sound of the machines made it difficult to hear what the two were saying, but it was clear from their facial expressions that they were engaged in some conflict.

Myŏngok approached them and shouted above the machine noise, "What's wrong?"

When the two saw their manager, they stopped arguing. Flustered, Hŏ Sŏnae returned to her weaving machine, leaving Kim Chŏngnam.

Myŏngok didn't think that discussing the matter on the factory floor was a good idea, so she grabbed him by the arm and said, "Let's talk in my office."

He followed her without a word. Even before Myŏngok could sit, Kim Chŏngnam requested that he be put in another shift.

"You want to work in another shift? Why?"

Myŏngok stared at him in confusion.

"Please just change my schedule. I can't work with her anymore," Chŏngnam replied determinedly.

"I would have to talk about this with the assistant manager...but why were you fighting with Sŏnae?"

"The weavers aren't supposed to just weave; they have to take care of the machines, as well. That's what we fought about."

"You're absolutely right. The weavers have to take care of the machines as if they owned them. Even so, you shouldn't fight with her. I will have a word with Sŏnae."

Just then, the morning shift assistant manager and the head technician entered the office. As soon as Chŏngnam saw his shift manager, he rushed out.

The assistant shift manager took no notice of Chŏngnam and asked the head technician about the detailed regulations of the technician proficiency exam for the repairmen. Myŏngok interrupted the men and called them over.

"Comrade assistant manager, I brought Chŏngnam into my office to talk about why he was fighting with Sŏnae, and now he wants his schedule changed. Do you know what's going on?"

The assistant manager nodded his head as if his suspicions had just been confirmed.

"Those two were lovers. But rumors have it Sŏnae's parents want her to get married to someone somewhere in Tŏkch'ŏn. Since then, the two have been fighting frequently."

"What? Sŏnae's getting married to someone in Tŏkch'ŏn?" asked Myŏngok. She didn't wait for an answer and asked another question, "Comrade assistant manager, is she really going to Tŏkch'ŏn to get married?"

"I'm not entirely sure."

"Send Sŏnae over here as soon as her shift is over."

The assistant manager agreed and left the office, but Myŏngok sat immersed in deep thought. *It takes at least five to six years to train a weaver like Sŏnae...Chŏngnam is a highly skilled, passionate comrade, who is attending technical college...why does she have to go to Tŏkch'ŏn to get married? I have to talk to Sŏnae.*

The time came for the morning shift to be replaced by the afternoon shift. There was only an hour to gather the output results from the morning shift and the output results for the entire day. As usual, the production manager started analyzing the results from the morning shift an hour before the two results needed to be combined.

The production manager returned to the office with a sense of anxiety.

"Comrade manager, the morning shift still needs to produce at least 300 meters of fabric, but I'm not sure if they can."

Myŏngok nodded. This was a common occurrence among the unskilled weavers who were not used to producing fabric with a new type of thread.

Nevertheless, Myŏngok could not just sit back and allow this to happen. For her, achieving goals were like pursuing Party-mindedness. No matter what happens, 300 meters of fabric needed to be produced within the next hour. Myŏngok stood up.

"Comrade head technician, go out there and find machines that have ten meters of thread left and attach them to thirty different machines. Let's hope that the thirty machines will be able to produce 300 meters of fabric in time. You look for machines in aisles 1 through 5, and I'll look in aisles 6 through 10."

The head technician stood up and left the office with Myŏngok. Soon, they found thirty machines and put competent repairmen to work on them. The head technician and Myŏngok did not leave the plant floor and assisted the weavers and repairmen.

The machines produced the remaining bundles of fabric well before the time was up. Myŏngok picked up the bundles and took them to the fitting shop. Time flew by, and the fabric continued to shoot from the machines. The head technician picked up the last bundles of fabric and carried them to the fitting shop, where he anxiously waited for the results from the production recorder.

"Comrade manager, we have 356 meters!"

Myŏngok let out a sigh of relief and looked at the head technician. "Good job, comrade."

Once the afternoon shift ended at five o'clock, the production manager gathered the factory's total output, recorded the data, and put the report on Myŏngok's desk.

Myŏngok glanced at the report and recorded any production problems in her daily planner to discuss in the managers' meeting. She was so focused that she didn't realize Hŏ Sŏnae had entered the office.

"Comrade manager, did you want to see me?"

Myŏngok looked up as soon as she heard Sŏnae's voice. She noticed how Sŏnae appeared slimmer and taller in her sky-blue two-piece suit, how she gave off an energetic vibe.

Only then did Myŏngok remember that yes, she had called for Sŏnae.

"Comrade Sŏnae, are you really going to Tŏkch'ŏn to get married?"

Sŏnae blushed at Myŏng-ok's direct question and then laughed at the absurdity of such thought.

"No. Comrade manager, I told my parents that I will not do that. Why would I leave my hometown to get married in Tŏkch'ŏn?"

"Then, why are you keeping your distance from comrade Chŏngnam? He's enthusiastic and a great comrade. And, in a couple of years, he will be a technician."

"Come now, comrade manager...I didn't do anything wrong. I wouldn't get angry without a reason. I got angry because he wouldn't take a look at the warning light on my machine."

Myŏngok felt relieved, as though rays of sunlight parted the dark clouds.

"So, comrade Chŏngnam was making a fuss over nothing! He even asked me to change his schedule..."

"What? He wanted to change his schedule? So ridiculous."

Sŏnae stopped smiling. Myŏngok noticed Sŏnae's solemn demeanor and said, "It's all right. I will meet with comrade Chŏngnam tomorrow. Everything's going to be fine. You must be tired. You can go now."

"I'm going to say something to him, too. I didn't know he was so petty," Sŏnae said, annoyed.

Myŏngok called her back and said, "Sŏnae, he's not being petty. When people are in love, there are all kinds of misunderstandings. Don't be too harsh when you talk to him— he's a good comrade."

Sŏnae laughed as if she had not been upset at all.

"Comrade manager, I know what you're saying."

Myŏngok felt relieved and smiled brightly.

The managers' meeting ended later than expected. Myŏngok left the meeting and rushed back to her office. She had to attend the wedding of Kim Sŏngch'ŏl's, a repairman at the factory. Moreover, he was the son of Tŏkbae, who worked in the raw materials department.

The year before, Kim Sŏngch'ŏl had been discharged from the army and dispatched to work as a repairman at Myŏngok's factory. He had been working for only half a year, but he showed great enthusiasm and diligence, capable of understanding his job better than most. He was beloved by others at the factory for being an earnest comrade.

Myŏngok walked into her office and saw that the production manager had been waiting for her.

"Comrade manager, they told me to tell you not to be late for the wedding. The assistant manager already left."

Myŏngok remembered that she had asked the production manager to pick up a wedding gift for Kim Sŏngch'ŏl.

"Comrade, what about the gift?"

"I picked one up from the factory gift shop."

The production manager pulled out a unique, handmade desktop clock from his iron container, along with a handicraft object that resembled Yi Toryŏng and Sŏng Ch'unhyang.[2]

---

2 These two characters are from the folktale called *The Tale of Ch'unhyang*, which is a story about a wife who remains faithful to her husband.

Myŏngok saw the gifts and was happy.

"The gifts look great! Let's wrap them up and go."

The head technician had to finish up some things left undone from the day shift, so Myŏngok and the production manager decided to go on ahead. The two left the factory with the wrapped wedding gift.

It was a clear night with a large full moon, but the streetlights and illumination from the tall apartment buildings overpowered the moon.

The two rushed past the factory dormitory and approached the Sanŏp intersection.

Myŏngok stopped in her tracks at the thought of preparing a quick dinner for her children.

"Comrade, take this and go on ahead. I'm going to make noodles for my kids. I'll see you there."

Myŏngok hurried home. She ran up three flights of stairs, opened the door and called out, "Ŭnhŭi!"

"Yes, mom?"

The eleven-year-old child stuck her head out from the kitchen and greeted her mother. She was holding a knife. Myŏngok was surprised and asked, "Ŭnhŭi, what are you doing?"

"I'm cutting green onions," she replied with a sense of pride.

"You're doing what?"

"Dad told me to try it."

"Is he here?"

"Yeah, he's helping Kyŏngsu wash up."

Myŏngok thought it was strange for her husband to come home so early. She recalled the incident in the morning and felt guilty. She peered inside the room and saw the children's backpack and sketchbook strewn across the floor. She threw her shoes off and rushed to tidy up the house.

At the factory, Myŏngok supervised hundreds of workers and oversaw the production of tens of thousands of meters of fabric every day, but at home, she was a housewife and a mother.

After tidying up the room, she opened the door to the bathroom and saw her husband washing their son's face. As soon as Kyŏngsu saw his mother, he boasted, "Mom, I beat Ch'ŏlnam."

"Hold still, let's finish washing your face first," said her husband.

Myŏngok asked, "How did you come home so early?"

"It's not unusual," he replied, and then he stopped her from coming inside the bathroom. "Don't come in. Tŏkbae's father stopped by just now worried that you weren't going to the wedding."

"I was on my way, but I wanted to prepare dinner for the kids."

"Ŭnhŭi bought some noodles. She can do things like this now. She's quite good at it."

"Really? That's good."

Myŏngok was pleased. She went into the kitchen, portioned out the noodles, and made the broth.

Her husband and Kyŏngsu came out of the bathroom.

"Honey, you have to go now. He really wants you to be there. Leave the housework to us."

Her husband's words were a reminder of the importance of her being a manager, but they were also a reminder of how he was willing to lessen her burden of the housework.

Myŏngok gleefully went into her room and changed into a dark green traditional dress.

As she walked out of the house, she felt grateful for her husband's sincere efforts to help her with the household chores. She realized that she'd been able to work as a manager for the past six years because of help and support from her husband. At times, he would get upset and be frustrated with her, but not because he was that kind of person. He was always concerned about her role as a manager and truly hoped that there wouldn't be any problems with either production or her relationship with others.

She realized that her frustration with her husband this morning was her own limited understanding of him and a feeble-minded attitude toward him. She believed that T'ansil's husband, too, was more than capable of understanding and supporting T'ansil.

The wedding was taking place nearby her home, on the second floor of the factory housing complex.

As Myŏngok entered the premises, she could hear the cheerful voices of inebriated guests. From the kitchen window, Sŏngch'ŏl's mother spotted Myŏngok and said, "You're finally here. Hey, Sŏngch'ŏl, your manager is here!"

Sŏngch'ŏl's father, Tŏkbae, rushed out to greet Myŏngok. The elderly man with many wrinkles smiled brightly.

"I was afraid you weren't going to come, but you're here!"

"Elder Tŏkbae, you look so happy. Congratulations."

Myŏngok bowed to the elder. Tŏkbae was overcome with emotions and he grabbed Myŏngok's hand.

"I know you're busy, but thank you for coming."

At that moment, Sŏngch'ŏl came out to greet Myŏngok. He looked taller and more handsome in his wedding suit.

"Comrade manager, you made it. Thank you for coming."

Myŏngok congratulated Sŏngch'ŏl and was dragged into the house by Tŏkbae. Inside the large house, there were guests sitting around the tables. The guests were all the workers from the factory.

Among the guests were Kim Chŏngnam and Hŏ Sŏnae, sitting next to each other. The same couple that had been fighting earlier in the afternoon. It occurred to Myŏngok that there was no longer any need to meet with Kim Chŏngnam.

On the tables, there were all kinds of delicious foods, soft drinks, and alcohol. The cheerful guests greeted Myŏngok as she entered the room.

After Myŏngok exchanged greetings with the guests, Tŏkbae led her to a table near the bride and groom where elders from the raw materials department were seated.

Myŏngok took her seat and admired the bride and groom. The bride looked beautiful in her golden traditional dress, and Sŏngch'ŏl looked particularly handsome and stately. Myŏngok turned to the guests and said, "Everyone, let's raise our glasses to the bride and groom. Cheers!"

The guests cheered for them and raised their glasses.

Myŏngok then poured wine into Tŏkbae's glass and congratulated him again. He gladly drank the wine and poured a glass for her.

"Manager, allow me to pour you a glass. I don't know if you remember, but when you were a schoolgirl, you used to come to the factory to look for your mom. I used to scold you by saying, 'Myŏngok, why have you come to the factory again? Go home.' And now, you have become the head manager, the pillar of the factory. Manager, please accept this drink from the man who used to scold you."

Tŏkbae became emotional as he recalled those days.

Myŏngok rose from her seat and raised her glass, "Elder Tŏkbae, thank you." Her voice was emotional, as well. "Sir, I do remember. You were the manager then, and you used to scold me. But you also used to help me with my homework and encourage me to do well in school. I will never forget those days."

Myŏngok looked to the bride and groom and the other young guests, who were engaged in their own conversation.

"Comrades, I would like to say something to the bride and groom and all the young guests here tonight. You must know and never forget who elder

Tŏkbae is and the other elders from the raw materials department. During the Korean War, they built air-raid shelters in the deep mountains and made military uniforms. Then, they erected the textile factory through hard work from the ashes of the war and turned the factory into what it is today. They are the true pillars of the factory, serving as managers, assistant managers, innovators, and highly skilled workers. We must respect them and never forget them. We must push the factory forward and find ways to develop it. We have to realize the honor and recognize the responsibility of producing fabric for our people, and let's continue to create better fabric."

Myŏngok was caught up in the moment as she gave the emotional speech, and the guests could not help but agree with her. The young workers stopped talking and listened to her, and the elders nodded their heads in agreement, reflecting upon the earlier days of their difficult but fruitful lives.

As soon as Myŏngok sat, an accordion player from the factory recreation center arrived. People both young and old were excited—dancing and singing along with the accordion music. They sang old songs, cheerful songs, and inspirational songs that gave them hope for tomorrow.

People were having so much fun that they didn't realize how late it had become. At last, the guests decided to go home and left elder Tŏkbae's house with joy.

Myŏngok joined the workers, who were walking back to their factory dormitory. They complimented her for giving a great speech, and they were surprised to hear her sing. Myŏngok joked with them, laughed with them, and talked with them the entire way.

Once they got to the street corner, Myŏngok bid farewell to the workers and found herself walking alone in the tranquil evening. She was exhausted from working all day, but invigorated by the wedding and overjoyed from walking with her workers.

She thought over the day's events. Yes, it had been a busy day. Well, every day was busy for her, what with having to supervise hundreds of workers and oversee tens of thousands of meters of fabric; there was never a day that went by that wasn't busy.

Yesterday had been as busy, and tomorrow would be as busy as today, and also the day after. However, amid this busy life, it was also rewarding and meaningful. If she were to take on a less stressful position, of a follower rather than a leader, then she would not enjoy her life and would find it meaningless.

She felt a sudden rush of excitement and picked up her pace. Her neighborhood was quiet and dark as the residents had gone to sleep, except for one
window on the third floor, her home. Perhaps her husband was reviewing his
lecture notes or reading a book. Whichever it was, Myŏngok was thankful that
he'd stayed up for her.

CHAPTER 3

FACE[1]

Kim Myŏngjin was born on August 25, 1942 in the township Ku, Kosŏng city, Kangwŏn Province. After graduating from high school, he enlisted in the Korean People's Army in 1960. While serving as a logistics officer, Kim regularly wrote and managed to publish several short stories in literary journals and newspapers. He eventually became a full time, professional author and joined the Writers Union of Chagan Province in 1978.

"Face" tells the life trajectories of two childhood friends interested in architecture – a gentle, sensitive boy nicknamed the "bride" and his assertive, handsome companion, nicknamed the "groom". The two friends eventually have a falling out over different visions of architectural composition, and go their separate ways. The "groom" becomes a successful architect, and the "bride" becomes a geologist. The "groom" is among the few who are commissioned to build a recreational center, but his blueprints are rejected by the city council for their lack of vision. The council decides on the blueprints of a young female architect. The young architect is revealed to be the daughter of "bride" who drew her blueprints with her father's help.

"Face" follows a prototypical narrative structure in North Korean stories that depict an experienced and confident character's opposition to a novel or revolutionary method which they eventually come to embrace. This trope is of

---

1 Kim Myŏngjin
   2009
   Translated by Immanuel Kim.

course reminiscent of what Katerina Clark dubbed the "master plot" of social-ist realism, in which a young ambitious worker eager to raise productivity by introducing new methods has to overcome the inertia of skeptical colleagues. Yet while Soviet socialist realism emphasized the dialectic between the hero's spontaneity and the consciousness of an older mentor who helps channel revo-lutionary fervor, North Korean narratives, as noted by Brian Myers, tend to emphasize spontaneity over consciousness. Common in production novels, this literary device became a staple of hidden hero stories where the unorthodox, unknown, and yet effective methods of the hero is scrutinized and challenged by an authority figure such as a manager or a Party official.

"Face" offers a variation on this classic theme, depicting how, through pas-sion and dedication, an amateur manages to surpass an established expert. Moreover, the story offers insights into class differences and social distinction, camaraderie, and appearances in the DPRK.

My son got a girlfriend. I'd thought he was too busy to date because he seemed so intensely focused on his job at the Provincial Department of Art Production, where he had been working since graduating from art school. But I eventually learned that he had been dating this girl... I suppose he is of that age now.

It hadn't been long since I found out about her. My son, Myŏngsu, had been working in Sŏjung district for over a month when I found a drawing of a woman among some of the sketches he brought back from work. Round, plump face, eyelashes that looked like a crescent moon, lustrous eyes, a slightly rounded nose, slender lips. I don't know if it was because of the beauty of her face, but somehow the woman looked very familiar.

"Who is this?" I asked.

Myŏngsu blushed and averted his eyes.

"Uh...I met her at Sŏjung district," he replied.

It was pretty obvious that he had fallen for this girl. He had never seemed interested in dating when he was in college or even after graduating. For him to have drawn her picture meant he must have really liked her. But I could see why he was attracted to her. Her face exuded charm and intelligence. In any case, the woman had clearly already captured my son's heart so there was no reason for me to disapprove of their relationship.

"Why don't you invite her over one day?" I suggested, smiling.

About two weeks later, Myŏngsu brought her to our house. I looked at her face as she lowered her head and bowed to greet me. She seemed a bit shy, with rosy cheeks. She looked exactly like the drawing, but there was also something about her that was all too familiar. I couldn't help but stare.

"What's your name, dear?" I asked.

"Sin Chŏnghŭi."

"And what do you do for a living?" I continued.

"I teach at the Sŏjung Architecture Academy."

Her voice was clear and strong. She said that she had come to the city with the train early this morning since she had some things to do at the educational training center.

"I see...," I replied, rubbing my chin and feeling satisfied.

I couldn't find any fault in her: she was beautiful, well-mannered, and had a good job. I might be a bit biased toward her because I worked my whole life as an architect and city planner, and her being a teacher of architecture created an affinity with her. I was happy at the prospect of gaining a daughter-in-law.

"Please, have a seat here," I said.

I already felt like Chŏnghŭi was part of the family. I asked her about her age, where she was from, and which university she attended. I nodded as she told me that she was twenty-eight years old, born in Sŏjung district, and had graduated from Pyongyang University of Architecture.

My wife brought some fruit for us to eat, and she too seemed to be pleased with Chŏnghŭi. I felt the same way. I was overjoyed at the way Chŏnghŭi brightened up our home. I offered Chŏnghŭi a slice of pear and asked, "What does your father do?"

"He works for the Sŏjung Geological Research Center."

"And what's his name?" I asked.

"Sin Hyŏngyu."

"Sin Hyŏngyu...Sin Hyŏngyu..." I muttered.

I'd heard that name before. But where? I couldn't remember. There are so many people with similar names that there was no way I could remember all of them. As I continued my conversation with her, that name stuck in my mind.

After Chŏnghŭi left, I sat in front of my desk and looked at blueprints. But for some reason, I couldn't focus on my work and kept thinking about that name. *Sin Hyŏngyu.*

I shook my head as if trying to shake off these useless thoughts, but just as I was about to take out some reference documents, it came back to me like a flash of light. I froze, startled.

Sin Hyŏngyu! That's right. His name was Sin Hyŏngyu, I thought.

I was so excited, my heart pounded in my chest.

Does that mean Chŏnghŭi is Sin Hyŏngyu's daughter?

Life is full of coincidences, but I had never imagined meeting Sin Hyŏngyu's daughter like this. I sat in my armchair and began to reminisce.

Forty years ago, when I was in high school, I had a comrade by the name of Sin Hyŏngyu. He had crescent moon eyelashes and a light complexion. His personality was gentle, and he would blush at the slightest comments, inspiring us to call him "bride." The nickname suited him perfectly. Sin Hyŏngyu and I spent a lot of time together, and so the other students nicknamed me "groom." It's true that I was virile and knew how to use my fists, but more than that it was because I always protected my "bride" when he was in trouble.

Hyŏngyu 's house was right next to mine, so we hung out all the time. We came to share a strong connection because we understood each other. We were full of dreams back then and would often talk about our aspirations for the future. Surprisingly, he and I shared the same dreams.

Was there a better job than being an architect? Everyone has to leave their mark on this world. Was there anything more glorious, anything more meaningful than to leave behind on this planet something you'd created? I planned to become the world's best architect by working hard and studying diligently. Hyŏngyu and I both shared this ambition. We studied together and helped each other in order to one day achieve our shared goal.

From that point on, "bride" and "groom" always stuck together. Wherever the bride was, so was the groom.

When the school day ended, we'd race to the library and read up on books related to architecture and blueprints. We talked day and night about different designs and styles. Every day our dreams of becoming architects grew.

One day we decided to apply what we had learned to the task of remodeling our school. I came up with the idea, of course, but Hyŏngyu was wholly supportive.

The plan was to redesign all of the classrooms, offices for teachers and staff, the gym, labs, and the cafeteria. We were only students, but we wanted to surprise our teachers with our design ideas so that one day if the school board decided to renovate the school, it could take our design into consideration. This would be a dream come true for us.

We got to work immediately. First, we studied the school grounds carefully. Then we unrolled the blueprints and talked about the changes until the wee hours of the night.

I began to realize, though, that we disagreed more often than we agreed. Anything he suggested, I would reject and vice versa. With every line I drew, I could feel Hyŏngyu 's disapproval. This was an unexpected development, because I had thought we shared the same dreams, read the same books, and held the same beliefs. At this rate, there was no way we would ever finish this new design for our school.

"Let's do this instead," I suggested, "You draw your design and I draw mine. Later, we can pick and choose the best ideas from each of our designs."

Hyŏngyu agreed.

I completed my blueprint over the weekend. I was gratified by my own designs. But even after two weeks Hyŏngyu had not finished his.

"Hey, what's taking so long?" I asked him.

Every time I confronted him about this matter, he would mutter some excuse, "Just give me more time." But this excuse went on for days. I was frustrated. I realized that I could not work with such a "bride." He was too sensitive and meticulous, not decisive enough. I'd been foolish to think that I could work with him, and I could hardly suppress my frustration.

After a whole month, Hyŏngyu finally showed me his design. I was completely disappointed. It looked nothing like mine. First of all, the classroom sizes were different. My classrooms were huge and bold, but his were small and cute looking. Offices for teachers and staff, the gym, and cafeteria...everything was off from mine.

"Why did you draw the gym like this? And if you put the offices here, what's that going to do?" I asked.

I commented on—and complained about—everything he drew. I couldn't believe that this was drawn by the same person I shared my dreams with. It seemed like he was an entirely different person from the person I had known.

Flushed, Hyŏngyu listened to everything I said and responded, "You think you're so good? Why do you look down on others?"

He was being defensive and not willing to listen to my advice.

I stormed out and shouted, "Hey, you're the bride, so you should just listen to what I say and not talk so much!"

"*What* did you say? Who do you think you are?" Hyŏngyu retorted.

We were on the verge of fighting. Neither of us wanted to back down. In the end, we never completed the design for our school. Our dreams and aspirations drifted away.

I realized then and there that we were different—different personalities, different ideas, and different behavior. Why hadn't I detected this earlier? We might have had similar dreams, but we couldn't work together. His girlish demeanor disappeared. He no longer looked like the sensitive, soft kid who couldn't assert himself. From that day forth, we were no longer "bride" and "groom."

After graduating from high school, I went to architecture college and Hyŏngyu joined the military. I was so furious with him that I had no desire to write him letters. He faded from my memory.

After college, I landed a job at the Department of City Planning. My dreams came true: I designed many plans for the city including movie theaters, a playground for children, various institutional buildings, and even residential houses. People complimented me everywhere I went.

They would say, "His buildings are as handsome as he is."

Every time I looked at my designs, I felt proud of myself and deeply satisfied. I was finally leaving my mark on this world.

I advanced in my career, becoming the manager of my department after a few years and then the supervisor of the entire company. People envied me, and I was very proud of myself. It had taken me thirty years to achieve this, always going forward, never deviating. It wasn't easy to reach my position, to succeed as I had.

On the other hand, what about Hyŏngyu? Things didn't work out for him. I heard from comrades that after serving in the military, he landed a job at a geological research center, a field completely different from architecture. He raised his family in Sŏjung district, working a job that required him to be on the road all the time.

When I heard the news about Hyŏngyu, I felt bad for him. He'd buried his youthful dreams. If only he had followed the same path I had! No, even then, he still wouldn't have succeeded. Those designs of his from high school were certainly not going to help him get ahead. Realizing this had probably led to him switching to geological research. My sympathy and pity for Hyŏngyu slowly faded away.

Our paths did cross once, a few days after I was appointed as the chief of my company. I was walking along the riverbank in Sŏjung district. I had just finished a meeting with the local workers and decided to take a stroll. At that moment, I noticed someone was staring at me and heading toward me. His face was ghostly white.

"Hey, aren't you Comrade Myŏngguk?" he asked.

He grabbed my hand and shook it with excitement. I was taken aback. Round face, light complexion...It was Hyŏngyu!

"How long has it been? I heard that you lived in this area, but I never expected to see you here like this," I responded.

Time had left my former "bride" unrecognizable. His shoulders were broader, and his body stronger looking. He was carrying a heavy backpack. It was so heavy that the straps dug into his shoulders. I noticed his disheveled appearance and his shoes, worn out from trekking through dangerous mountainous paths.

"Anyway, what do you have in your backpack?" I asked.

"Oh, these? These are samples of ore. I got this from Mount Ch'ŏnma and need to analyze them," he replied, pulling his backpack up and chuckling.

For an instant, as he blushed, he looked just like he used to back when students called him "bride."

Hyŏngyu said, "I heard that you got promoted to supervisor of the Department of City Planning. I was so happy for you. Congratulations, truly."

It was a bit awkward for me to receive this kind of compliment from Hyŏngyu. I felt like I was the only one of the two of us who'd succeeded in life, and so I tried to be humble.

"Well, there's nothing wrong about being a geological researcher—it's an important job. You must have found plenty of new veins," I said.

I didn't want Hyŏngyu to feel ashamed of himself. It must not be easy to look up and see someone else on top of the mountain of success.

Hyŏngyu replied, "While people like you build up from the earth, people like me dig the earth. It's not easy searching for jewels buried underground."

For some reason, I felt a bit empty as Hyŏngyu chuckled and said these words. He was right. There is no easy job. I simply wished that he would be the best at his job and become successful one day.

Hyŏngyu apologized for holding me up like this without offering any hospitality. He grabbed my hand and said, "Let's go to my place. It's not far from here."

I begged off, telling him that I was busy at the moment but promising to stop by some other time. And with that, I left.

I forgot about the promise, and after many years the memory of Sin Hyŏngyu had faded away.

But what a surprise it was to now see his daughter at my home, and with the prospect of her becoming my daughter-in-law. Life somehow finds a way to surprise us.

A few days later...

I got dressed in front of the mirror in the morning before heading out to work. I combed my hair with mousse and sprayed on some cologne. It had been my morning routine for as long as I could remember. Perhaps it was this kind of care and attention to myself that helped me to look youthful, even now that I was nearing sixty. People had told me that I looked seven or eight years younger than I really was, something I didn't mind hearing.

I smiled with satisfaction. It was the smile of a man who had accomplished something significant: I had been working on a design for the past several months, and it was finally going to be complete.

It was a redevelopment of the streets in Sŏjung district. The town had built a huge factory not too long ago and the population consequently increased. So, there was a lot of work to be done. I decided to take on the project, having already done several similar projects in the past, and thinking that this past experience would make the job an easy one. The city planning was being done at a rapid pace.

However, as I was about to complete the city design, something unexpected happened. Someone from Sŏjung district had put together a few designs, which the officials from the province asked me to take a look at.

What was going on? I was nearly done with the city planning and now the town wanted to look into somebody else's designs. It might have been a coincidence, but something didn't seem right. I didn't know who had made these designs, but this person must not have known that I was already doing the city planning. Whoever it was, coming from a small town like this, the designs were probably just going to be very amateurish, I thought.

I figured I would just go down to the city planning office later when I had the time and sort things out with them. But actually, busy as I was, I soon forgot about it entirely.

Then came the deadline to submit the new city plan. I had been going over my plans for the past couple of days, and I felt that they were fine for a small town.

I remembered the compliment that I heard in the past: "His buildings are as handsome as he is." I expected to hear those compliments again.

Instead, I suffered a bitter and unanticipated blow to my plans. That night, something dramatic happened. My plans were rejected by the town council. The reason given? My plans were too similar to the ones used in another town. They claimed that my ideas were not creative and that I was only aping existing work.

I hung my head. I had been over-confident in my work, thinking that I would be the envy of the city. But instead, I'd ended up receiving this kind of criticism...

After that day, I could not bring myself to smile. Depressed, I endeavored to engage in some self-reflection.

A city planner's first set of designs is always done carefully and with much creativity. There is research involved, passion, and a lot of effort. You must set high standards for yourself in order to receive compliments such as "talented architect" or "someone with a bright future." But these compliments might go to your head to the point where you think you are the best, and that's when you stop working as hard and become lazy. In reality, you are left behind as the world progresses.

I reexamined the designs for Sŏjung district carefully. I was shocked. There were errors everywhere. What the council had criticized—the lack of creativity and the reuse of existing designs—was evident. I could not believe how complacent I had become. I had spent time primping my face in the mirror every morning, but I hadn't given the same attention to my heart.

I set the blueprints aside and fell into deep thought. I didn't have the confidence to restart the design. Would a revolutionary project, in line with the needs of this new century, ever materialize in that old, rigid head of mine?

It was at that moment that I remembered that some designs had been submitted to Sŏjung district. While I hadn't given them much thought before, now I would have to consider them again. Who would have guessed that my plans would be rejected? What an unusual turn of events.

But I wasn't certain that those other plans were any good either. I would have to take a look at them before passing any judgment. It was nonetheless strange that the town council had decided to accept these design plans rather than rely on a professional company. In any case, I was uneasy about all this.

Anyway, I hopped on a train and went down to Sŏjung district.

It was a beautiful autumn day. Outside the window, there were trees changing color and fields turning golden. I opened the window and could smell the fragrance of ripe fruit. It was the type of landscape that filled with joy the heart of anyone who looked at it.

As we approached Sŏjung district, I was uneasy again. I wondered what the designs looked like and who had made them. For the council to reject my proposal and accept the one from one of the town's own citizens meant that this person must have at least a modicum of talent. Many thoughts filled my mind.

I then also remembered that Sin Hyŏngyu lived in Sŏjung district, and that not too long ago I had met his daughter Sin Chŏnghŭi, who graduated from Pyongyang University of Architecture. And there was also the need to get the wedding prepared... So many thoughts weighed heavy on my mind.

The train arrived in Sŏjung district. The Vice Chairman of the Army Committee greeted me at the station and escorted me to his office, a large room on the second floor.

"Please, have a seat," he said.

"Actually, I would like to see the designs immediately," I said, unable to contain my impatience.

The Vice Chairman pulled out a thick stack of blueprints and placed them on the table. There were designs for wide streets lined with distinct buildings of all shapes and sizes, and plans for a town cultural center, student association center, volunteer centers, residential houses, and many more.

At first, I merely skimmed through the plans, but I couldn't deny the fact that these designs were innovative and had a distinct character. Each building was unique and different from the others, while maintaining a cohesion of style and patterns. The construction materials were locally sourced. What was interesting was how the architecture of every building was adapted to the geographic location of the district. For instance, the roofs were designed specifically to handle the rain and snow.

But the most pleasing part of the plans was the student association center. It was designed to reflect the bright and cheerful attitude of the children and was a tall building that reached the sky. The architecture alone seemed inviting; it was a building that would speak to children.

The Vice Chairman looked at me with much anticipation and asked, "So, what do you think?"

"It's nice" I replied.

I responded robotically, trying to contain my excitement. I quickly paced around the office. I hadn't expected to see such extraordinary designs. It was as if a miracle had happened. I couldn't believe that such ideas had come from this remote mountainous town.

"Who drew these?" I asked.

"A teacher from the architecture college, Sin Chŏnghŭi. She's a young teacher," the Vice Chairman said, pouring me a glass of water.

"Did you say Sin Chŏnghŭi?"

Upon hearing the name, I froze. I recalled her soft voice, but it felt as if she were calling out to me now with a thunderous cry. The Vice Chairman noticed my shocked expression.

"Do you know her?" he asked.

"Uh, right, that is...."

I blushed and stuttered a vague response. I didn't know what to say.

"Would you like to meet her?" he asked.

He looked at me as if he were trying to read my mind.

So, Sin Chŏnghŭi is the one who designed this. She has accomplished something that her father couldn't. I wanted to meet her and congratulate her. I also wanted to ask how she came up with these designs.

"Yes, I would like to see her," I replied excitedly.

"Great. I've already called her."

The Vice Chairman left the room. I heard footsteps in the hall and knew it was Sin Chŏnghŭi.

Someone quietly knocked on the door before entering. Chŏnghŭi had rosy cheeks, and hair that fell along her face.

"How are you?" she asked.

She brushed her hair away from her face as she greeted me. She looked beautiful and vibrant. I rose and shook her hand.

"It's so nice to see you again," I said.

Chŏnghŭi blushed.

"Comrade Chŏnghŭi, I just saw your designs. They look incredible."

I wanted to suppress my excitement, so I took a long pause.

"When you came to my house last week, why didn't you say anything about these designs?" I asked.

"Oh that...well...I didn't want to bring this up in our first meeting," she replied.

"I didn't know you had this kind of talent."

"I'm not sure if I'm qualified yet to receive that kind of compliment," Chŏnghŭi said, blushing. "The credit should really be given to my father."

"Your father?" I asked, shocked.

I'd thought the ideas were Chŏnghŭi's, but they were actually Sin Hyŏngyu's. The same man whose designs I'd found disappointing back in high school, the same man I had forgotten over these years, the same man who works for the geological research center, the man who I thought had given up on architectural designs. It was both unexpected and unbelievable. But it was the truth. Chŏnghŭi was sitting in front of me with the blueprints spread across the desk.

"Comrade Chŏnghŭi, could you tell me more about your father?" I asked.

I sat across from her and gazed at her face, recognizing the face of my dear old friend.

"There isn't much to say," she said with her head lowered.

I insisted one more time, and then she proceeded to talk:

"I thought I knew my father well...his dreams, aspirations, and the things he loved. I always thought that his entire life revolved around his geological research. When I graduated from middle school, I realized that he had had other dreams. I didn't know what I wanted to be. I thought about being a dancer or a researcher.

One day, my father approached me and told me, 'I would like you to be an architect. This used to be my dream. But, after military service, I was placed in the geological research center because they needed people there. Thereafter, I committed to this work and found meaning in it.'

As a geologist, my father found important minerals that our country needed and brought joy to the Party. Our nation awarded him for his distinguished service."

I was deeply moved. I had thought that Hyŏngyu simply toiled up in the mountains; I never imagined that he did such great work for our country. I'd thought that I was standing high on the mountain of success and could look down on him. But now I realized that he had been standing on a higher ground than me all along.

Chŏnghŭi continued, "But it seemed like my father had some unfinished business. He would often sit at his desk and draw something. I finally realized what he had been drawing.

"He said, 'Whenever I walk the streets of this small town, I wish there were nice modern buildings. It's important to take care of your own town. Doing so is a great service to the country. Of course, our town is a bit different from other towns because it's in the mountains. But we can't sit around and expect the country to do everything for us. That's why I've been drawing these designs.'

"My father diligently drew those designs and came up with a great plan for this town. I didn't understand the technicalities of the blueprints at the time, but I understood his heart. He loves this town and wanted to make it look like other modern towns. That's how his dream became my dream, and that's how I went to architecture college. I finished what my father had started."

I was overcome with emotion. I never knew Sin Hyŏngyu was this passionate.

Chŏnghŭi checked the time on her watch and stood up.

"I..."

"Do you have to be somewhere?" I asked.

"I have a class now."

"Ah yes, go teach."

I felt an emptiness inside. I wanted to hear more about Chŏnghŭi and her father...

"I'll see you later," Chŏnghŭi said and bowed.

As I walked her out of the office, we agreed to meet again the next day.

I reexamined the blueprints in the office. I wanted to make sure I saw the correct plans. I might have been too excited at first. I needed to scrutinize these closely to confirm my assessment. Student association center, cultural center, residential houses...

The more I examined these plans, the more excited I became. I hadn't made a mistake earlier. My instincts were correct: these were good designs, and the more I looked at them, the more new things I discovered. I recognized the value of these designs, which made me want to know more about Sin Chŏnghŭi and her father Sin Hyŏngyu.

The next couple of days were going to be busy. I would have to meet with the town council members and Party members to go over Sin Hyŏngyu's designs and blueprints.

It was evening. I sat in the office alone, deep in thought. I needed to compose myself from the excitement I'd felt over the past couple of days.

The passing of time had made me forget an old friend. I used to look down from the mountain of my success and see Sin Hyŏngyu, but I had come to a point where I would have to see him eye to eye. The thought of it made me feel ashamed of myself. His passion-filled designs that reflected the modern generation forced me to take a good look at myself. I realized that I had become lazy and old-fashioned. On the outside, my face may have been clean, but on the inside I was rotten. I had not kept up with the times. And now I needed to set aside my designs and support Hyŏngyu and Chŏnghŭi's innovative plans. I needed to turn my life around. I had always judged people based on my standards, but from now on, I would judge myself based on the demands of the era.

Chŏnghŭi said she would come by in the evening.

I looked out the window as the sun set. I wanted to hear the rest of the story from Chŏnghŭi.

I heard a knock at the door.

She's here!

I turned to the door and said, "Come in, please."

The person who came in was none other than my son, Myŏngsu.

"What brings you here," I asked.

"I came down here to paint more landscapes," he replied, smiling.

"Is that so? Don't you have to see Chŏnghŭi?"

"I was just with her."

Myŏngsu's face turned red. Perhaps it was because he went to see his girlfriend before coming to see his father. I didn't want him to feel bad, so I showed him the blueprints that Chŏnghŭi had designed and told him about our meeting.

"Chŏnghŭi is good, but her father is also very talented," I said. "I'm so glad to have seen these blueprints, but I'm more pleased to have met great people in this town."

I was speaking my mind freely. Myŏngsu was listening intently and said, "I heard something from comrade Chŏnghŭi...do you want to hear it?"

"Sure," I said, nodding.

Myŏngsu shifted his position in his seat and proceeded to speak.

"After Chŏnghŭi graduated from architecture college and got a job as a teacher, her father was more excited than anyone else. He felt that she would be able to complete the designs that he had started. He spent most of his time in the mountains, but whenever he would return, he would look at Chŏnghŭi's designs and help her with them. He reminded her to be mindful of the town's geographical location and apply the latest technological skills that she'd learned from college. He guided her nearly every step of the way. Whenever she felt defeated, he would reprimand her and encourage her to continue. There was this one time when the two were designing the student association center..."

After many drafts, Chŏnghŭi showed her father the designs.

What's he going to think of them?

Hyŏnggyu put on his glasses and examined the designs. Without a word, he lit a cigarette. Chŏnghŭi was nervous because her father hadn't said a word yet.

"What were you thinking as you drew up these designs?" he asked.

Chŏnghŭi didn't know how to respond.

"Did you imagine the children entering this center?" he asked.

Chŏnghŭi lowered her eyes. Hyŏngyu paused for a moment, and then proceeded.

"When you meet someone for the first time, you look at their face. The first impression is always important. You can perceive that person's personality, heart, and thoughts just from the face. Architecture is the same. This design is not good for children. Don't you think that the face of this building should be inviting to the children, bright and cheerful? But your design doesn't show that. It's too rigid and hard."

Chŏnghŭi's face turned red. She was upset with herself for disappointing her father.

Hyŏngyu realized that he had upset his daughter.

"I think I went too far..." he said softly. "A few days ago, there was an article in the newspaper about the grand opening of a student association center in Tongsan district. It looked amazing. You don't have to copy it, but do go over there and take a look at it. It might help you."

Did he just say Tongsan district? Chŏnghŭi thought. *Tongsan district is several hundred kilometers away. It will take me a couple of days to go there and back. But if it is what he wants me to do, then I guess I should go.*

"Yes, father."

Although she had agreed to go, but she was so busy teaching at the school that she never found the time to make the trip. She also wondered if it was absolutely necessary to go that far.

Hyŏngyu would call his daughter from his research center in the mountains to see if she had progressed with the designs. Her answer was always the same: "I haven't found the time to go there yet." And with that, she was able to buy more time. Hyŏngyu also realized that she must be busy with her work.

One night, it rained heavily. Someone knocked. When Chŏnghŭi opened the door, she saw her father drenched from the rain.

"Father! What are you doing here?"

Chŏnghŭi rushed to get her father out of wet clothes and dried off. Hyŏngyu drew a big smile on his haggard face.

"Take a look at this!" he said.

He took something out of his coat, something that was wrapped in a plastic bag. When Chŏnghŭi opened the bag, she was surprised. It was a drawing of the student association center in Tongsan district. It meant that Hyŏngyu traveled hundreds of kilometers to Tongsan district to sketch the center, in this pouring rainy evening...

"There is so much to learn from that building," he said.

"Father!" Chŏnghŭi cried. She choked up and buried her face in his arms.

As much as it pained her that he'd gone to such trouble on her behalf, it also made her realize that he had a true passion for architecture, and that he would go the end of the earth to discover beautiful designs.

"The sketch that her father brought was a big help to her. The building was outstanding, and it provided her with a clear direction as to how to design her own center," Myŏngsu said, ending his recounting of what had happened.

After hearing the story, I gathered the blueprints on the table. I felt a new sense of respect. These weren't just ordinary blueprints.

I fell into deep thought. When we were young, Hyŏngyu's sensitive and quiet personality had eventually put me off. I couldn't even stand to look at his pretty face anymore. But I realized something different about him today. He was committed to his geological work, digging the earth to find new minerals. He had lived a life of passion that derived from his childhood dreams, dreams that would one day bloom. He appeared to me like a different man, a new man, a beautiful man who embraced the times he lived in.

Just then, I heard footsteps approaching the door. Someone knocked softly and entered. It was Chŏnghŭi.

"Sorry I'm late," she said.

Adorably, she blushed with embarrassment.

"I just heard from Myŏngsu about what happened between you and your father," I said.

"Oh, I see..." Chŏnghŭi muttered as her face turned red.

"Comrade Chŏnghŭi, I would like to see your father. I haven't seen him in a while. He must've changed a lot."

"Do you know my father?" asked Chŏnghŭi, surprised.

Myŏngsu was also surprised. Unable to contain my excitement, I paced around the office.

"Of course, I do! We used to hang out so much we were inseparable. We shared the same dream..."

"Really? It would be so nice for the two of you to see each other again," Chŏnghŭi said. But then, her face got solemn. "I don't know how to say this, but my father left to conduct research a few days ago...he's not home at the moment."

"Is that so?" I replied, feeling a bit sad for not being able to see him. However, one could feel his breath and personality in these blueprints, so much that it was no different from meeting him.

I smoothed out the blueprints on the desk. I felt like I was having a heartfelt conversation with him:

Hey Hyŏngyu. I got to see the real me through you today. You criticized me harshly, but I needed that. Who would've thought that someone like you, the gentle, sensitive "bride" would ever have the courage to berate me like that? I'm really happy today. I got to discover who I am because of you.

The beauty of a person is not the face, but the heart. True beauty is found not in someone who is complacent but in someone who continues to improve oneself and heads in the direction of progress. I realized that true character is built on such thoughts.

"My father isn't home, but my mother is waiting for us. Please come to our house," Chŏnghŭi said with her head lowered.

I smiled and said, "Yes, let's go. Let's go and make wedding arrangements, as well."

The way Chŏnghŭi and Myŏngsu gazed at each other made me happy.

"Let's go," I insisted, and followed behind my son and Chŏnghŭi.

COMMUNITIES

CHAPTER 4

NEIGHBORS[1]

Ch'oe Sŏngjin was born on October 27, 1949 in Kusŏng, North P'yŏngan Province. He started writing and published his first short story while serving in the Korean People's Army. He later attended the Kim Hyong Jik College of Education in Pyongyang, famous for its literary training program that recruits amateur writers – often termed "literary correspondents" (*munhak t'ongsinwŏn*) – and prepares them for a professional writing career. Now a member of the North Korean Writers Union's central committee and a recipient of the prestigious Chosŏn Literary Award, Ch'oe has established himself as a major figure of the North Korean literary establishment and is known as a prolific and versatile writer. He notably gained recognition for stories about bold and tenacious characters, such as "The Bridge" (*Tari*, 1987) in which a researcher risks his life to develop a new mining method despite the opposition of his manager, "The High Soaring Tower" (*Nop'i sosŭn t'ap*, 1992) about workers who erect an impossibly high tower in the midst of a typhoon and *Express Train to the Future* (*Miraehaeng kŭmhaengryŏlch'a*, 2018) about a teacher's push for digitization in education.

In "Neighbors", however, heroism is not about the actions taken but rather the ones avoided. In a middle-class apartment building, neighboring families prepare for a holiday picnic, playfully vying to see who can bring the most

---

1 Ch'oe Sŏngjin
   1991
   Translated by Benoit Berthelier.

unique and abundant dishes. One neighbor, employed at the state's food distribution system, faces light-hearted nudges to "contribute" something special from his job. However, when, on the day of the picnic, he arrives late with a truck full of rations, the jovial atmosphere turns tense, as neighbors fear they might've inadvertently prompted him to pilfer from the state. But the thought of theft, it turns out, had never crossed the man's mind and the rations he brought were for the local labor brigade.

The North Korean public food distribution system was responsible for providing every household with food rations the quantity and quality of which were based on a number of factors such as the number of family members, their occupation and political standing. The system started becoming increasingly unreliable from the 1980s before collapsing during the famine of the mid-1990s. While public food distribution was still functional at the time "Neighbor" was written, the story hints at the fact that theft and mismanagement were not unheard of and shows that people complemented the state's rations, for instance with food obtained from relatives in rural areas. With a keen eye for the finer details of social distinction, Ch'oe Sŏngjin also tells us that even under a state that officially strives to build a classless society, North Korean neighbors too worry about keeping up with the Joneses.

There are five different families living on the seventh floor of our apartment building, and the men of each household all have different jobs.

The head of the family in apartment 1 is a product quality control inspector. I live in apartment 2, and I am a journalist. The older gentleman in apartment 3 used to be a worker at a factory making mining equipment but is now working as a consultant for an iron casting plant. He's a war veteran and also served as a lay judge for the district. The head of the household in apartment 4 has recently been made director of the district's food distribution, and the young guy from apartment 5 drives a freezer car.

We had all moved in on the same day to this newly built apartment building four months ago and, since then, we'd all developed decent relationships with one another, but gathering everyone together at the same time was tricky. The quality inspector often had to travel for work and I, just this year, had already spent more than six months away, living in a sawmill in the north of the country to collect information for an article I was writing. All the others were as busy. The freezer car driver's job, for example, had him traveling around all day and he frequently didn't return home until late at night. The man working for the food distribution system had to bounce from place to place like a jumping bean. The old gentleman from apartment 3 always kept himself busy overseeing the complex production process of casted products, such as new drill types—already a difficult task— but on top of that he also served on the local municipal court.

Despite all our busy schedules, on August 15th, National Day, everyone managed to gather together with their families at the freezer car driver's home for the first time since we'd moved in. We complimented his wife, who had graduated from a cooking school, for her excellent food. And over the course of the day, we came to decide that, for the next holiday, we would all go together with our families to the Mirim Dam for a picnic.

This was how it all started. It was the quality inspector, a portly man— who claimed he was getting fat even though he barely ate and only drank cold water— who raised the idea of going to the dam, his long face beaming with excitement from the liquor. He said that these days the landscape there is breathtaking and that there were two new pleasure boats that could take you all the way to Ponghwari and back while you enjoyed the view. That's why people in the know, he added, opt to go there rather than to Moranbong or Taesŏngsan when they have a day off. After advertising the dam enough to pique our curiosity, he revealed his plan, which was for all of us to prepare well in advance and to go and enjoy ourselves with our families in Mirim for the upcoming Foundation Day, the anniversary of our Republic's creation.

"Today was nice but we have to keep setting the bar higher, right? I mean, we can't spend National Day just sitting inside with a bottle of soju, don't you agree? Aren't we, the men of the 7th floor, just as good as anybody else? Just look at this young man here, he's a freezer car driver! Need I say more? And the old gentleman from the mining tools factory, he's been a hardworking man all his life and now because he sits on the local municipal court, is there anything in the district he couldn't get his hands on? And then of course there's also our man here in charge of the food distribution system, he only has to lift a finger and *wŏn*! It will be done! Just like that! We don't want to be petty or miserly, right? Let's show everybody what we're really capable of!"

He had mentioned all of us one by one, but clearly the question "We don't want to be petty or miserly, right?" was meant for the man in charge of the food rations.

There was no doubt about it. The freezer car driver was just starting in life, but he was a generous guy, the type to share with his neighbors if he ever got his hands on some fish or other things like that. The quality inspector was also kindhearted, and he was always giving out some local delicacy or other that he'd procured during his business trips to the countryside. But the man in charge of the food distribution system hardly ever did anything like this.

Although, there was this one thing. One day, several of the men from our floor were leaving for work and the quality inspector asked him in jest if it wasn't about time he showed us what a guy in his position was really capable of.

The director frenetically waved his hands. "Oh no! Please. Don't say that. I'm just a lowly director, and not a very good one at that." His modesty likely meant either that he wasn't in a position to help his neighbors or that we shouldn't even think of ever receiving anything to eat from him. Slyly laughing at the sight of this naïve guy turning red and confused from a little joke, the quality inspector apparently started to think that he could up the ante. As soon as we had parted ways with the food distribution director, he came up to me and whispered:

"My dear journalist, this guy is always acting like he's poor and has no clout at his job. What do you say we give him a hard time? Then maybe the cheapskate will be a bit more generous?"

From then on, every time the quality inspector encountered the director, he started really teasing him. He would say that even though the director was in charge of the food distribution, his heart was smaller than a baby chicken's, asking him if he really thought he could live with us on the same floor if he didn't even care about his neighbors.

And it was the quality inspector too, who had come up with this idea of a group picnic among neighbors.

His proposal was met with approval by everybody. A bit tipsy, we all shouted excitedly: "All right!" The old foundry worker even promised to show us all his fishing skills that day. He said that it would be trout season and that everybody who went to Mirim to fish loved it, but that he himself had not had the time to do so.

The wives and children were particularly happy about the quality inspector's proposal. My wife and my daughter, who was in her fourth year of primary school, were so happy they did not know what to do. Indeed, as I was almost always away on business, I could only very rarely take them out even for a stroll in the park or the streets.

My wife started preparing for the picnic quite early.

It seemed that all the wives saw the preparations as a happy burden.

With still another week to go before the holiday, my wife already seemed to be putting food aside for the picnic—some of the specialties that our relatives in the countryside sent us, along with special ingredients she'd tracked down after searching in every store.

When I realized what she was up to, I said, "Honey, there's no need to do all that already. The food store will certainly have all the things we need on the day of the holiday. It looks like you're preparing a giant feast!" But as was always the case when she had something particular in mind, she would not have it any other way and paid no attention to what I'd said. She pointed out that since all of the families from our floor would be together at the picnic, there would naturally be a tacit competition to see which household was the best. Did we—the house of a respected journalist—really want to come in last? "Our family has to prepare more than the others and even if we do that, we're not guaranteed to get so much as a consolation prize." According to her, everybody on her floor was already actively preparing for the picnic. Since it was the first picnic we had organized since we all moved in on that 7th floor, it seemed that a competitive spirit had quietly taken hold of us all.

Every night, our daughter gave us a news bulletin of our neighbors' activities. At Sukhŭi's apartment next door, they had put such and such specialty from the South in the fridge. To another of the apartments, a grandfather from Sinp'o had sent an extraordinarily huge octopus…

The kid was drawing circles on the calendar every single day and counting down the days until Foundation Day on her fingers. When I returned to Pyongyang after leaving the sawmill workers up north, she had already drawn eight circles on the September.

Foundation Day was tomorrow.

Having watched the news report of the commemoration events on TV at the office and at home, when I finally made it back, it was as if the holiday had already started. In the kitchen, my wife was busy with preparations and had laid out all the delicacies that grocery stores specially stocked for the occasion. And my daughter, Oknim, was in her room laying out new clothes, her hat, and her hiking bag.

That night, I slept fitfully. The aroma of fried food and sounds of chopping emanated from the kitchen. Apparently, my wife was intent on filling an entire truck with food.

This energy that women have is really nothing to joke about! Even after cooking all night for their husband and kids, they are still fresh and joyful as if they are not even tired.

I woke up late the next morning, and indeed my wife looked nothing like someone who'd been up all night. She'd put on her best clothes and make-up and was now arranging my daughter's attire.

Naturally, I started to think that we should have this kind of picnic more often. It had been a long time since I'd seen my wife so splendidly dressed. She was wearing a stunning multicolored *chŏgori*[2] over a light velvet skirt and had put her hair into a bun. She looked ten years younger. They say that a woman's forties are the prime of her life, and I guess that is true.

"Honey, up, up! Now! And you, what are you doing again with that book?"

My wife, who was nagging our daughter for her crumpled skirt, got mad at me as soon as she saw me looking for the novel I kept by my bedside. I left the book where it was.

She kept telling me to hurry, because everyone else, even the old gentleman from the foundry, was about to leave.

But just as we were leaving the apartment, one more thing delayed us: surprisingly, it was alcohol. The bottle of Songsan liquor from the grocery store lay on the floor in a corner of the living room. Songsan was a new product, the result of our district workers' labor, and the local foodstuff factory had recently begun mass production and distribution of the Songsan to people on Foundation Day. I asked my wife why we were leaving the bottle behind. In reply, she asked if I was really thinking about bringing such a thing to an event like this. She opened her bag: inside were several bottles of liquor with absolutely splendid labels. How and where had she gotten her hands on such rare liquor? But for this holiday, I still wanted to take the unassuming Songsan liquor bottle because it symbolized the good work of our district's laborers. I especially wanted to pour a drink of that liquor to the old gentleman from the foundry, who was a pillar of our district and had done so much to improve the lives of its inhabitants. Eventually, I convinced my wife to bring the Songsan liquor instead of the long-necked bottles she had packed.

In the hallway, we ran into the couple from apartment 5, the freezer car driver and his wife. Both were usually of a quiet disposition, and people said they were like brother and sister. But they were now having an argument, as all young couples sometimes do. The man had come out the door wearing a handsome suit and his new wife followed behind him, telling him he had forgotten to wear his medal. She took out a third rank medal of National Valor. When the young man realized she was serious about having him wear it, he suddenly turned his gaze to me. His face became red, and he quickly whispered to his wife:

"People are going to make fun of me. It's not a commemorative event so why would I wear this. People will think I'm bragging."

---

2 The upper part of a traditional Korean outfit.

"What? How could you say this about a medal! And isn't today commemorating the founding of our Republic? You *must* wear it!" she urged.

As I was watching these two, my heart suddenly filled with emotion.

The young wife was right. After all, wasn't the meaning of today's holiday that all citizens of our country should bless the Republic? And wasn't this medal the symbol of the young driver's clean conscience and diligent labor, of his contributions and sacrifices to our motherland?

"Comrade driver, if your wife wants you to, you should wear it. A medal is a great honor." I could not help but sound a bit solemn, as I spoke the words.

The quality inspector's family came out of their apartment, also ready to leave. They were quite a sight, this family: the father, his face already red, was followed by his wife in splendid attire, and his sons were all strong and stout like him. Every one of them was carrying multiple bags or baskets. The eldest, a senior in high school, carried a brand new boombox. He had not bothered to adjust the volume, and so the melody of *Yangsando* blared out, filling the hallway. The wife, who was not quite as refined as her clothes, screamed even louder than the music towards her apartment door to call for her youngest. The kid, known to be a prankster, emerged carrying a weird bag covered in zippers and a guitar as tall as he was.

The freezer car driver took in the sight of this rowdy bunch and turned to me with a mischievous grin.

"Amazing!" he said.

"Haha!" I laughed sympathetically. It occurred to me that in the wrong place and at the wrong volume, even good music can sound atrocious. I was reminded of that saying according to which music prevents aging, but noise actually shortens life. As I was thinking that it would be nice to lower the boombox's volume, the driver just kept on looking, amused and surprised, at the quality inspector and his family who were descending the stairs loudly.

It was actually quite a sight. Even though my wife had stayed up all night, we'd only prepared two small bags, and the driver and his wife had packed even less. Since he was a delivery man, I'd assumed he'd prepare more, but his wife was carrying only a single bag. The quality inspector's family, however, was really something else.

The quality inspector was the first one to reach the bottom of the stairs. He screamed at us to come down quicker. A bus was waiting for us, ready to go to the Mirim Dam. The quality inspector knew the driver and had arranged for him to take us. With a filter cigarette stuck in his mouth, the driver was urging us to get on the bus as if he had some pressing matter to attend to.

"Thanks to the family from apartment number 1, we've got luxury trans-
port! We'll have to return this favor somehow!" said the wife of the gentleman
from the foundry gaily, as she moved her corpulent body up the bus steps.
Visibly satisfied, the inspector replied:

"Oh, please don't. In fact, it's our comrade driver here that you should be
thanking."

"You're right, of course. Thank you, comrade driver!"

The wife from apartment number 3 thanked the driver, and everybody else
followed suit. The atmosphere was warm and joyful.

Her husband, the older gentleman from the foundry, sat alone puffing
silently on his cigarette. Out of all the men on our floor, he spoke the least.
He'd taken part in the war, the post-war reconstruction, the Ch'ŏllima movement, and the Great Construction of socialism. He'd lived through all the glorious steps of our revolution. His children were grown and had families of their
own, and so he was now living out his old age with his wife. The only visits
he received were from his married daughters, who came to see him one after
the other. As it was just he and his wife, the bag of food he'd prepared looked
accordingly basic. Nonetheless, the disassembled parts of his fishing rod stuck
out of the corners of his bag. He was dressed in high-quality fisherman's attire
with a grey jumper and a straw-hat. It seemed to me that he was more excited
about the prospect of fishing than about the actual picnic. It was also obvious, though, that his wife was overjoyed at the chance to escape her lonesome
routine. She mingled with the young couples and the children, laughing and
chatting and brightening the atmosphere.

Yet the bus still could not leave because of the family from apartment number 4. For some reason they were the only one who hadn't shown up yet.

"*Cha*, it looks like the food distribution guy is making some really sumptuous preparations," grumbled the quality inspector with a slightly exasperated
tone as he glanced up at the seventh floor.

The bus driver consulted his watch and said that he had things to do.
Furthermore, everybody was impatient to see the scenery at the dam, so they
started complaining about the food distribution director being so slow.

"Maybe he's already dead drunk?"

"No, that's impossible. It must be that since it's a holiday, he just slept in
late."

"I see that guy every morning cleaning up the yard. He's always the first to
wake up so it wouldn't be like him."

"Maybe he left already?"

"That might be it. Their place was quiet all morning."

"So, we're waiting for nothing. Maybe the young guy from apartment 5 can do all of us a favor and go check on them."

The freezer car driver went up to apartment number 4 and came back down with the wife and children, but the chief was nowhere to be seen. His wife, a petite woman with an exquisite grace about her, said that her husband had left at dawn for his workplace because he was worried over some truck issue. They had been waiting for him, but he still had not come back. When they heard this, a shadow passed over her kids' faces. They were disappointed that their dad was the only one missing on a day like this. Seeing them like that made me feel uncomfortable.

Really, on a day like this you have to forget about your work and just make your kids happy, Comrade food distribution director! Where did you go? I thought.

Since we didn't know when he'd be back, we couldn't wait any longer. We all hopped onto the bus with his family and left.

On the road, we could see the streets and their holiday decorations, and from every street rolled wave after wave of splendidly dressed people. The flags of our republic, adorning every public building, were fluttering slowly in the cool breeze. Flags also hung from the windows of every house. It was a sea of flags evocative of so many memories. But as we sat in the bus, our small party was not exactly happy. Of course, it was because of the director of the local food distribution system. His kids sat in the back and kept looking behind the bus in hopes their father would be following. And naturally, they were making the mood inside the bus quite awkward. I too, in my mind, started to curse the food distribution director.

By the time we arrived at the lake, a couple of hours had passed with still no sign of him. And still, we couldn't start the picnic without him. It would just have been too hard on his children, who were already so disappointed. We were worried and annoyed and did not know if the atmosphere would ever lighten up. The quality inspector must have sensed this too. He waved his two hands in frustration and shouted:

"*Cha*, since he left because of a truck issue, that means he'll come back with a truck full of food. Wait and see. In any case, it's clear that the director is going to surprise us." He turned around and looked at the kids from apartment number 4. There was something strange in his eyes, something like the friendliness needed to raise the spirits of all the people tired of waiting. And surely, his words had the same effect as putting grease on a squeaky wheel.

"Ha, a whole truck full of food, I'm telling you. How nice!"

"Since he's in charge of the food distribution, it's the least he can do."

"But what are we going to do with it?"

"What are you worrying about? We can give our newlyweds here a second marriage banquet, right?"

"That would be nice. But I don't know... are you sure he'll bring a whole truckful of food?"

"*Cha*, no doubt. Trust me. Now, let's wait and see!" said the quality inspector.

"Let's wait then. Whatever happens, today's picnic will be extraordinary."

Everybody was excited and started chatting. It was as if we were finally going to ride the happiness cart.

But even though I let myself get taken in by the pleasant chatter, something, in a deep corner of my heart, made me feel uneasy, because I was worried that the director might actually have gone to the food distribution warehouse to grab things for us.

It was, of course, unlikely that he would come with a "truckful" of food, but since he was responsible for a fairly large distribution center, he could have swiped a few bottles of liquor, some candy or other things like that. The director was an earnest and honest man, but if he had taken the quality inspector's teasing too seriously, he may have gone too far. And it would be really stupid if he ended up being late for that reason.

As I was dwelling on these thoughts, the old gentleman from apartment number 3 left in search of a fishing spot. The usually quiet freezer car driver was whispering something to his beautiful young wife, and in an attempt to raise the spirits of the wives and children, the quality inspector headed towards the wharf where the pleasure boat was moored.

On the wharf, young workers from a construction company that had received the red flag of the Three Revolutions[3] were waiting to board the boat. The quality inspector elbowed his way through them and went up to the captain's cabin as if he was going to try and negotiate something with him.

The inspector was a man of action and always full of energy. He was the type of person that finds happiness in always putting himself out there to help others. Those people, like vitamins, give our lives a much-needed vitality.

But I still couldn't entirely erase the anxiety that remained in a corner of my heart.

I went to find the old man from apartment number 3 by the water. For some reason, I wanted to be near him.

---

3 A distinction for institutions that exemplify technical, ideological and cultural revolutions.

He sat behind his fishing rod, his line already surrounded by small ripples in the water.

"Look here. I'm going to get a big one," he said.

He turned to me and smiled.

"Sir," I said.

"What?"

He took in the somber look on my face. I wanted to ask him what he thought about the food distribution director and whether he reckoned the picnic was going well. But after meeting his gaze, which brimmed with warmth, I gave up on the idea.

I couldn't share such worries with a man so pure and upright, a man who was always so kindhearted and thoughtful.

It would be extremely disrespectful to speak rashly and pass judgement on somebody else in front of this elderly gentleman who had been through so much during his life.

He didn't ask me for an answer.

He had remained silent, but became suddenly animated as something slowly moved over the water.

"Haha, would you look at that," he said while carefully lowering his voice. "Aren't those ripples?" he observed. "Some trout must be having fun over there. Looks like it smelled the bait. Don't come up to the surface, go down. Down! Hey! Bunch of dummies looking for floating bait. Go *down!* There's plenty to eat down there!"

The ripples on the surface of the water looked unremarkable to me, but it seemed that the old man could feel the movement of the fish as if he could see them with his own eyes.

He seemed completely absorbed in his fishing.

In the high blue sky, the sun had risen, huge and glaring like a fireball.

The day was truly beautiful, sun rays smashing against the waves and rippling on the water before breaking into gleaming flashes of bright light.

The little red lacquered float attached to his line, which had been resting at the surface, suddenly plunged underwater and disappeared, as in a game of hide and seek. The old gentleman grumbled in response, but did not budge. He was lost in his thoughts.

Dumbfounded at first, I finally shouted to him, "Sir!" Startled, he pulled on his rod, but it was too late. The fish had eaten the bait and disappeared.

"You've missed your first catch" I said, feeling sorry.

But the old man didn't seem particularly upset. He simply rearranged his rod and cast his line again. He sat calmly and then spoke these unexpected words:

"This quality inspector is a good man, but his jokes go too far. Somebody should tell him not to make those pleasantries in front of the comrade from the food distribution system. I think he ended up making this earnest man worry for nothing."

I was confused.

"But that guy, the director, is a good person," the old gentleman added.

He had perfectly grasped the exact nature of my earlier silence. He truly was a thoughtful and sensitive person. I couldn't think of anything to say.

Suddenly shouts rose from where the wives and children were. The quality inspector was surrounded by them but eventually came out. It looked like something good had happened.

"Eh, it was tough, but it's all arranged," said the quality inspector, as he briskly walked towards our fishing spot. "They only have room for twenty people, so if we let the boys from the construction company board there won't be room for us. So, I asked them to be understanding and give us their spot instead." He mumbled something about getting on with it and looked at this watch. Two wrinkles appeared on his otherwise smooth forehead. "*Cha*, why isn't that guy coming already?" They said the boat would leave at eleven."

"Since the man from apartment number 7 has responsibilities, it's possible that he got busy and won't be able to make it," suggested the freezer car driver who had somehow appeared by my side. There was a rough edge of irritation in his voice, which was usually mild and soft-spoken.

I too felt somewhat uneasy.

"Say, neighbor..."

"What's going on?"

The quality inspector had asked this carefully, as if he had noticed something of the strange apprehension in my voice. I spoke, but my voice came out unexpectedly softer than usual:

"I just wanted to say this. Today's a joyful event for everyone isn't it? If we get on that boat first and leave the comrades from the construction company behind, they'll be really disappointed. It's just my opinion, but I don't think they should be giving us their spot. We should be the one letting them get on the boat. What do you think?"

"That's right," said the old gentleman from apartment 3 as he held onto his fishing rod. I understood how the freezer car driver must be feeling, so I turned my eyes towards him.

"How about our newlywed over here?" asked the quality inspector.

"Let's do it."

The quality inspector seemed unperturbed. "All right. It looks like you all agree so I'll go and cancel," he said decisively, waving his hand quickly and turning his gaze to the young driver: "Since it's what the masses want."

He didn't seem to intend any subtext as he spoke. Immediately, the atmosphere lightened. Just our simple mutual understanding, which might not seem like much, was nonetheless such a pleasant thing.

"All is well then," mumbled the old foundry worker mystifyingly. He took out a pack of Kyŏngch'uk cigarettes from his pocket. After offering one to each of us, even the young driver, he stuck one in his mouth. Then it happened. His eyes, which had never let the red float out of their sight, suddenly widened and beamed with a radiant light. He pulled the rod back right away.

The rod bent as if it were about to break, and the circular movements of the line made it clear that a fish had been caught. The old man kept his cool and slowly reeled the fish in with a few swift and precise moves.

"It's a trout! Oh! Look at that guy! Yes, hmm, it's a big one too."

White foam appeared on the surface of the water. Caught by human ingenuity, the large trout was being pulled, wriggling with great energy, towards the bank. As soon as it hit the water in the bucket, it began to writhe and bounce.

"Take it to my wife and have her cut it up and serve it raw. With such a good start, I won't have any problems catching five or six more," the old man with visible satisfaction. He pulled a new cigarette from his pocket and threw his line back in the water.

Then, something extraordinary happened. Before the old gentleman could even light his cigarette, he had caught another big trout. The fish just kept coming, and not even thirty minutes later he had already caught four.

According to the old man, an entire hover of trout had come to celebrate the holiday. In any case the flapping fishes made the picnic a sight to behold.

"I thought you had only brought your fishing rod in your bag, but it looks like you're actually the person who brought the most food to this picnic!"

"He's a working-class man, of course he knows how to make something out of nothing!"

"If he went to one of those fishing clubs, he'd be made president for sure!"

Everybody was laughing and congratulating the old gentleman.

The women then moved to a flat, pebbly area to arrange a kitchen and build a fire, their hands flying with industry. The quality inspector, who had just canceled our tour on the pleasure boat, moved in and started giving out instructions.

"He chose the wrong job. He's made to be a restaurant owner," whispered the freezer car driver as he put a trout onto a spit.

I laughed. "Yes, it sure looks like it."

Nonetheless, the uneasiness in a corner of my heart remained.

I kept wondering, *Why is the director of the food distribution system still not here?*

The sun was already high above our heads. It would soon be time to have lunch. I was impatient to see him come, yet paradoxically, I also dreaded his arrival. I would never have thought that I could become so anxious over such an ordinary person.

I came to realize more clearly what it was that I wished of him. The old gentleman and the young guy from apartment 5 must have been feeling exactly the same way. That was it. It was clear that the two of them were also thinking about the food distribution director, who, for some reason, was late to our party.

Our odd protagonist finally arrived around lunchtime as we were waiting for our lovely wives to serve the food. Even his arrival was somewhat out of the ordinary. His son, hitherto dispirited by his absence, was now shouting: "Mother! Father has arrived!" Everybody looked towards the road. One of the trucks used by the food distribution system was approaching. The director opened the door and stepped out.

When I caught a glimpse of all the plastic crates full of glass bottles and the cardboard boxes through the truck's open doors, I felt as if giant walls were crumbling around me. The director's children, unaware of what was going on, were simply happy to see their long-awaited father, but it seemed to me as if everything around us were covered in darkness. I could only feel an unspeakable scorn for this man who had betrayed the trust of the district's people – his neighbors. How could such a thing happen to us? To our lives? How?

I looked at the people around, or more precisely at the men, whose expressions looked full of judgement. The old gentleman from apartment 3 searched for his pack of cigarettes with shaky hands. The freezer car driver whispered surreptitiously to his wife. What about the product quality inspector? Was he happy about what he had done? About what his silly jokes had made the director do? I searched him out as angrily as someone who has had his heart stolen.

The inspector was standing a ways away, by the water. He now looked completely exhausted and empty. When the food distribution director moved towards us, the inspector looked at him with terror and collapsed on the grass.

I could clearly see his face becoming somber. He was no different from the rest of us, after all.

He must have felt as we did. But what were we going to do now with this food distribution truck?

The director's son, excited, grabbed one of the boxes inside the truck. But the director stopped him right away:

"Hey there buddy! This isn't for you!"

The director walked toward us. He looked at the food and then at us. He seemed a bit taken aback, since we were standing there, quiet as if held in suspense waiting for some solemn verdict.

"I'm sorry I made you wait," he said. He must be misinterpreting our long faces. "Last night, as our daughter was coming home from work, she saw a group of young guys from a labor brigade setting up their tents in our district. I thought that if they had just been dispatched there, they probably wouldn't have prepared anything for the holiday. That's why I went to work this morning and tried to organize something... Anyway. They're also living in our district for the time being, so we can't let them have a bad holiday."

He looked as if he was trying to find an excuse. "Sure, they could have come after or before the holiday... but since they're a labor brigade..." It was impossible to blame him for what he'd done! No, I felt admiration for him. He'd worked since dawn to gather foods for these young men! Everybody else stayed silent. They too must have been reflecting deeply on the situation. And then, a cry of joy arose from somewhere close by. Then the sound of a gong— *ch'aeraeng ch'aeraeng*! Everybody turned their heads towards the noise. Further up the river, on a meadow bathed in blazing sunlight, was one of the small temporary buildings used by the brigade. A white ball sprung above the roof. The sound of the gong and the young boys' shouts were all rising from there. For some reason, this was the first time that I'd noticed the building.

"So, you're saying that everything inside that car is food for the comrades in the labor brigade?"

"Yes. Well, to be honest, I was worried that the picnic would start late just because of me, so the driver told me not to worry and gave me a ride here."

"Such good people. You're all such good..." The old gentleman could not finish his sentence, as if he had suddenly felt uneasy. His swollen cheeks were trembling, and he swallowed heavily. After a while, the old gentleman eventually took the director's hands between his own and spoke with a voice that was both hesitant and slightly annoyed:

"I can't... And you were saying you couldn't do your duty properly as a director... Don't you ever say something stupid like that again. You're the most upright man in our district. Those kids in the labor brigade, they're no different from us, from the people from our floor. Of course, we're all the same."

My heart grew full as I listened to the old gentleman's words. In the director's head, the people from our floor, just like the labor brigade, all counted as "residents of the district," whom he had to care for.

As we were waving the truck goodbye, somebody reminded us that it was time to have lunch.

We all sat together with the wives and children, like a family, on the clean pebbled ground.

Our holiday meal was really something. Nothing less than a sumptuous feast. Bulgogi, fresh vegetable dishes of all kinds, plates of boiled beef, colorful fruits, and all sorts of local delicacies from the provinces: squid, pickled vegetables... And in the middle of all that, raw fish slices from the trout that the old foundry worker had caught in the Taedong river and that his wife had prepared.

"It's fantastic!" shouted someone happily.

The older gentleman looked around at the food and shook his head.

"No, all of this is women's stuff. Whatever you say, for us men—a "

Suddenly, the sound of the women's protesting voices exploded. Startled, the old man waved his hands.

"Men are all like that. They can't help themselves if there's liquor. I hate having to sit next to a drunk old man."

One after the other, all the women protested. Only the young lady from apartment number 5 remained silent. Embarrassed, she covered her mouth.

Just as the women's outcry was calming down, the food distribution chief opened a small plastic bag.

As everybody was looking at him, he pulled two bottles out of the bag. Their simple label only read "Songsan liquor".

"Maybe it won't be good for our comrades here..."

His face became red as if he were ashamed. "I'm in charge of the food distribution system and I'm your neighbor, but even if you're trying to be polite you can't say that this is much..."

Everybody turned silent. What was there to say? Even if he had said nothing about the origin of these two bottles of Songsan liquor, we all knew where they came from. They were the bottles he had been supplied with by the food store for the holiday, like everyone else.

The silence lasted for a little while longer until the old man from apartment 3 started to speak:

"Listen now, comrade. Don't be like that. What are you apologizing for? How do you think this picnic would have turned out if you had showed up here with food from the national supply? Food that was supposed to go to our people? It would have been terrible, I tell you that."

The corners of his eyes were wet and twinkling. . His speech had made the atmosphere more serious. but he smiled happily and looked around at us all.

"*Cha*, what are you waiting for? We've got to celebrate this Foundation Day! I didn't come empty handed."

The old man buried his hand in his older leather bag and took out another bottle with the Songsan liquor label.

"Oh no, what was I thinking? How could I forget?"

I suddenly remembered the incident from earlier in the morning. I turned to my wife and gave her a meaningful look before searching for my bag. Everybody took out their bottles of Songsan liquor at almost the same time.

"Look here now, comrade. You always say that even though you're in charge of the district's food distribution, you 'can't do your duty properly', but you're not a lousy director. You're living well, you're living a proper life."

The old man from apartment number 3 turned towards us:

"Comrade, this Songsan liquor is the first liquor to be mass produced in our district. It's a first, but I'm also sure that our country will grow richer. Why am I so sure? Because of people like the food distribution director here, who work for the people with all their hearts. Our Republic has given birth to such workers and its future is bright!"

The wives started pouring the liquor. Hurrah! To the Republic and its prosperity! The glasses, aloft above our heads, sparkled in the sunlight.

As we were toasting, I suddenly noticed the quality inspector, who was staring at his glass, unable to move. He looked lost in his thoughts. Strangely, seeing him like this made me even more happy. I gave him a nudge, then turned to the group and shouted:

"*Cha*, come on drink up. It's good stuff."

A pleasant melody poured out of the boombox. From the wharf, we could hear the long sound of a siren. The boat, splendidly covered in flags and other adornments, was leaving the riverbank and heading out to the blue lake. On it, the young guys from the construction company, beautifully dressed, waved back at us. The medals hanging from each man's chest caught my eye. I suddenly remembered the young wife of the freezer car driver and how she had hung the medal on her husband's chest. I started to think about the meaning of the flag on this medal. The sea of flags I had seen on my way to the picnic rose in my mind's eye. Among the numerous thoughts that these countless flags brought to mind, I thought about the people I had spent the last few months with—these simple and ordinary sawmill workers, who were no different from my neighbors. Working hard, diligently, every day of their lives. Even today, silently, in the distant forests of the North, their labor was making our country richer.

CHAPTER 5

HOPING FOR LUCK TO STRIKE[1]

Han Ungbin was born on October 10, 1945 in Longjing, Jilin Province, China and moved to the DPRK with his family shortly after the country's establishment in 1948. Like many other writers in this anthology – and in North Korea – Han did not start his professional life as a writer. A coal miner, he wrote fiction during his spare time and published his first piece "One Fine Holiday" (*Ŏnŭ han hyusik nal e*, 1973) by sending it to the literary journal *Chosŏn munhak*. His publications as a "literary correspondent" for the journal led to his selection for a training program at Kim Il Sung University in Pyongyang, which offers amateur authors a pathway to a professional writing career. Han gained prominence for his short stories about the everyday life of middle-class characters, before shifting his focus to novels in the 2000s and drawing inspiration from real-life figures like long-distance runner Chŏng Sŏng'ok and "unconverted long-term prisoners" — northern loyalists incarcerated in South Korea.

"Hoping for Luck to Strike" is representative of Han's early body of work as a short fiction writer in which, as South Korean critic Chŏn Yŏngsŏn notes, heroism is achieved by preserving or maintaining the mundane. There is, "nothing extraordinary" about the protagonist whose work is likewise, in his own words, "nothing out of the ordinary". Yet, his ordinary existence is disrupted by a number of seemingly trivial events: a business trip to a rural

---

1 Han Ungbin
   1993
   Translated by Benoit Berthelier.

province, the prospect of getting a new, larger apartment, and an attempt to find a husband for his wife's younger sister. The story unfolds in a lighthearted way as the naïve and clumsy hero's attempts to solve each of these problems fail, before he realizes, in a final epiphany, the futility of trying to change things in an already optimal system.

Despite its humorous tone and a conclusion akin to advocating for the passive acceptance of authoritarianism, the story implicitly highlights numerous endemic issues within the North Korean "socialist eden". The protagonist's attempt to give an expensive liquor to a state employee in charge of housing assignments is framed as a friendly encounter between strangers but objectively amounts to little more than plain bribery, insinuating that "ordinary" people trying to get better housing need a privileged relationship with those in charge of distributing it. Similarly, his plan to marry his sister-in-law to a city boy is more than just casual matchmaking: it is the only way to get her to move from her rural village and into a city with better living standards. Marriage is, for rural women (rural men marrying urban women must bring their wife to their village), one of the only avenues for geographic and social mobility in a country with strict controls on internal migration and urban population quotas. Even the business trip that opens up the story, with its vague and seemingly mundane objective of collecting "additional materials" is more problematic than it seems. In a country in which a factory's supply of materials is managed by central planners, a lack of materials is a sign of planning failure. It is up to individuals to tap their personal network to fill in the gaps in the system with a parallel system of supply and demand. Published in 1993, the story can therefore also be read as highlighting the banality of corruption and inequality, the shortcomings of the planned economy and the emergence of parallel economies shortly before the systemic collapse of the famine years.

For the first time in ages, I was to go on a business trip. Given that I'm not really the traveling type and I rarely go on vacation, there was a good reason for my sudden and uncharacteristic departure: the factory urgently required additional materials.

Nobody could have been happier than my wife to learn I was going away. While it might seem odd for a wife to rejoice over her husband leaving the house, the real reason for her excitement was my destination.

"Honey," my wife urged me, "don't stay at a hotel. Stay with my parents."

My in-laws lived in the very village I would be traveling to. I clicked my tongue.

"What? Do you think I'm going there for fun? Do you know how far your parents' place is from the factory? It's eight— no, over *nine kilometers!*"

"You call that far?" she said. "Just take the bus and you'll be there in no time."

At this point, I knew the best thing to do was to stay quiet. If I said anything more, she would just get angry and accuse me of not caring about her family. Then she would ask what they had ever done to me and would end by reproaching me for not caring about her. Of course, when I'd first learned that I had to go to that village, the thought of visiting my in-laws had actually popped into my head. People say that there is nothing more pleasant than enjoying your in-laws' hospitality—and I had indeed experienced it quite a bit already throughout my marriage. Plus, there was my wife's younger sister, who always followed me around calling me "Brother-in-law! Brother-in-law!"

"And my parents will be so surprised to see you," my wife said, interpreting my silence to her advantage. Her face lit up as she spoke, as if the plan for me to stay with her parents was a foregone conclusion. She went on, "And can you imagine how happy Yŏngok will be to see you? She says that she misses you every time she writes us a letter … Oh and honey, this time please also take the picture with you."

"What picture?"

"Come on. You saw it the other day. Just a minute, where did I put it?"

My wife rifled through her bag before she finally found it in the front pocket. "Here it is!" she cried.

It was only then that I remembered. The photograph was of a tidy-looking young man with chiseled facial features. The story that went along with the picture came back to me. He was purported to have a good job and a good personality, and you could tell from the picture that he was in fine health. But the crucial thing was that this particular young man had seen Yŏngok last year when she came to visit us, and that she'd made an impression on him. He would be a very good match for her, and considering that getting married was a priority for Yŏngok, my sacrificing a day over it felt like a trivial matter.

"Good, I'll give it to her!"

I said this robustly as I slid the man's picture into my pocket.

My wife was so happy with my assurance that she had nothing to add.

She said only, "I'm sure our little Yŏngok will like him!"

I was in total agreement, of course.

After that, the rest of the evening progressed peacefully, with nothing but cordiality between us.

But there were two things that still weighed on my wife. The first was that since I was going on a business trip, I would be unable to deliver all the gifts she'd prepared for her family. (From my side of things, this was a relief.)

The other regrettable thing, according to my wife, was that my absence would prevent us from making any progress at all on our housing situation. New apartment buildings had recently been constructed downtown, and she was insisting that we should try to get a place there.

"You should go to the Housing Assignment Department, too. If you just sit around and do nothing, they will never know about our situation. Don't you know that the crying baby gets the milk?"

The crying baby gets the milk...I had nothing to add to this. My wife, who had delivered and raised our child, is the expert in that department.

But for someone like me, who is neither outgoing nor eloquent, walking into the Housing Assignment Department, where I wouldn't know anyone, would require quite a bit of courage. What was I supposed to say? Where was I supposed to start? Almost every night, my wife nagged me about the apartment situation, which often led to an argument.

But that night, dinner came to an end without too much strife. A visit to the Housing Assignment Department would simply not be possible while I was away visiting my in-laws—a fortunate reality, from my perspective.

Not that I didn't want to move to a new apartment or think that having an extra room wouldn't be nice. I might even have wanted it more than my wife, but I didn't like to rush into anything.

For one, I'd always had some hope—a hunch—that somehow luck would be on my side and everything would work out in the end. This is how I've always dealt with everything. Now that I thought about it, I'd always been a hopeful person, and my hopes had almost always materialized in one way or another— even if sometimes a bit late.

Lying in bed, I thought about my wife's younger sister. Yŏngok was twenty-three. When had I last seen her? I'd gone to my in-laws' place around the end of last year, so it must have been a little over six months ago.

She'd walked nine kilometers to the station with me to see me off because I'd missed my bus, thanks to my mother-in-law's excessive hospitality. She'd stuffed my luggage with all sorts of packages and when the suitcase was filled to the hilt, she moved on to preparing another bag with yet more items.

"I'm telling, you, wait a bit!" my mother-in-law had insisted. "You men have no idea. When you're in the city, you'll miss all these things."

Did she imagine that the city was a place with no grass and no fields, only apartments and people? I tried to refuse, but she thought I was just being nice and trying to spare her the trouble.

You could tell that she found pleasure in showering her children with her generosity, so in the end I gave in. And even Yŏngok, who had visited us many times and knew that we were not lacking for anything in the city, urged her mother on to pack more things into the new suitcase.

"Put this in, too! And that!" Yŏngok cheered.

I missed the bus during the birth of yet another piece of luggage. And that's how I ended up walking to the station with Yŏngok. The road was a mountainous path flanked by small vegetable fields on both sides. Yŏngok was truly happy. She asked question after question, regaled me with stories about the village, and laughed about absolutely trivial things. If a comrade we met on the road asked where we were going, she answered proudly:

"This is my brother-in-law! I'm seeing him off!"

She knew every person we encountered.

"There's really no one you don't know, is there?" I asked.

My remark puzzled her.

"How could I *not* know them when we all live in the same village? Don't you know everyone who lives in your city?"

"In my city?" I said, "I don't even know my neighbors!"

"Oh!" she cried. "How is that possible?"

She was genuinely surprised and could not understand. "How do you live without knowing each other?"

I laughed.

"Come live in the city and you'll learn soon enough."

"What do you mean? How could I ever live in the city?"

"If you get married to a city boy you could."

"Oh!"

She laughed gayly. After walking for a bit in silence, she asked, "How could someone like me go to the city?"

"What do you mean, Yŏngok?"

"Well, I'm just a country bumpkin. By the way, did my mom pack the boiled eggs?"

For the remainder of our walk, we dropped the issue of her moving to the city. She laughed and chatted about other things, which made me happy. When we reached the station, her smiling eyes filled with tears.

"Brother-in-law, when are you coming back?"

"Guess I'll have to come back soon."

"Come often. Okay?"

The moment I saw these two clear eyes filled with tears, I decided to find a way for her to come live in the city with us. When I returned home and talked to my wife about this, she confessed that she had long harbored similar ideas but hadn't said anything because bringing a country girl to live in the city is socially frowned upon. But she had been trying hard to find ways to have her sister come up regardless. The picture of the young man was a result of these efforts.

Since that evening, every time I received a letter from Yŏngok saying that she missed us, I took it as a sort of plea—her asking me to arrange a marriage. I saw her tear-filled eyes looking at me, beseeching me. All right! I've made up my mind. I will take the time to go visit her, regardless of how busy and tired I am. This is important to her! I fell asleep, my heart somewhat calmer now that I'd made up my mind. Yŏngok, I thought, be patient: Help is on the way!

The next morning, I went to the station and looked for the clerk my wife had told me about over breakfast.

"There will be a lot of people at the ticket booth, so just go to the lobby. My comrade will be there. She'll take care of your tickets," my wife said.

"How will I know what to do?" I asked, confused.

My wife took out a small piece of paper and handed it to me. "I wrote everything here. I also wrote down her name, so just go there and give her this paper."

Women really are a thoughtful bunch. Imagining how she must have stayed up all night to prepare for my departure like this brought tears to my eyes. It's this kind of thing that led to that saying: "Though not through blood, marriage is the closest relationship."

Sure enough, the station was quite crowded. All the many seats were occupied, and people who hadn't gotten a seat lingered in the lobby, looking for a vacant spot. The ticket booth was even more crowded, so I headed toward the information point. The clerk, whom my wife had told me about, greeted me with a friendly and professional smile. She glanced at the paper and looked delighted.

"Please wait here," she said.

Everything was going perfectly. As I glanced about for a seat for myself, a group of people simultaneously stood up and walked over to the ticket booth, as if they were giving up their seats for me. I quickly sat down, and all my worries disappeared.

I pitied everyone else who hadn't been as lucky in finding a seat so easily. A man came up to me and asked, "Did they say if they started selling tickets for the train to X already?"

That was my train. I shook my head and told him, "I don't really know."

"What train are you taking again?", he asked.

He seemed puzzled by my answer.

"Haven't you got your ticket already?"

"No, I, thought ..." I trailed off while looking in the direction of the place where I expected my clerk to return to help me. "I, um, asked somebody," I told the man.

"Ah, is that so?" he said, before running to the ticket booth.

I stretched my legs. How comfortable. I didn't have to worry about tickets like other passengers did. I was filled, once again, with gratitude for my wife. It would have been terribly complicated to get tickets in this maelstrom. Overcome with satisfaction, I closed my eyes. But I soon opened them again. Surely, the clerk must be looking for me by now?

She was nowhere to be seen. Also strange was that the crowd of people had almost entirely disappeared. You could see empty seats here and there. Maybe all those people had only come to greet or say goodbye to other passengers? The lobby became quiet.

A man approached me and asked, "Is there still a lot of time left?"

I turned to him and noticed he was the same man who'd talked to me a moment ago. I was confused.

"Did you buy your ticket?" I asked him.

"Yes, I bought it."

I was taken aback.

"That fast?"

"There's almost no one in line!"

I looked over at the ticket booth. There were only three or four people there. I scanned the lobby. The clerk was still nowhere to be seen. What was going on? Why was she so late?

The man asked me, "Did you buy your ticket?"

I avoided answering too directly: "Well, yes..." I said, trailing off.

He sat down next to me and kept bouncing his leg. Why was he shaking his leg like that? People have the oddest habits. He was fumbling with his tickets and even started humming.

Crap! Did the clerk forget about me? Maybe she told me to follow her when I first met her? But I distinctly remember her telling me to wait. Why was she so late?

"Aren't you going to get your ticket punched?" the man sitting next to me asked.

"Please go ahead," I said to him. "I'll stay here a bit..."

He smiled and nodded as if he understood.

"In that case, take your time," he said.

Take my time? Our train was leaving in just ten minutes. And the ticket gate was going to close in less than five minutes.

There was hardly anyone left in the lobby. The ticket line was completely empty. Why wasn't the clerk coming? Had she forgotten about me? The work of a clerk is to answer endless questions from the patrons and direct them here and there. She could very well have forgotten about me. If she did forget, that would be a disaster. Would I be able to leave today?

When the hand of the wall clock showed less than five minutes until the train's departure, the clerk at last showed up with my ticket. Without thinking to thank her, I took the ticket and immediately ran toward my gate.

A loud announcement over the PA system echoed in the lobby.

"Passengers to XX, please come to the platform immediately. The train is approaching the station."

I ran until I reached the gate. The young lady checking tickets there looked up and glared at me.

"Sir, where have you been? The train will leave soon."

"Sorry about that," I said,

I hurried out of the gate, but she shouted for me to return.

"Sir! You have to get your ticket punched!"

"Ah, right," I said.

But I couldn't remember which pocket I'd put my ticket in. Only after rummaging through all of them did I find it.

"You were supposed to get your ticket ready before coming to the gate."

"I'm so sorry," I said.

I turned around to leave, but the young inspector's angry voice stopped me again.

"Sir! Aren't you going to take your ticket?"

"Ticket?"

I realized that I had left the ticket in her hand. I snatched it back.

"Hurry now," she said. "The train is about to leave!"

"Yes, yes. Sorry."

Behind me, I heard the young ticket inspector snicker, "I've had it with all these idiots."

I narrowly managed to make it onto the train but there were no empty seats left inside.

"You couldn't get a seat?" someone asked.

I looked down in the direction of the voice. It was the man I'd met at the station. He was comfortably seated and even had his newspaper spread open. His expression was sympathetic, his leg was bouncing.

Instead of answering him, I merely smiled awkwardly. He scrambled to make room for me beside him.

"It's not much, but you can sit here," he told me. "This passenger said he was getting off in an hour," he added, gesturing to the man sitting next to him.

I gently placed my butt on a small piece of his charity. The more I thought about it, the more absurd it all seemed. If I had not met my wife's "acquaintance" and just bought the tickets, would not everything have gone smoothly and without any fuss? I had to apologize three times to a young ticket inspector who was even younger that my wife's sister, and—on top of it all—I got called an "idiot." I'd narrowly managed to board the train, and there was nowhere to sit except for the little piece of seat that this man with his annoying leg-shaking habit was offering to me out of pity. And now there I was, squeezed next to him. I felt like I was the butt of some sort of joke.

The wind blowing through the train's window chilled my cheeks. At the same time, I realized I was drenched in sweat. Without really knowing why, I began to laugh.

After an hour had passed, the other passenger vacated his seat, finally allowing me to sit comfortably. I leaned back and began exchanging superficial courtesies with my leg-shaking companion. Where are you going? Where do you work? Etcetera.

There was nothing extraordinary about me. I was an employee at a factory that was not particularly big, going to a factory in the middle of a rural village that was also not particularly big. My work was nothing out of the ordinary—collecting materials.

On the other hand, what the man told me left me completely stunned. So much so that his habit of shaking his leg no longer seemed quite as annoying.

"I work at the Housing Assignment Department," he said.

I replied, "The Housing Assignment Department, you say?"

"Why is that so surprising?" he asked me. "Do you know anyone there?"

His question flustered me a bit. I couldn't very well tell him that the Housing Assignment Department was the subject of many heated conversations between me and my wife. I tried very hard to appear like a person who didn't know anything about the department at all.

"Ah, the Housing Assignment Department," I said in an offhand way. "You must be very busy."

"Well, normally we're not that busy," he told me, "but these days, with the whole construction of new apartment buildings, we're in over our heads. The workers are working overtime to finish up, and *we're* working overtime to assign the apartments. Properly selecting residents is not a simple task."

"I bet," I said in an absentminded kind of way, while furiously sorting my thoughts. The Housing Assignment Department, the very place I couldn't bring myself to visit because I lacked the courage. And now, just like that, the Housing Assignment Department was sitting in front of me!

It would have been hard to arrange this kind of opportunity even if I worked at it. I decided that it would be better to get acquainted with my companion first and then go visit him at his office. But you cannot become friendly with someone just by exchanging a few words. On a train, friendship grows at the same speed as the locomotive and vanishes just as fast when it stops.

In my luggage, there was a bottle of the expensive Koryŏ Ginseng Liquor (my wife had put it there) that I was going to give to my father-in-law and a cheap bottle of Taepyŏng Liquor that I planned to give to my business associates. I thought I might become more acquainted with this man over a bottle of Taepyŏng Liquor.

"This train ride is a bit boring," I said as a passing remark.

"It is what it is. Train journeys are always boring," my companion replied with the tone of a philosopher. He kept shaking his leg compulsively.

"Well then, we'll have to make it interesting."

As soon as I said this, I put my hand in my bag and grabbed the smooth neck of the bottle.

"Here... let's have a drink..."

As I pulled out the bottle, I ended up in an embarrassing predicament. The thing I grabbed was not Taepyŏng Liquor but the expensive Koryŏ Ginseng Liquor that I had planned on giving to my father-in-law.

"Wait...Isn't that something you brought for some special occasion?" my companion asked.

"Don't worry about it," I quickly answered, trying to hide my frustration.

I had only planned on serving my companion a cheap cut of meat but ended up offering him an expensive steak instead. But by then, it was too late not to switch the bottles.

"Ah, please don't open it. I can't hold my liquor."

"Neither can I. It's just to pass the time..."

I felt sorry for my father-in-law and the image of my wife's sulky face crossed my mind, but I also thought that this was for the best. Maybe this Housing Assignment Department's employee would be impressed by this Koryŏ Ginseng Liquor and would not forget about me. He would remember me by the colored label and the golden tint of the liquor.

However, he held my hand as I was about to open the cork.

"Come on. We shouldn't ruin the trip for others inside the train with the smell of alcohol. We should drink something refreshing like this."

He took two bottles of soda out of his bag.

To be honest, for a poor drinker like me, this was much more pleasant.

"Ah, I feel so bad…" I said.

I was now the one getting treated.

But with every cup of soda we poured, I felt this was for the best. And the gorgeous bottle of Koryŏ Ginseng Liquor looked even more refined and outstanding among the pedestrian soda bottles.

Up until now, our conversation had been boring and awkward, filled with long stretches of silence. But now we were chatting and laughing without allowing silence to creep in. If we had nothing to say, we would just offer each other a drink: Okay, drink up! No, no, you first!

The situation in South Korea, the reconstruction of Angkor Wat in Cambodia, the slums of the starving world, the huge crowds of the unemployed in capitalist societies and even the gangs of New York were topics we put up for discussion and analysis.

"The things that are happening in this world… Really," I said.

I let out of a sigh of lament when I was interrupted by an announcement from the loudspeakers that caught me by surprise.

"We are now arriving at Tŏkhŭng station. Passengers boarding off the train, please exit on the right without rushing."

But it was impossible not to rush. Tŏkhŭng was the station where I was supposed to get off. The train only stopped there for one minute, and it had already entered the station.

I must have missed the previous announcements while I was talking with my companion.

I hurriedly grabbed my bag and stood up.

"Are you getting off?" my companion asked.

He was visibly surprised by my abrupt behavior.

"Yes. Getting off. Well then, it was a pleasure…"

I still had a lot to say (I still had not said a word about the apartment!) but there was not a second to lose.

"Hey! Hey!" my companion cried, "You forgot to take this!"

He held aloft the bottle of Koryŏ Ginseng Liquor.

"No, you keep it. I'll come visit you sometime later," I answered.

I ran towards the exit. As soon as I set foot on the platform, the train started to move as if it had been waiting for me to get off. The bottle still in his hand, my companion looked at me from the window.

I waved my hand. He waved back.

Very well done! Now, when I go to the Housing Assignment Department after my trip, I thought, he will greet me with open arms.

My bag was lighter, now that I had given away the Koryŏ Ginseng Liquor, but so was my heart. If my wife could have seen me today on that train, she would not have been able to suppress her admiration: "Wow! I didn't know you could be so crafty!" she would exclaim. I think every husband in the world must have this foolish side to them that yearns for compliments from their wives.

"Really well done!" I said to myself.

I repeated it one more time. This was the first time in my life that I had orchestrated a "diplomatic" success. I headed towards the factory.

"Is comrade An Kyŏngch'an here?" I asked.

The young receptionist looked at me with beaming eyes and said, "He is away on business. Where are you coming from?"

"What?"

I completely ignored her question. Only the words "away on business" resounded in my ears like a clap of thunder.

"When did he leave?"

"About five days ago. He's coming back tomorrow."

I sighed in relief.

"How can I help you?" she asked, looking at me intently. Her gaze made me blush. A middle-aged man like myself blushing because a young lady was gazing at him might sound odd, but the real reason for my embarrassment was that she asked me that question as if she knew why I'd come to see An Kyŏngch'an.

"I – It's just that, well… He's an old friend. In that case, I'll come back tomorrow."

I gave this evasive answer before rushing out of the office. I was disappointed. Without him, my business trip was unnecessary.

Only after I'd walked out of the office did it dawn on me that things might actually have turned out for the best. Since I had to wait until tomorrow to attend to my business, I could go visit my in-laws without having to feel guilty for wasting the company's time on personal matters. I would also be able to discuss the marital issue with Yŏngok. I was supposed to sleep at a hotel, but I could just spend the night at my in-laws' instead. Their place was about nine kilometers away, but at least I wouldn't be charged for room and board.

"It's a bargain for me, my company, and the country!"

I spoke aloud, as if subconsciously hoping to be overheard. All that was left for me to do was to go to my in-laws' and take care of this family business.

Yŏngok was certainly a lucky young woman to have someone like me, I thought.

But when I got to the bus stop, the bus had already left. A person told me that I just missed it:

"Over there, do you see the one making the turn?"

Over in the distance, I saw the yellow and red-striped butt of the bus going around a mountain bend.

I plunked myself down on the bench. The next one wouldn't come for another few hours. It would be better to walk there. It was only a nine-kilometer walk through the mountains. I would have to go around the mountainside, down into the valley and up a ridge, but even walking slowly it should not take me more than two and a half hours.

It is rare for men my age not to be fond of their younger sisters-in-law. Even people who do not have good relations with their in-laws have a special affinity for their wife's younger sister and would go to great lengths for her happiness.

I stood up from the bench.

Just the memory of my trek to my in-laws that day is enough to send shivers down my spine.

I had been walking for about half an hour when the capricious mountain weather changed, and rain started to fall. I quickly ducked under an alder tree on the side of the road. At first it sheltered me from the rain, but as time passed, the rain started to pour down like the Waterfall of the Nine Dragons in Mount Kŭmgang. I looked like I had walked under the end of the eaves of a house on a rainy day and been hit in the face by the water pouring from the gutter. My surroundings were completely empty, without a single person in sight.

I had no choice but to come out from under the tree and continue walking. My clothes were soaked.

Thankfully, the rain soon stopped, and sunlight pierced through a rift between the clouds. But soon, clouds again covered the sun, and the wind started to blow. Such treacherous weather in these mountains! Even the sky was as rugged and craggy as the ground. In a single hour, the weather had already changed two or three times.

Soaked and windswept, I began to shiver.

I didn't really know why the road was so slippery, but I nearly fell every ten steps or so. People who are used to taking very long walks will already know this, but almost falling can be worse than actually falling.

"Damn it!" I cursed with every step. Everything in my sight added to my anger: a rock curled up like a dumb bear, a boringly straight larch tree, a shabby dog soaked by the rain running around aimlessly, the water from the stream and its deafening noise...

A crow standing in the middle of the road flapped its wings and flew to the top of a telephone pole. Looking down at me suspiciously, it cawed.

Mixed with the sound of the wind, the sound of the stream and the sound of the rain, its cries sounded like "Where are you going, where are you going?"

The crow kept repeating his call, as if it was waiting for me to respond. I got angry and stamped my foot, but without even a nod, that clever fellow resumed his cawing.

I glanced at the crow and grumbled.

"I'm going to my in-laws, you idiot. It's because of my sister-in-law that I look like a mouse soaked in water."

Just then, as if telling me to get going, the bird cawed again before flying away.

I muttered, "Stupid bird."

I may have said those words merely to break the tedium of silence, as I had not encountered a single person to talk to on the way. Silence can be harder to bear than noise. The deafening sound of the valley's stream and the wind only made the silence deeper and I started to feel as if my own existence had become a part of this wind and water that did not possess the ability to speak.

This is how I ended up conversing with a crow, not like in a children's story or a folktale where it's all imaginary but in reality.

What was strange was that after venting my anger at the crow, my heart felt somewhat lighter. I was not going through all this trouble for myself, but for someone else (even if it was my sister-in-law)! The thought gave me comfort. Maybe the martyrs of times past, both famous and obscure, had felt this comfort too.

I also pictured my wife clicking her tongue, her tender heart aching as I would tell her the story of my arduous journey. As a husband, I fall in the "foolish" category and part of me always longed to be the object of my wife's sympathy.

Actually, I wished that the rain would start pouring again and that the wind would just keep blowing until I entered my in-laws' house. I wanted to show them the kind of hardships I had gone through to get here...

But by the time I reached the brook at the foot of my in-laws' hamlet, the wind had stopped and the air turned warm with sunlight. It was a nice evening with a slight breeze. No one could have guessed the kind of horrible weather I had just encountered.

"Damn it!"

For no reason, everything felt terribly unfair to me. I looked down at my shoes and my pants, both covered in mud. In any case, I would have to clean myself up. Making my way through thick willows I went down to the brook.

There was a red tractor in the middle of the stream and between its wheels, I saw two pairs of legs in the water. Two people were washing their hands and feet.

I crouched down on the opposite bank of the river, slightly upstream from them. While cleaning my shoes, I innocently looked at the two pairs of legs between the wheels. Both of them had rolled up their pants. One pair was dark-skinned, thick like a pole and looked as strong as a wooden barrel. The other one was slender yet soft and full of suppleness. It seemed as if the water of the stream was flowing more carefully when it reached their side. A young woman, for sure. At this very moment, Yŏngok was probably somewhere also finishing her day at work and washing her legs like this.

I started washing the dirt off my pants. If I were to enter my in-laws' house right now, everyone would have been in an uproar. Yŏngok would cling to my arm and jump for joy.

"What brings you here? Why didn't you tell us you were coming!" she would shout.

"I came for you."

"For me? Oh my! What are you talking about?"

"Just look at this picture, and you'll know what I mean. You'll like him."

Musing in my own imagination, I reached into my pocket. You could tell that I was scowling from the reflection in the stream. Inside my pocket, the picture was soaked by the rain and was crumpled like an old piece of paper. The handsome young man's face was now in a permanent scowl, even worse than mine. He looked as if he had lost an eye, and his nose was shaped like a stairway reaching down to his mouth.

What am I going to do with this?

In front of the tractor, the two people continued to splash water on themselves, indifferent to my predicament. The water drops were filled with crimson sunset and fell down on the stream with a sound of laughter.

"Clean your face," said the woman.

The voice sounded somewhat familiar. "Could it be?"... As the thought crossed my mind, I started listening more carefully.

"No need," said the man. "The real face of a driver is his tractor. Who knows, my mother-in-law might like that face better."

"Mother-in-law? Since when do you have a mother-in-law, comrade?"

The voice really sounded like Yŏngok.

"Of course, I've got one. It's your mother comrade."

"Oh my!"

The man, with his maple leaf-like hand, scooped some water and splashed it on himself, followed by "Ah, so refreshing."

"I'm going," the woman said.

"What? Where?"

"Let go of my hand," she insisted.

"Are you seriously going?"

"I told you to let go... People will see us!"

"Then hurry up and answer"

"Fine! I'm not going! I'm not going!" she said.

There was a delightful laughter...

"Comrade, really!" she cried.

Again, the lively sound of water splashing.

I let out a sigh. Looking at my reflection in the water, I realized I had been smiling without even knowing it. A literarily inclined quill would have written that their love was in full blossom. The only thing left for this young couple to do was officially proclaiming their love at the altar.

Of course not. It couldn't be her. Definitely not. My sister-in-law was going home where she would wait for me to bring her good news. But as I stood up, something the young man said made me flinch.

"Comrade Yŏngok!"

Yŏngok?!

Yŏngok was the name of my sister-in-law.

Aghast, I stared blankly at the two pairs of legs that appeared side by side under the vehicle. These supple legs had already walked their own path and found love.

"What's wrong?" she asked.

"Won't your big sister and her husband say anything when they learn about us? You said they wanted to take you to the city..."

"The city? Who said that?"

"Didn't you?"

"Me?"

"You know, that time when I came to bring the grain fertilizer."

"Oh my! Is that what you're talking about? I was just joking, that's all. How would that even be possible? If it were you comrade, wouldn't you want to live close to your family?"

"Well sure but..."

"I'd prefer if my sister and my brother-in-law both came here and lived with us. Isn't it great here? The next time I'll see them, I'll tell them to come live with us."

"Well said! And I'll stand by your side and support you!" he said.

What?!

I didn't realize it, but the picture had slipped out of my hand and was now floating down the stream. It was only when Yŏngok said, "Oh my! Whose picture is this?" that I realized what had happened.

I saw her hand pick up the picture from the water.

I hid among the willows as fast as I could. I had no other choice.

"Oh my, he's really funny looking. He looks like an idiot," she said.

Avoiding their eyes, I went back on the road and plodded toward the village.

My clothes were soaked from the rain and stuck to my body making a splashing sound every time I moved. My legs were shaking as if they were about to collapse, and I was shivering. It sounded like she was saying "Oh my, my brother-in-law is an idiot."

A cow on the side of the road stared at me and mooed loud enough to scare me. The dogs from the neighboring houses started barking. The chickens that had been lingering on the road scattered in all directions clucking uncontrollably. A grey cat arched its back and jumped like a shadow over a water-filled rut left by a cartwheel. Here and there, the dogs came outside the houses, barking aggressively. One of them was howling elegiacally, its head raised towards the sky, another one was barking so angrily it sounded like it was coughing, and a third one was yelping as if it were trying to suppress a fit of laughter. Without even realizing it, I myself started laughing too. It felt as if the cow and the chickens and the dogs all knew my troubles and were laughing at me for going through all the trouble for nothing.

"My goodness?! Who do we have here!" my father-in-law shouted, running toward me. "What brings you here all of a sudden?"

"Ah, I...am here on business and I thought I'd stop by..."

I did not have to give any other reasons than my business trip.

And I could also use the trip as an excuse to explain why the bag that my father-in-law had offered to carry was so light. After giving away the Koryŏ Ginseng Liquor, the bag did not feel that heavy anymore. Maybe the importance of things depends more on their value than on their weight. I felt sorry for my father-in-law. But he would surely be happy to know that our apartment situation had taken a big step forward because of the liquor. Besides, what is a bottle of Koryŏ Ginseng Liquor compared to a nice apartment...

At that moment, the kitchen door opened, and my mother-in-law ran out.

"*Aigu*! Who do we have here! I did think it was strange when the telegram came…"

I was startled.

"Are you saying someone sent you a telegram?" I asked.

"Yup that's right! Got it today, right here."

I was deeply moved. My wife was really something. She sent a telegram to tell her mother to prepare for my arrival… Such perfect solicitude could only bring tears to my eyes. I will have to do something to make her happy when I get back. The news of our apartment situation's big step forward should do the trick for sure…

"Here ya go."

My mother-in-law handed me the telegram. Obviously, it must just have said the train number and the time of my arrival.

But what was written on the paper was beyond my imagination:

"Got the apartment. Come back ASAP. Sŏnok."

Sŏnok? That's my wife's name all right. But what was this about getting the new apartment? My companion from the Housing Assignment Department who I met on the train and the bottle of Koryŏ Ginseng Liquor suddenly came to my mind. Could it be that the bottle of liquor had already worked its magic?

On the other side of the twig gate, one of the dogs that had chased me earlier (that fellow really had a nasty character) was barking incessantly. It raised its head to the overcast sky and looked as if it was staring at the clouds and laughing, rather than barking away at me. Unconsciously, the expression "laugh with one's head thrown back toward the sky"[2] sprung to my mind. For some reason, I also had the impulse to look at the sky and laugh.

My companion must still be on that train. It was obvious that the new apartment had to do with something other than my "diplomacy." So, what happened? "Shit! You damn dog!"

Scared by my father-in-law's loud voice, the dog skirted away but barked again as if bursting into laughter with its head pointed towards the sky.

"Can you believe that mutt? So loud," said my father-in-law.

---

2 *Angch'ŏndaeso* (yǎng tiān dà xiào): an idiom of Chinese origin. The expression originally refers to an episode of Sima Qian's Historical Records. Asked by the king of Qi to negotiate military assistance from the state of Zhao with just a few pounds of gold, the scholar Chunyu Kun threw his head back towards the sky and laughed. Comparing the king's attitude to that of peasant sacrificing a pig's trotter in hope of a good harvest, the scholar explained that it is ridiculous to give a little and expect a lot.

"Let it go," said my mother-in-law. "Let him laugh."

One after the other, the events that occurred since I left this morning passed before my eyes. The trouble I had because of the train ticket, the sliver of a seat in the train I received out of "charity," the Koryŏ Ginseng Liquor, the kilometers of walking in the rain, the picture that had floated away on the stream, and the telegram telling me we had gotten the new apartment... In the end, I had not waited in vain for luck to strike.

Why did things turn out this way? Everything I did and worried about turned out to be a waste of time. But this luck just appeared out of nowhere. I didn't have to do anything. But could I really consider this luck? I guess you could also call it coincidence... Perhaps all the times I've strangely hoped that luck would strike, I had really been hoping for some kind of magical coincidence...

The clear sound of a song suddenly grew closer, shaking the sunset-filled sky.

Our country gives us houses, and laughter blooms like flowers
Our country gives us rice, and we have no worries

Yŏngok stood between the green vines of cowpeas, and her red headscarf looked bright like fireworks. Why was the light so dazzling... *It's thanks to this great country...*

I closed my eyes for a moment. The hope that luck would strike... This hope was not a coincidence. I realized that my life was no mere coincidence. From the day I was born in this blessed country, everything has been given to me.

The kindergarten, school, the hospital and also my new apartment...

When children need something, their parents take care of it before they even ask.

The Great Leader and the Dear General who have made these strokes of luck an everyday thing... If we forget even for a moment to respect our leaders, we will end up becoming ludicrous beings, much like I have today. A person who looks at a dead leaf and assumes that the entire tree is dead would not be much different from the three blind men who went to see an elephant... [3]

The music of the song shook my heart like a bell.

Thank you, thank you, Our Party, thank you

---

3 Reference to a famous tale about three blind men touching an elephant to learn what it is like. Each touches a different part of the animal. When they compare their observations, the three men end in total disagreement as to the appearance of the elephant.

CHAPTER 6

SEVENTEEN PEOPLE'S LAUGHTER[1]

Kim Chŏng was born in January 1940 in Myŏngch'ŏn city, North Hamgyŏng province. He graduated from Kim Il Sung University in 1974 after majoring in children's literature in the Department of Language and Literature. After graduation, Kim quickly rose to prominence and was invited to join the April 15 Literary Production Unit, a select group of writers tasked with producing short stories and novels about the lives of the North Korean leaders. Drawing from his training as a children's literature author, Kim would go on to write a fictionalized account of Kim Il Sung's youth (*The Anchor is Drawn*, *Tach'ŭn ollatta*, 1982) and the lives of other members of the ruling family. He was also one of the editors of Kim Il Sung's memoirs (*With the Century*, *Segi wa tŏburŏ*, 1992) and has, since 2001, served as the chair of the April 15 Literary Production Unit.

Published in the late 1980s at the peak of the Hidden Hero movement in literature and political discourse, *Seventeen People's Laughter* illustrates many hallmark traits of the genre. The hidden hero of the story, Pak Suhyŏn, is a man willing to sacrifice not only his own welfare, but also that of his family, for a great good. Pak stands out less for his extraordinary musical skills than for his willingness to submit to simple utilitarian arithmetic: the summed happiness of seventeen people is greater than the happiness of a family of three. Pak's personal attributes, such as his fame, position, and abilities, are likewise

---

1 Kim Chŏng
   1989
   Translated by Immanuel Kim.

overshadowed by his deeper understanding of their relative unimportance compared to the collective.

While it might be tempting to portray this as typical of a collectivist society eager to suppress individual distinctiveness, the hidden hero trope, to the contrary, delineates a distinct dynamic between the individual and the collective. This aspect is further underscored in the depiction of Migyŏng's personal maturation. Originally unable to accept seeing her father being taken away from her, she comes to understand the selfishness of her actions through individual introspection. This clash between a parent devoted to a larger cause and a child resenting their absence is itself a common trope of hidden hero stories and one that served as the central plot of the 2007 movie *A Schoolgirl's Diary* (*Han nyŏhaksaeng ŭi ilgi*), one of few North Korean films to have been released internationally.

On Moran Hill in Pyongyang, when you head down towards the South from the Ŭlmil Pavilion, there is a small area called "Outdoor Stage" on the side of the road. It got its name about twenty years ago. The workers from our factory started coming here to spend the September 9 holiday (the Day of the Foundation of the Republic) each year, and now it has become something of an official annual event.

Every year, we would hold a talent show at the Outdoor Stage featuring various and pretty decent acts by people we had invited. Elder Pak's magic tricks and Kim Chindo's voice performances and imitations were quite popular, for instance, and unique enough that you could not have found them at similar events organized directly by the factory.

Unfortunately, there was no one to accompany these performances with a musical instrument such as an accordion. We once had a young curly-haired man at our factory who played the accordion exceptionally well, but he never trained anyone else and was transferred to the district youth league a few months later. From that point on, our factory was never the same. There was another young man who had played a bit in school, but he was not quite good enough to perform in front of everyone at the talent show.

So, we had to make do and mixed songs with vocal percussions. Even then, the Outdoor Stage would get packed with people. The stage was at the corner of the main road, so anyone who walked down from the hillside would stop by to watch the show. Many of the audience members would jump in and participate in the performances.

Three o'clock in the afternoon was the peak time, and the audience would cheer "Great!" "Awesome!" to Kim Chindo's vocal percussions. People danced and had a great time.

By the time everyone got up to dance, Kim Chindo had already lost his voice. Two comedians came up on stage and tried to imitate a trumpet sound going *ppamppala ppamppa, ppamppala ppamppa*, but it was not good enough to keep the party going.

I missed the young curly-haired man who'd played the accordion. Everything had been better when he was still around. The dances were nice, but how much nicer would they have been with music! Back then, what had attracted all those people to our "Outdoor Stage" wasn't as much the dancing as the music of the accordion.

But all we had left now were our mouths to sing with. Even though our workshop at the factory had a thirty-year history, we were reduced to dancing to the rhythm of a lone vocal percussionist. We danced, but without proper music, something was amiss.

I kept these thoughts to myself and mechanically started following the flow of the other dancers. But after a short while I suddenly let out a shout:

"Hey!".

I had just discovered, among the crowd, a man with an accordion around his shoulder. He was chatting with a woman and seemed to be enjoying the festivities. I assumed that the two were married.

I have to get him to play somehow, I thought.

I rushed toward the man, not caring about the people I bumped into along the way.

He wore large, thick glasses that made him look like an intellectual. He appeared to be in his late forties, a bit too old to be lugging an accordion around. His face was pallid and thin for someone with such warm eyes. His large forehead gave him a bookish charm. He wore a thick navy-blue jacket and a snow white dress shirt which made him stand out among the crowd and the leafy nature surrounding us.

I wonder what he does for a living? He doesn't look like a professional player. A professional wouldn't just walk around with an accordion to a festival like this. I bet he's the kind of guy who wouldn't refuse to play.

Possibly realizing that I was going to request that he play a song, he adjusted his accordion and gave me a wary look.

I didn't greet him; I just grabbed his arm and said, "Comrade, sorry to do this to you, but do me a favor. Could you please play us a song?"

"A song? We were just passing by," he replied.

He smiled as a sign of refusal.

I pulled on his arm harder than before and said, "Comrade, I beg of you. Please do us this one favor."

"I'm sorry, but we were just stopping by on our way to the Ŭlmil Pavillion. If I were alone, I would do it. But you see, there are three of us here," he said.

The third person was a young girl in her teens, standing behind her parents. She glared at me with piercing eyes.

But I wasn't about to give up on this stranger. With my other hand, I grabbed his accordion so that he couldn't get away.

"Wow, you're really putting me on the spot," he said.

He looked to his wife and daughter for help to get out of this awkward situation. If one of them did not refuse and remained neutral, then the balance would tip in my favor.

Fortunately, his wife cracked a smile, which was an indication that she didn't mind. But his daughter demanded that they leave, which did not help the situation.

"Dad, let's go, *now!*" she cried.

She tried hard not to make eye contact with me as she pulled on her father's arm.

The decision was now this fellow's and his alone. If his daughter continued to insist on going, then he would most likely listen to her. I didn't have any trick up my sleeves to deal with kids her age. In fact, I didn't have any other method of convincing the man other than holding on to his accordion strap with all my might.

At that moment, Kim Chindo approached me and whispered into my ear.

"Hey chief, you're barking up the wrong tree. Do you know who this is?"

"No, who is it?" I asked.

"This is the famous music conductor, Pak Suhyŏn," he said.

"Really? How wonderful and fortunate we are! Hey guys, welcome our guests," I shouted.

Kim Chindo read my mind and started making goat sounds with his mouth.

Young women standing around the family started laughing and giggling so hard their bodies bent backwards. As they laughed, they glanced at the young daughter who had not changed her facial expression a bit. *Lighten up a bit, girl. Enjoy the fun. Tell your father to join our workers.* This was the message that was whispering in their eyes. All the people surrounding us were giving the young girl the same look.

Pak Suhyŏn's eyes grew big and he was about to crack a smile, but then he realized what he was about to do and shut his mouth tightly and turned his head away. His daughter was completely unmoved by the entertaining spectacle. The look on her face said it all: "Goat sounds aren't funny."

But then the daughter, just for a moment, got distracted, and I took that opportunity to successfully drag Pak Suhyŏn onto the stage.

The workers stopped dancing and began clapping for him. Two workers filled a tall sparkling glass with beer and offered it to Pak Suhyŏn as if this were some kind of formal ceremony, saying, "We, the seventeen workers at this factory, cordially present you with this from the bottom of our hearts."

I handed the two glasses of beer to Pak Suhyŏn, one for each hand. He didn't take it because his daughter was crying out to him from behind us: "Father!".

"That's my daughter telling me not to drink," said Pak Suhyŏn. "She's been saying this for the past two months. Some silly person must've told my Migyŏng to stop me from drinking beer or any alcoholic beverage. If I drink this, I won't hear the end of it. So, I regretfully return these to you."

Pak Suhyŏn took a gulp from each glass secretly and then made a show for his daughter of handing the glasses of beer back to us. It was funny to see a spoiled child police her father, but also charming that a middle-aged man like him would be intimidated by his daughter.

Just then, Pak Suhyŏn began playing the accordion. The melody of "Ongheya" rocked the Outdoor Stage. Our workers held hands and danced to the music, shrugging their shoulders to the beat. The dance moves were different from before when the only music came from someone's mouth. Music from the accordion had the magical power to invigorate and energize the people to dance with larger movements. It reminded me of how our workers operate the machines with great rhythm.

I had never heard anyone play the accordion so wonderfully in my entire life. When the young curly-haired man had played for us last time, he had managed to give all the young guys and girls a good time, but this was much more skillful and entrancing. I couldn't believe how someone could move his fingers like that and how expressive he was while playing. I didn't realize that my mouth was agape with wonderment.

The veins in Pak Suhyŏn's hands bulged as his hands fluttered over the accordion like a light, free bird. He moved his body freely to the music, and his facial expression perfectly captured the sentiment of the song, something that a musical instrument could not do alone.

The most important thing was that he did not refuse to play any of our requests. Seventeen of us requested seventeen songs, and he played all of them with all his heart. He played as if her were performing in front of thousands of people.

At times, he would keep the rhythm with his right hand and play the keys with his left hand. At other times, he would tilt his head back and stomp his feet on the ground to keep the rhythm for the dancers. He didn't care how he looked while playing. He lost all inhibition and moved to the music. He was a nationally renowned music conductor, but at that moment he was just one of us.

Beads of sweat rolled down his face, and soon his entire body was drenched in sweat. He took off his jacket, loosened his necktie, and played the accordion more passionately than before.

The music drew more people onto the dance floor. We also pulled Pak Suhyŏn's wife onto the dance floor.

As the festivities reached their height in excitement, and the people's laughter got louder, I kept looking over at Migyŏng and I began to feel anxious. No matter how hard others were dancing or how good a time they were having, she was not.

Even though I knew it was pointless, I gathered some rice cakes and other sweet candies in a container and went over to Migyŏng. Maybe festival desserts would lighten her up.

"These are our specialties around here. This one here was made by the cell Party member's wife, and it's incredible. Try some," I said.

I set the container down and handed her a rice cake.

Migyŏng didn't want cakes and she scowled at me, pursing her lips to show that she was never going to eat these or speak to me. Her slender chin quivered, and then she looked away.

I was relieved that she wasn't going to talk. But then I saw her eyes welling up with tears, and my heart dropped. *Uh oh, this isn't good. What's going on?*

"Hey Migyŏng, why are you crying?" I asked.

Not knowing how to handle the situation, I stood with my hands on my waist.

She didn't want to show me that she was crying, so she quickly wiped the tears away and glared at me again.

"Mister, who the hell do you think you are to take my dad away..." she muttered under her breath. I couldn't quite hear her, but I understood what she was grumbling about.

How could I argue with her, really? She was right. On this joyous holiday, I had kidnapped her father and ruined a family outing.

"Comrade Migyŏng, feel free to criticize me. I deserve it," I said.

I stretched out my arms like I was going to embrace her in order to get a conversation going. But my congenial gesture was not working on Migyŏng. Tears welled up in her eyes as she stared above the pine tree line. She muttered something and then began her complaint.

"Mister, you have completely ruined our plans. Today was the first day in ten years that we've had a family outing. We were supposed to go to Moranbong…"

I was surprised to hear the words "ten years". Factory workers like us go to Moranbong frequently and enjoy a day out, but to hear that a musical artist and his family hadn't been to Moranbong in ten years was surprising.

"What does your father do during the holidays?" I asked, sitting down next to Migyŏng.

"He goes to the concert hall. His day off is on other days, but I'm at school on those days. During the holidays, he has to work," she replied.

"I see. Yes, the concert hall needs to be open during the holidays."

I began to imagine what it would be like to turn on the house lights and invite the audience into our capital's concert hall. People flood the amusement parks and picnic areas while the concert hall plays music for everyone.

"But Migyŏng, how did your father find the time to go to Moranbong today and not the concert hall?" I asked.

I was hoping she'd tell me something, even if she were railing at me while she did.

She furrowed her brows in thought, and then spoke in a faint voice, "My dad hasn't been to the concert hall because he's been sick. Doctors told him to stay home for a few months, and so he handed his baton over to someone else. We thought that we were going to stay home for the holidays because he's sick. But he woke up this morning and told us that we're going to Moranbong. I was so happy I felt like dancing. But then…"

"Ah, but then this foolish old man interfered with your family outing," I confirmed.

Feeling guilty and sorry for Migyŏng, I stood up and cut through the dancing crowd and got up on the dance floor. I stopped Pak Suhyŏn from playing any further and whispered into his ear, "Mr. Conductor, I heard that it's been ten years since you had a family trip. I'm really sorry to hear that."

"There's no need to be sorry," he whispered back. "When else would I play the accordion? It sounds like Migyŏng revealed some family secrets. I wouldn't pay too much attention to that kid."

"I say this because your daughter doesn't look too pleased."

"Come on, comrade chief. If that's the case, you shouldn't have called me up here in the first place. I don't care if you kick me out, I'm not leaving."

"Are you having fun?" I asked.

"Of course! Don't worry about Migyŏng. I'll have a word with her. She's not as stubborn as she looks."

With his accordion around his shoulder, Pak Suhyŏn walked over to his daughter.

"Are you mad, Migyŏng," asked Pak Suhyŏn.

He folded his legs along the slope of the hill, placed the accordion in front of him, and rested his arms on the accordion. He looked at Migyŏng carefully.

Migyŏng didn't say a word and only fiddled with a blade of grass.

Pak Suhyŏn continued, "Then, should we go and have our family time?"

"You do whatever you want," she replied. But she didn't get up. Just moments ago, she had expressed strong feelings to me, but now she was being very flexible with her father.

Pak Suhyŏn took his middle finger and lightly flicked it on Migyŏng's forehead and laughed.

"Whatever I want? That's great. I'm glad you said that. There are three of us, and there are seventeen of them. Isn't it better if seventeen people have fun rather than just three?"

He didn't wait for his daughter to respond. He stood up and ran back to the dance floor. Everyone witnessed the father-daughter exchange and cheered when he returned to them.

He's right. That's the right way of thinking. That kind of thinking is the jewel of our society, and it has made our life happier and brighter, I thought.

Pak's words echoed in my head, and I couldn't seem to leave Migyŏng by herself.

Yes, let's all go to Moranbong this time next year.

Then a year passed. Factory workers and the locals were out at the Open Stage on September 9, as always. It was a little past noon and hordes of people gathered again, just like the year before. The silly skit we'd prepared, called "Pair Figure Skating," turned out to be a huge hit.

Kim Chindo played the role of the male figure skater, and another man, one of our factory's newcomers, dressed up like a female figure skater. When Chindo lifted the other man and twirled him in the air, people were in tears, stomping their feet and bursting out in laughter.

The year before, as Pak Suhyŏn and his family were leaving, he'd promised to return on New Year's Day with his accordion. But I didn't count on that, and thought he was only saying it to be nice. Or, even if he sincerely wanted to come back to our festival, perhaps when the time came, he'd be tied down with work, or Migyŏng might not allow him to come back.

The Party cell secretary had told us that he'd arranged for someone to be trained to play the accordion. But the guy he picked was a new worker from the boxing club who had no desire to play a musical instrument. He had been recommended for musical training, but it had already been two months and nothing had come of it.

We had no other choice but to dance to the music coming out of Kim Chindo's mouth as we usually did.

But there was a miracle. As we were dancing the *Tondollari*, we heard the sound of an accordion heading our way. I didn't have to look in the direction of the music; I just knew that it was Pak Suhyŏn.

"Conductor Pak Suhyŏn is back!" our workers cried.

Kim Chindo stopped making noises with his mouth, the people stopped dancing and headed toward sound of the accordion.

"Hey, that's not Pak Suhyŏn. It's his daughter," said Kim Chindo, pointing for me to see.

We couldn't believe our eyes. It was Migyŏng playing the accordion.

I rushed over to her and embraced her.

"Migyŏng, it's so great to see you. What brings you here?" I asked.

She didn't say a word but only laughed. This was the kid who had reproached me last year by saying, "Mister, who the hell do you think you are to take my dad away..." with tears running down her face. And here she was now standing in front of me. I could hardly believe it was the same stubborn kid. She had grown and matured in the past year.

I placed my hand on her head and looked around. *If the daughter is here, surely so is her father*, I thought. But I couldn't find Pak Suhyŏn, which was strange.

"You came alone? Where is your father?" I asked.

A shadow fell over Migyŏng's face. She lowered her head, and in a faint voice, she said, "Father passed away."

Everything got quiet.

Pak Suhyŏn passed away? What a tragedy, I thought.

I felt like a vice was crushing my heart. Rather than weep, my body ached with the pain of his loss. I placed my hand on her shoulder.

"When did he pass?" I asked.

"March, this year," she replied.

"I can't believe this. He had so much energy when he played the accordion last year."

"When he was here last year, he probably already knew that it was a terminal disease. My mother and I were the only ones who did not know about it.

If we had known, we wouldn't have made him come here. He knew he didn't have much time left in this world, and so he did what I wanted."

We listened solemnly and fell into deep thought. Last year's festival and performance was Pak Suhyŏn's last performance, and we were his last audience.

"But Migyŏng, what made you come here today," I asked.

I removed my hat and looked into Migyŏng's tear-filled eyes.

She dabbed her eyes and stared into empty space.

"One day, my father held my hands and said, 'It looks like we won't be able to go to Moranbong again this year. I can't seem to keep my promises...' After he passed away, I kept thinking about what he said. So, I decided that on September 9, I would come out to see you and your workers. I really missed you folks."

She turned and looked at me with a sense of determination. She smiled again. Her smile was as innocent as the child she was, but it was also a pure smile that showed signs of maturity. This past year had changed her beyond recognition, physically of course but also mentally. Following her father's spirit, she stood amid the seventeen workers to celebrate the holiday.

How did she mature so much in just one year? The human heart is truly beautiful, I thought.

I looked up to the sky and felt grateful to our country for raising such wonderful people.

"Mister, come and dance!" Migyŏng called out to me.

The people at the "Outdoor Stage" were dancing in unity to Migyŏng's performance.

Someone hung a garland around Migyŏng's neck. It was a garland that had been prepared for Pak Suhyŏn's return.

CHAPTER 7

THE ACTOR'S LAST CLASS[1]

Born in Kobe in 1945, to Korean parents, Kang Kwimi completed her primary education in Japan in one of the Korean schools run by the General Association of Korean Residents in Japan (*Chosŏn ch'ongnyŏn*), an organization of diasporic Koreans in Japan (*zainichi*) with close ties to the Democratic People's Republic of Korea. At 16, Kang moved to Pyongyang, as part of a repatriation program sponsored by the North Korean and Japanese government. She studied literature at Kim Il Sung University and made her literary debut in 1982 with the short story "Where I Grew Up" (*Nasŏ charan'got*), about *zainichi* Korean students struggling to come to terms with their identities as Koreans in Japan and the idea of a single "homeland" in the context of national division. Her subsequent works have continued to explore the fate of the diasporic *zainichi* community, drawing a stark contrast between the discrimination endured by those who remain in Japan and the prosperous lives of those who choose to return to their homeland.

"The Actor's Last Class" is representative of Kang's works on the *zainichi* diaspora and their narratives of homecoming. The story is set during the "Great National Migration from Capitalism Towards Socialism", a repatriation movement which, from 1959 on encouraged Koreans in Japan to migrate to North Korea. Roksan, an aspiring actor, refuses to follow his family back

---

1 Kang Kwimi
2005
Translated by Benoit Berthelier.

to Korea and remains in Japan to pursue a career in film. After a rival actor exposes his Korean heritage, the protagonist finds himself excluded from the film industry and forced to take on a job as a human billboard, dressed in a clown costume. Faced with failure and contemplating suicide, he eventually moves to North Korea where he becomes one of the nation's most prominent actors.

The *zainichi* diaspora holds a prominent place in North Korean culture, and "The Actor's Last Class" aligns with the common portrayal of the diaspora as victims of Japanese discrimination and capitalist exploitation; a marginalized group that can only achieve true success upon returning to their socialist homeland. In that regard, it is worth noting that Kang's own biography, as a successful returnee author, is as essential an element of her literary work as her written words.

There is also more to this short story than a crude, propagandistic contrast. "The Actor's Last Class" is one of the only stories in this volume to expand the notion of community beyond national borders. While the text seems to unequivocally separate Koreans from Japanese and avoids questions of cultural or ethnic hybridity among the diaspora, the pervasive theme of acting, whether as a Japanese historical figure in a film or as a respectable salaryman, is used to raise deeper questions about authenticity and identity as performance.

"Our dad is the best!"

Pak Roksan heard his daughter's joyful voice coming from the room downstairs, followed by his sons' shouts of approval. He was sitting alone upstairs holding a tiny picture in his hand. "Honey, what are you doing here by yourself?" asked his wife upon entering the room. She looked worried.

She had a good reason to be. That very day, the Supreme People's Assembly had decided to grant Pak Roksan the title of People's Actor of the Democratic People's Republic of Korea after he had received praise from Kim Jong Il for his role in the film series *Nation and Destiny*.

His wife didn't understand why he was sitting alone like this instead of sharing the family's excitement on this day of celebration. But as soon as she saw the picture that Roksan was holding, she was taken aback. "Honey, on such a happy day… Why would you…". She couldn't finish her sentence. Her eyes filled with tears.

The picture was Rembrandt's *Return of the prodigal son*. It wasn't the original, not even a good reproduction. It had been torn out of an art magazine and framed.

It was a painting of a father shedding tears of joy as he embraces his son who kneels before him in rags. Rembrandt's masterpiece was a depiction of the biblical story about a prodigal son who had run away from home, about a son who had become a beggar but whose father had nonetheless welcomed him back with open arms. The picture had been printed on cheap paper and now, after several decades, it had become so faded that even the expression of the father's happy face had become hard to decipher. It nonetheless made Roksan's wife cry every time she saw it.

"Honey, please come over and sit here," Roksan urged, gesturing with his hand.

She wiped her tears and sat down.

Outside, trams, buses and cars zipped by at full speed one after the other. Headlights illuminated the asphalt road still wet from the early summer rain, and streetlamps lit up the large billboards that were lined up like walls. With those lights floating by, the road seemed to flow like a meandering river.

"You asked me why I would think about that incident on a day like this. But it is precisely days like this that make me think about it. How could we forget what happened then?"

His wife once again wiped the edges of her eyes.

"I thought about it today too..." she confessed.

Both looked again at the photograph that Roksan held in his hand.

A father embracing his prodigal son who came back after becoming a beggar... As they gazed at the painting, so typical of Rembrandt, they recalled a street in Kyoto. That was more than thirty years ago.

Streets in Kyoto were also full of lights. And they too resembled the flow of a meandering river, with the headlights from cars speeding down the road.

But it was a river of sadness and despair.

Kyoto Station, summer Juche 52 (1963).

The train station was crowded with Korean compatriots. Some were going back to the fatherland, while others were simply seeing them off. All their hands were waving the flag of the republic. People embraced each other and exchanged warm farewells.

"Safe travels! We'll see you in the old country!"

"Goodbye! We'll meet again for sure!"

The station seemed like it was being rocked by waves of emotion and exaltation—these compatriots were going home, to their native land, a land that was calling them back through the unprecedented historical event that was "The Great National Migration from Capitalism Towards Socialism." [2]

One middle-aged woman, however, seemed livid and devastated. As she was about to board the train, she shouted the name of her son at the top of her lungs:

"Roksan! Roksan!"

Alongside the mother, a fifteen-year-old boy also cried out, "Big brother! Where are you?"

They were Roksan's mother and little brother. They had lost sight of him on the platform in the large crowd. The train whistled as it was about to depart, and the outpouring of joy and the clamor of emotions on the platform swallowed up the mother's and little brother's desperate cries.

The train started to move. Everything had been loaded, and the train slowly departed the station.

They'd searched for him without success and eventually left on the train. The flood of people who had earlier gathered to bid the travelers farewell was gone. The station was silent.

Leaning against a pillar on the platform, Roksan looked at the train in the distance and wiped his tears.

Mother, forgive me, Roksan said to himself.

The following night, he called the shelter for repatriates in Niigata.

He heard his mother sobbing on the other end of the phone.

"Roksan, come to me. It's not too late, the repatriation boat hasn't left yet. You can still take an express train. How will you survive alone in this country? Come, I beg you."

His mother's tearful voice was breaking his heart, and, for a while, he did not know what to say. He needed a moment to pull himself together:

"Mother, please forgive me. I have to do this. But when I become successful, I will definitely come see you."

Roksan's mother gripped the phone while she cried. Her voice traveled through the phone line across hundreds of kilometers before coming out of the receiver:

---

2 From 1959 onwards, the North Korean government organized, with the help of the International Red Cross and the Japanese government, a repatriation campaign targeted at people of Korean descent who resided in Japan. Out of the 600,000 members of the diasporic community, an estimated 90,000 moved to the North.

"It's impossible. Impossible... Roksan, just thinking that we lost your father in this country is enough to break my heart, so how could I ever leave you here? Let's all go back together. I'm begging you."

"Mother, please forgive me. I'll tell you everything once I succeed."

"Roksan!"

"Mother, good... goodbye."

And so, at twenty years of age, Roksan bid farewell to his family and stayed in Japan.

He wanted to become a famous actor. It had been his dream ever since he was a child, when he would go to a nearby film studio and wait for any up-and-coming actor to pass by. He would follow the actors and ask for an autograph. He ended up having several notebooks filled with autographs. And if he ever saw a movie being shot on a street, he would forget to eat and haunt the set for hours. One time, hanging around a movie shoot, he didn't come home for almost four days, causing his family to be extremely worried. His friends nick-named him "movie buff." His frantic film fever left such a strong impression on the film studio people that after he graduated high school, he managed to get a job there running errands and cleaning the equipment. He held the lowest position, even among the studio's errand boys, but that only invigorated his desire to become an actor.

Even the illustrious Shakespeare started as a doorman in a theatre, and didn't he become a world-renowned playwright? If so, couldn't Roksan become a famous actor by starting as an errand boy?

One day, as he was busy carrying equipment to prepare for a set, someone from the studio spotted him. No ordinary employee, it was Tanigawa, a director famous across the whole country, someone who couldn't be bothered to spare a glance at an ordinary person. Actors tried to get his attention. Actresses did their best to look appealing when they walked by him.

It was this Tanigawa who was looking at Pak Roksan.

When Roksan noticed Tanigawa's gaze, he froze in his tracks and stood like a funerary stele. He had no idea why the man he had revered as a god for so long was looking at him.

Later, Tanigawa told his people:

"His thick eyebrows are as beautiful as a flying dragon. His piercing eyes are absolutely mesmerizing. His nose has a remarkable allure, and with his tightly clenched lips his face has a very masculine appeal. What's more, he is incredibly tall and has a virile physique. I have to say, he is a handsome man, the likes of which are hard to find. Even if you looked in all corners of Japan, you would be hard pressed to find someone like that."

He was in the middle of casting parts in an ambitious, big-budget historical movie that was to be shot in a few months. As soon as he saw Roksan, his head was filled with an irrepressible feeling of joy. And that is how, from an errand boy, Roksan got the opportunity to become an actor.

For the time being, Tanigawa gave him a small role.

Roksan had dreamt of being an actor for a long time, and, when he was a child, his comrades marveled at his ability to perfectly reenact the scenes from any movie. He was therefore able to act brilliantly for this minor role.

"Not bad. You're good. But try to be even better," said Tanigawa, patting Roksan on the shoulder.

The director really liked Roksan's performance.

Thereafter, even when he had to travel far, Tanigawa brought Roksan along and helped him improve his acting.

"You lack the correct way of expressing your feelings. You still have a long way to go."

Tanigawa was quite demanding, and he could be hurtful and insulting to those who did not do exactly as he said.

But Roksan was gladly willing to endure the treatment. Don't they say that the sweetest fruits grow from the bitterest roots? If it could make him a famous actor, he was ready to go through much worse.

His skills improved day by day.

Soon, he signed a formal contract with the film studio on Tanigawa's recommendation.

His heart was about to explode like a balloon. He had managed to reach a path that was now wide open before him and would lead him to realize his childhood dream.

It was around that time that his father, who had been a driver, died suddenly in a car accident. One morning, just like that, Roksan's family lost its breadwinner.

They wondered how they would manage to survive.

His mother, at last, decided to return to Korea. She had no reason to stay in the country that had taken her husband from her.

When he was still alive, his father had once spoken of going back to Korea, but Roksan had nonetheless not anticipated his mother's decision to leave Japan.

If I missed this chance, this unique chance to fulfill my hopes, all my dreams would be ruined. I cannot pass up this opportunity, thought Roksan.

And so, he hid behind a pillar at the train station and watched his mother and brother leave.

Now alone, Roksan rented a room in the house of a woman who was Tanigawa's distant cousin.

This woman was no less a cinephile than he was and, because she'd heard from Tanigawa that Roksan would soon be the lead in a big movie, she gave him a special deal on the room.

Roksan had asked to rent out the cheapest room available, a small storage room in the attic. But the woman had given him a much more comfortable one, facing south and well lit. She took care of him as if he were a young master from a well-to-do family.

It was as if the doors of hope had opened up before him. In his dreams, he saw himself as the celebrated lead actor in a critically acclaimed movie. He also saw his mother filled with joy as she learned of his success.

But something unexpected happened. The morning when Roksan came to see Tanigawa after he received the movie's script and spent the night memorizing it, Tanigawa's eyes were cold like a block of ice. Without even asking him to sit, he looked at him suspiciously and asked:

"Yamada-san, is it true that you are a Korean?"

Up until now, Tanigawa had always talked to him in an informal way, without using honorifics. Roksan was stunned to hear him speak in honorifics and even more terrified by the nature of the question.

Roksan answered with a question:

"Who told you this?"

Tanigawa took a meticulously folded piece of paper out of his pocket. It was an anonymous letter:

"This Yamada Roggusan (this was Roksan's Japanese name) that you like so much is a *senjin*.[3] What kind of person are you to support the career of a *senjin*?"

There was no need to ask who had written this. It must have been one of Roksan's many competitors who was vying to get the role.

"Is this true?" shouted Tanigawa, slapping the letter.

Roksan looked at the letter. The words on the paper painfully pierced his eyes.

He lowered his head.

"No! I'm not a *senjin*. I'm Korean! I'm Pak Roksan!"

As if he were taken aback by his attitude, Tanigawa remained silent for a few moments before opening his mouth:

---

3 Derogatory terms for Koreans in Japanese, abbreviation of *chōsenjin* (Korean person).

"Yamada-san, as you know this is a historical film about Japan… So, in a historical film about Japan… having a Korean play the lead role…"

And that is how Roksan, on the verge of becoming an actor, saw his dream pop like a soap bubble. He also got fired from his job as an errand boy at the film studio. But he did not really care. How could he run errands there if he could not become an actor anymore?

As soon as he got fired, he faced a chain of difficulties. His landlady, who had heard the story, removed him from his sunny room and placed him in the storage room in the attic. She started treating him not like a young master but more like a servant. After a few days, she nervously pressed him to pay his rent and he had to spend his days outside, returning to his room only at night, like a thief. He went everywhere looking for a job, but in this stone-cold country there was no one to help a young penniless Korean. The landlady eventually kicked him out of his room. He took what few belongings he possessed and ended up in the streets. Food quickly became a problem. For the first time, Roksan realized the true meaning of an old saying: "Of all ailments, hunger is the saddest and the hardest to endure".

He became one of those creatures that roams the streets with nowhere to go. But he could not bring himself to beg.

One day as he stood in the corner of a street, crushed by hunger, somebody put something in his hand.

Surprised, Roksan opened his eyes. His benefactor was a clown, with a pointy hat and a polka dot costume, wearing a sandwich board covering his chest and back. A clown, the lowest of all street scum, with his face full of grotesque make-up, was the one who gave him charity.

Offended, Roksan ran after him.

"What the hell is this? I'm not a bum!"

Roksan took the money and threw it at the clown. After briskly walking away, he realized that he might have been unkind. Was not this man a human being too? He ran towards him to apologize.

However, far from being hurt by Roksan's attitude, the clown went his way laughing. The melody of the song he kept singing rose up in harmony with the bell he was ringing:

Don't ask any question
Just look at my billboard

It seemed as if he were saying: I am not a man, I am just a billboard.

Ah, I've reached the point where even a street clown takes pity on me, Roksan thought.

That night, Roksan paced up and down an alleyway lined with restaurants and did not know what to do. Without him even noticing, hunger had guided his steps in this direction and now prevented him from leaving.

Sushi restaurants, noodle restaurants...

Dizzying neon signs blinked all around him.

It seemed that all the food and dishes in the world were gathered in this alleyway.

Roksan was standing as if his feet were nailed to the ground in front of a sushi restaurant. Between the two black curtains hanging from the front door, one could clearly see the inside of the restaurant. In the kitchen, a cook, with a towel tightly tied around his head, was preparing *maki* rolls with mystifying dexterity. He first spread a black sheet of seaweed paper glistening with oil on a bamboo mat. Using a spoon, he then adroitly covered it with rice as white as snow and lined it up with yellow bits of omelet, lightly boiled green spinach, cucumber, grilled eels... He quickly rolled the bamboo mat and finished the roll in one go. With a large knife, he sliced the whole thing and placed it on a white square plate.

*Ah, if only I could eat just one of those rolls. If I had kept the money that the clown gave me earlier...*Roksan thought.

His mouth watered, and his stomach growled loud enough to be heard from kilometers away.

Before he even realized what he was doing, he'd grabbed the curtains and entered the restaurant. All he could see was the sushi on the white plate. The cook raised his head when he heard the curtains open, and his eyes were now turning into flaming torches.

Roksan looked at the cook's mouth opening wide and just when he thought he was hearing people shouting "Thief!" two hands from behind grabbed his shoulders like a tight vise.

I'm caught! As the thought crossed his mind, everything turned black before his eyes. He suddenly remembered Jean Valjean, who had spent nineteen years in prison and lived his entire life hiding from the police because he had stolen some bread.

But the man who grabbed Roksan's shoulders did not shout at him. Instead, he spoke in a soft tone, "Why! Why would you open the curtains and rush into the restaurant like that? Look at how surprised people look."

It was an older man, much beyond his fifties. He pushed Roksan into the restaurant.

"Here, have a seat."

The cook sighed with relief. He glanced at Roksan from top to bottom as if he still suspected him, then asked the older man:

"Is this guy with you?"

"Absolutely. Young people are feisty you see…"

Like a puppet, Roksan let the older man guide him to his seat and sat down. It took a while before he could finally ask:

"Sir, who are you?"

The older man cracked a smile and said, "I'm Korean like you, young man."

Roksan was puzzled and asked, "How did you know that I was Korean?"

"I knew it when I saw you on the street refusing to beg."

"On the street?"

Roksan did not remember seeing an older man anywhere.

"Where did you see me?"

At that moment, the waiter came with two plates of *sushi*.

"Eat. We'll talk more later…"

Roksan emptied his plate in a flash. The older man pushed his plate toward Roksan, who ended up emptying that plate too.

"And now, I'd like to hear how a young lad like you ended up in this situation."

Roksan told him his entire story without hiding anything.

Hunger had made him lose his mind, so he was very grateful to the older man for preventing him from becoming Kyoto's "Jean Valjean." But more than that, he had seen in the old man's eyes—these slightly wrinkled eyes that now looked at him—a warm benevolence and a deep wisdom. And he had mentioned that he was a Korean like him.

When Roksan finished his story, the older man let out a long sigh.

"So now, you're all alone without anywhere to go? What are you going to do?"

He didn't know how to respond.

The older man remained silent. He closed his eyes for a second, then asked without reopening them:

"Young man, would you do something if I asked you to do it?"

"What is it?"

The older man opened his eyes and smiled:

"Don't worry about it. It's not thievery, begging or gambling. It's not a scam either. What do you say?"

Roksan looked again straight into the older man's eyes and said without hesitating:

"I'll do it."

"All right. Then come to my house tonight."

"Sorry?"

"You can't sleep on the streets, now can you? We may be further south than in Korea here, but for people who don't have a home, it's colder. That's life in a foreign land, isn't it?"

And so Roksan followed the older man to his house.

They were greeted by his daughter who must have been about the same age as Roksan.

The older man and his daughter lived together in this small house.

Rembrandt's *Return of the Prodigal Son* was stuck on a wall with a tack.

Beginning that very night, Roksan would experience unforeseen joy and surprises along with shame, despair and failure.

His first surprise came from the older man's daughter.

"Come on, say hi," he told his daughter. "It's a young guy who works with me in the company's sales department."

As he bowed to say hello, a shout of surprise escaped her mouth. "Oh my!" Roksan looked up and shouted, "Myŏngmi!"

Yes. It really was Myŏngmi from high school.

Myŏngmi... At school, she was the only girl whom he'd ever felt close to. He met her when he was a sophomore.

She'd been a transfer student from another school. She sat next to Roksan, as that was the only empty seat. They ended up becoming desk buddies.

She whispered, "My name is Akemi (Myŏngmi). Thank you in advance for your help."

Roksan never quite fit in with the other Japanese students, so he only nodded without even turning his head.

Two weeks later, during English class, the teacher suddenly announced that there was an exam. The students started to grumble and sigh with frustration.

The exam started.

Roksan always scored the highest in the class and had no difficulties answering every question.

There was still time before the end of the test, so he stole glances at Myŏngmi's answers. She answered almost all of them, except for one. She bit her lips anxiously. Roksan took pity on her. So, he wrote down the answer on the back of his exam and showed it to her. Myŏngmi's eye lit up and she wrote down the answer right away. That day, out of thirty-five students, only Roksan and Myŏngmi got a perfect score.

At the end of the class, Roksan strolled towards the river with his bag on his shoulders. Someone approached him from behind and said "Hey!" It was Myŏngmi.

"Thank you so much for helping me this time. From now on, I'll study harder to make sure I don't end up in a similar situation again."

"You're welcome" said Roksan gruffly. He continued walking. Myŏngmi followed him and kept talking, even though he hardly paid any attention to her.

"Roksan, you're Korean, aren't you?"

He stopped walking and quickly turned his head towards her. The question irritated him, as he had been trying hard to hide the fact that he was Korean.

"Even if that were true, what's it to you?" he spat with a dirty look.

Oddly enough, Myŏngmi's smile became even more radiant.

"It's just that I am Korean too."

"What?"

"If you hadn't been Korean, I think I might as well have thrown my test in the trash today."

Only then did Roksan look at Myŏngmi's face again.

When she smiled, her whole face brightened up and had a playful air. There was a liveliness in her eyes that looked lovely to anyone who talked to her. The bridge of her nose was high, and she had a slightly prominent upper lip that gave her a very peculiar impish look. Now that he looked at her again knowing that she was Korean, she gave him a much better impression.

"Let's team up and do better than the Japanese students!" she cried.

Without knowing why, his eyes filled with tears upon hearing Myŏngmi's innocent and vivacious words.

This is how their friendship began.

Myŏngmi told Roksan that her father worked in the sales department of a company.

On the day of their graduation, they walked along the riverbank.

"Today is the last day we take this path," she said.

Roksan felt his heart tighten.

Whenever they took this path home, Myŏngmi spoke nonstop, chirping like a skylark. But that day, these were the only words she said. The rest of the way, she walked in silence.

After walking along the bank for a while, they reached a fork in the road. The sound of the wind rustling through the birch trees weakened, the chirping birds flew away and all became quiet around them, as if someone had been whispering to them.

Myŏngmi, visibly disappointed, let out a long sigh before she spoke:

"Well, looks like the time has come to part ways."

"Looks like it."

Their eyes met.

There were many things shining through their passionate eyes, but they stood there unable to decide whether they should speak or not.

"What are you going to do now?" she asked, breaking the silence.

"Well… for the time being, I'm not quite sure. But I want to become a famous actor one day."

"A famous actor?"

"If I succeed, I'll find you."

"Promise?"

"Of course!"

And with that, they parted ways. That had been some time ago.

Roksan was utterly embarrassed to stand before Myŏngmi, without a job or a home, particularly when he had boasted that he would come find her once he had become a famous actor.

But Myŏngmi, entirely unaware of his situation, was thrilled and could not stop talking to him.

"Father, I remember when we graduated, Roksan said he wanted to become a famous actor. And now he's working with you?"

Roksan wanted to find a mouse hole to hide in, but the older man smiled calmly.

"Don't you know? Do you think one can become an actor without money? Roksan works at the company to earn money for his acting classes."

"Hey! Is that so?"

Naïve Myŏngmi believed her father and did not ask any other questions. Shame and despair prevented Roksan from raising his head and he could only let out a sigh of relief. But this was only the first act of this tragic comedy.

The place where the older man took him the next day was not the sales department of some company but the advertising service of a department store that was so far away from their house that they had to change subways twice just to get there.

There was nobody else in the room when they entered. There were only two pointy hats and two clown costumes hanging from the wall.

Taken aback, Roksan wondered why the older man had brought him there. But once he had scanned the room, he noticed the older man taking off his clothes and donning the polka dot costume. When he was done, he told Roksan:

"Come on, get dressed."

"Excuse me?"

"Luckily for you, the other clown became half paralyzed after a stroke. So, there is a free spot for you."

"What?!"

It is only then that Roksan realized that the clown who'd given him money the day before was actually this older man, Myŏngmi's father. His whole body was shaking with shame and distress. He narrowly avoided the fate of Jean Valjean, but it was now the life of a clown that awaited him.

"Never! I... I... I can't do such a thing! How could I do something like that in front of people?"

Roksan stopped shouting as soon as he realized he couldn't bring himself to reject the man who'd showed him such kindness and hospitality.

The older man did not flinch. He chuckled, took Roksan's hand, and sat him down next to him.

"Young man, listen to what I have to say. You and I, we have no other path to follow. You and I, we share the same fate. I wanted to be an entrepreneur. A few years ago, I cut all ties with the *ch'ongnyŏn* organization.[4] How could I have done business properly here if people knew that I was Korean?... But the business I started went bankrupt not long ago and here I am now, a clown...

"You must have seen the picture from Rembrandt at our house? It shows a father embracing his prodigal son, who became a beggar, and preparing a fatted calf for him. But you, like I, do not have such a father. Even our fatherland would never take back prodigal sons like us. Our country that strove to achieve independence when it was in the fierce claws of the Japanese bastards; our country that managed to fend off those American bastards in a bloody war... How could it ever forgive us? I couldn't even bring myself to ask for forgiveness... So, I wear this costume."

A tear rolled down the older man's wrinkled cheek.

"In life, all sorts of things happen. But one should never forget one's fatherland. Even if you're tempted by ten thousand treasures, by glory or money, by honor or staggering success. If you get taken in by those things and forget, even for a moment, about your fatherland, you're betraying the country that gave birth to you. If you lead such a life, you can only end up stuck in the mud up to your neck. Regrets always come too late. When I realized that, it was already... late, too late. You can't relive your life."

---

4 *Chaeilbon Chosŏnin Ch'ongnyŏn haphoe*, a North-Korea affiliated association of Korean residents in Japan.

"So, I put on this costume and I carry those advertising billboards around the streets. I could not dare raise my head in front of people or my fatherland, so I put on this costume and I smear my face with make-up... It's the way it is. I reap what I've sown, it's my fault."

The older man spoke with a defeated voice. He seemed to have given up on everything.

Roksan, who had stood still looking down at the floor, took off his clothes quickly and threw them in a corner.

"I, too, will wear this costume," Roksan declared.

And so Roksan entered the second act of this tragic comedy. He became a clown, the lowest of jobs, for the lowest of dregs.

Day after day, the two men strode across the city, ringing their bells, their grotesque faces covered by make-up, dressed up in their polka dot costumes and wearing their pointy hats, carrying large advertising billboards on their bodies. Tears ran down his face, but he did not need to wipe or hide them. Nobody would see, nobody would even know that tears and sweat were rolling down his painted face, for he was not a human being anymore. He was a moving advertisement.

He expected his mother to appear suddenly on the corner of some street and scold him: "Roksan, you brat, you abandoned your mother and stayed in Japan to become a clown?"

When I walk down the street
Wearing my ridiculous costume
With my pointy hat, I ring my bell
And the leaves of the willows by the road,
Softly stroke my cheeks

When he saw his old schoolmates in the street, he would quickly turn his face away. Even though he knew that they wouldn't recognize him under all his make-up, his body shook with shame and despair whenever he saw someone he knew, and he would always try to avoid them as fast as possible. The older man, however, always remained calm. He never got angry nor surprised—he seemed above such things.

"See boy, people who pass by with a mocking smile are no different from us. Do you think there is a single human being who does not wear a mask? Displaying a smile that isn't really there, pretending to be happy... Don't be ashamed of your face. Once we've become clowns, we're not people anymore, we're just advertising billboards. Walking advertising billboards. Billboards don't get angry. They don't get sad. Act like you have no feelings and no expressions."

"Does your daughter know about your work?"

"What are you talking about? If she found out about this, she might try to kill herself. You must keep this secret at all costs."

He had Roksan promise this over a hundred times.

Roksan, too, did not want Myŏngmi to find out.

The older man chosen to work in a distant place so that he would not cross paths with Myŏngmi.

Later that night, they took off their clown costumes and headed home with more falsehoods. They greeted Myŏngmi and exchanged some fake stories about their day over dinner.

One day, as the two were working, the older man asked Roksan, "I've dragged you into quite a difficult predicament, haven't I?"

Roksan chuckled sadly.

"It's okay. I think of it as being in an acting class."

The older man laughed.

"People are actors, and the world is a stage, as Shakespeare used to say," Roksan added.

The older man walked a few more steps in silence, then said, "I hate those who've turned the world into a stage and people into actors!"

This outburst was quite unlike him. He was usually calm and collected in all circumstances. Roksan halted and said, "What did you say?"

"I hate them! I hate them a hundred times, a thousand times!"

He exploded because he was father forced to lie to his own daughter. The daughter whom he had taught that "a lie is the worst of all things." The rage of an old man who didn't know what to say to his child anymore when he came back home to his role as a father.

Even for an actor, comedy is only enjoyable on stage. Having to be an actor even when you're at home, having to turn your own home into a stage, was a cruel thing.

Roksan could not say anything. The older man walked in silence.

"There's one thing that bothers me," said the older man.

"What is it?"

"I have a grown-up daughter at home. We now have a young man like you living with us. People notice these things. Rumors are spreading and that's no good."

Roksan's face looked as if it were on fire. He spoke extremely fast and stuttered:

"I – today I will l-l-look for a room to rent. Right away!"

The older man smiled and grabbed his arm:

"No need. If you had to go somewhere else, we'd both be sad, my daughter and I. So, I think I found a solution. But I don't know what you'll think."

"S- so what is this solution?" Roksan asked.

"How would you like to become part of our family?"

"What? But I...so..."

"What a doofus you are. I'm asking if you'd like to marry Myŏngmi," the older man said.

Roksan stopped in his tracks. He was already deeply fond of Myŏngmi.

"Rea...really?" Roksan stuttered.

"So, you're okay with it?" the older man asked.

The older man laughed and so did Roksan. This might have been the only time when they both laughed heartily and happily on their way back home. That night, the older man once again made Roksan swear he would keep their secret.

The old man did not live much longer after that. One month after Roksan and Myŏngmi got married, the older man passed away from a cardiac disease, without even leaving a will.

Perhaps it was because they had sensed this tragic end somehow that Roksan and Myŏngmi had rushed to get married.

The two were now alone in the little house.

Roksan's life started becoming more difficult.

In the mornings he left home wearing a dignified expression and, after having wandered all day in shame and bearing the insults and scorn directed at street clowns, he returned home at night and made up lies. It was a difficult life, lying to his wife.

It had been easier when his father-in-law was around. He would speak on behalf of Roksan and change subjects when the situation was not favorable.

But now, Roksan had no way to avoid his wife's curiosity.

She pressed him with very precise questions to know how his work in the company went and she would not stop before she heard an answer that satisfied her. He would sometimes pretend to be in a bad mood and to not want to talk, or he would pretend to be sick and keep his mouth shut.

Once, as they were sitting face to face at the dinner table, his wife stared at him with her eyes wide open and asked him:

"What is that under your ear?"

"Under my ear?"

His heart dropped when he looked at himself in the mirror. There was still some of his clown make-up stuck under his ear.

"Where did you find this make-up?"

Roksan awkwardly tried to find an answer.

"Ah, that, yes of course. I've started an amateur theatre group at the company to practice my acting. I thought it might motivate people and increase sales. That's why I put on this make-up today."

"Is that so? In that case, why didn't you tell me sooner?"

Roksan acted like there was nothing to it and said, "It's nothing to write home about. I was going to tell you after I've become a real actor."

"Oh my, is that true? You're taking acting classes on top of your work? You're close to achieving your dream!"

Naïve Myŏngmi was overjoyed.

That night, as soon as his wife had fallen asleep, Roksan cried quietly.

From that day forth, he had to come up with stories about his amateur performances. It was truly pitiful.

And so opened the third act...

"Really, during those days, I had no idea what you were doing. I was deeply troubled ... I was afraid too... Especially when you went hiking."

Upon hearing these words, Roksan let out a deep sigh.

Lively voices of his children and the music from the television filled the house, but he reminisced about the past.

A journey to the past... the hikes...

Hiking was a hobby that Roksan picked up after hearing about his mother from a compatriot that he met on his way to work.

The compatriot coincidentally ran into Roksan on the street, grabbed his hand and said, "Say, I'm just coming back from the fatherland, and guess what, I saw your mother in Pyongyang?"

"My mother?"

Roksan grabbed his hand. Ever since they had parted ways at Kyoto Station, he had continually thought about her, and whenever he faced hardship or loneliness, he would call out to his mother for help in his head.

"She's extremely worried about you. Hurry up and write to her."

The compatriot wrote down her address for him.

Roksan held the paper in his hand and felt as if he was going to break down crying.

"Pyongyang, Pothong River district, Sinmi district, 25th block, stairway number 6, 4th floor, room 8."

Ah, mother! My dear mother and brother! Roksan thought.

He wiped his tears as he read the address from which his mother's scent seemed to emanate.

He wanted to write to her straight away. But what would he write about? He could not tell her that far from having become an actor, he was now a clown and a human billboard. If his mother had known, she would have fainted. But he also couldn't lie to his mother.

That night, after coming home, he spent a long time looking out the window towards the east, towards Pyongyang. The fatherland, far to the west. The fatherland, where his mother was thinking about him.

The song his mother used to sing to him when he was a child still echoed in his ears:

Sailing in the blue sky and the Milky Way
On a very small white ship with no mast
Nor oars, a rabbit and a cinnamon tree
Go and go boldly towards the western land

Maybe the composer of this nursery rhyme too had found himself stranded in a foreign land and spent his time crying and remembering his beloved fatherland in the west. Western land… Western sky…

But what he saw through the window was not Pyongyang's sky. From Kyoto, where he was, it was impossible to see Pyongyang's sky.

He looked for Pyongyang on a map. From where would he be able to see the western sky, the sky of Pyongyang where his mother was? He spent the night looking for such a place. Pyongyang was on the 39th parallel. Roksan's eyes looked for cities in Japan on a similar latitude and eventually stopped on a place called Honjo in Akita prefecture.

"Here!"

Flanked by the East Sea, the town was almost perfectly aligned with Pyongyang.

When he was off work a few days later, he left for Honjo.

"Honjo you say? I've never heard that name before in my life. Why would you go to such a place even though you've got no friends or family there?" asked Myŏngmi.

Roksan simply answered that he had to go there on business for his company.

That day, he took the train and when he arrived, he hiked up into the mountains. He reached the highest summit and for a long time looked at the western sky that spread across the sea. On the other side of the sea was

Pyongyang and his mother. From this point, there was nothing blocking the view, and he could fully contemplate the sea and the western sky.

"Mother, your undeserving son, Roksan, has come to greet you. I hope you can forgive your son, who ended up a clown because he did not listen to you. How could a horrible person like me ever face you again? Mother I can only respectfully salute you and beg for your forgiveness."

On his next day off, he went to Honjo again. And on the next one, and the next one… He could not have overcome the loneliness and the despair had he not done so. To his wife who grew increasingly suspicious, he answered that it was just that he had been hiking a few times in the mountains near Honjo and that it was his favorite place.

"Oh really? You never told me you liked hiking and that you liked this place. When did you start hiking?"

"Isn't there a saying that the late-night winds blow the hardest? People often become passionate about a hobby they start late. And in a way, hiking too is like an acting class."

Roksan hated himself for his ability to lie so blatantly and calmly.

Maybe it was his life as a clown that ended up making him impervious to everything. Even when he donned his pointy hat and pranced around the streets, he did not feel the same shame, despair and regret he once had. Once you have fallen into the trap, you are there for life, no matter how hard you try to get out.

One autumn day, as Roksan was getting ready to leave for Honjo again, his wife desperately tried to stop him.

"I heard that a lot of snow had fallen over there, why would you go hiking there? What would you do if there's an avalanche? You think that going hiking is like going on an expedition? You can't go there!"

"An expedition?" Roksan laughed. "Fine, let's call it an expedition."

The impishness that usually filled his wife's eyes was all but gone.

"And I hate it when you laugh like that. That empty, crazy laugh. Do you think I'm a child? What kind of person would go hiking and climbing mountains like that all by himself? What would you do if you run into a bear or a tiger…? I won't allow it. You'd better join some hiking club and go there with other people."

"I wouldn't be hiking for the same reasons as them."

"How could you have different reasons for going hiking? Don't people more or less all want the same thing? Getting some fresh air, enjoying nature, exercising a bit?"

Roksan could not stand this no longer. He told his wife everything.

Tears flowed from his eyes as he told her the reasons for going hiking. She, too, cried.

"Honey, in that case, wouldn't it be better if we just went back to Korea? Is there anything that ties you to this country or to your company? Why don't you think about going back if you miss your mother so much? I miss my mother too. She passed away while giving birth to me, and I've always lived with my father. I would like to call someone 'mother' for once."

Roksan shook his head.

"I can't go. Neither you nor I... Didn't your father say so? We've committed a crime against the fatherland."

Myŏngmi wiped her tears. She put Roksan's hiking clothes in his bag and changed the subject.

"So how is work these days. You always say that everything is fine but you're not getting any raises... Aren't they cheating you?"

"Cheating me? What are you talking about?"

"Nothing. I worry that's all."

Roksan let out a sigh of relief.

But their lives were about to enter the play's final act.

One day, Myŏngmi came home with two reasons to be happy. Her heart was almost exploding with joy. Without telling her husband, she had sent her mother-in-law in Pyongyang a letter and just received an answer. Furthermore, she had gone to the hospital because she was not feeling very well and received some happy news. Her heart was racing and she couldn't wait to share all this happiness right away with her husband.

However, when she reached the address where her father and her husband worked, she was flabbergasted. There was no company there. From what people told her, there had never been a company there. How was it possible? Was she on the wrong street? She walked around all the streets in the area but still couldn't find her husband's company. It was nowhere to be found.

She suddenly felt afraid.

A fake company? What kind of person is my husband? And my father? No, it can't be... but... Myŏngmi thought.

She was terrified and confused. As she stood in the street without knowing what to do, she met a former schoolmate. Her confusion only got worse when the classmate told her that he had seen her husband several times coming in and out of a street opposite the station where there was a department store.

This was really far from where they lived.

Neither her husband nor her father had ever mentioned that street's name. Without even thinking, she got on a tramway and headed there. On that street the department store and the other shops were packed together like the suckers on an octopus' tentacle...

When I walk down the street
With my funny polka dot costume
And my pointy hat, I ring my bell

There was a clown carrying an advertising billboard. A coffee shop was playing a sad song, and the clown was prancing around to the music's rhythm. His face and his laughable costume... Myŏngmi stared at him for a long time. She wondered how this person must have felt, now that he had given up the face he was born with for this one that was barely even human. What could he be thinking about when he met people's scornful looks? Had the clown made his face so grotesque-looking to get people's attention, or to hide from people? He must constantly be looking for a mousehole to hide in...

A pack of children had encircled the clown and ran circles around him while singing:

Dance, dance! Clown, clown!
Sing, sing! Clown, clown!
Clown, clown, clown, clown
Dance on all four!
Jump on two legs!
Clown, clown, clown, clown

The clown, as if used to their mockery, ignored them and kept walking. What kind of life was that, to be constantly submitted to ridicule and insults?

As Myŏngmi was thinking like this, the clown's behavior abruptly changed.

One minute he was hopping around, the next minute he suddenly turned around and started running.

"What?"

As if by instinct, the children chased after the fugitive like a pack of young dogs. They chased him and screamed and threw rocks, rotten tomatoes, and empty juice cans at him. The fleeing clown quickly turned his head around to look behind him. At that very moment, a sharp bit of scrap metal flew towards his face and hit him on the forehead.

"Ouch!"

Myŏngmi ran towards him. The children ran away and scattered. The clown held his face in his hands. Blood was dripping between his fingers.

"Oh my goodness, you're bleeding!" she cried.

He had a wound shaped like an L on his forehead.

As if he felt no pain, he pretended not to see Myŏngmi and continued on his way.

"Hey! Excuse me! Hey, you!" she shouted after him.

The clown didn't turn around, acting as if he didn't even hear her. He rang his bell and sang:

As a young man, the billboard clown
Got in all sorts of trouble
But don't ask any questions
Just read the billboard

Myŏngmi looked at his retreating back with tears in her eyes. When she noticed the sun was about to set, she hurried back home.

It was already night when she got back and, forgetting why she even went out in the first place, she just sat on the floor, still, absent-minded and terribly suspicious. There was nothing she could do as anxiety and fear festered inside her.

Her husband came back late and very drunk. Until then, he'd never touched liquor. Myŏngmi was surprised to see her husband drunk, but even more surprising was the bandage wrapped around his head.

"Honey, what happened to you?"

She followed her staggering husband to the bedroom and made him lie down.

"Honey, how did you get hurt?"

"Yeah, yeah. Not hurt... just a bandage"

"What are you saying?"

"Today... I played the role... of someone wounded on the forehead... yes, that's it... the acting class... that's why I came home... without taking the bandage off... aren't I cool... eh?"

She put her hands on her husband's forehead. He grunted.

"Stop lying!" she yelled.

Myŏngmi quickly undid the bandage. When she saw his forehead, she screamed. There was an L-shaped wound surrounded by makeup which had not been washed off.

"Ah!"

Myŏngmi collapsed. She felt as if the whole world was turning upside down. Yes. This clown was actually her husband. He must've been shocked when he saw her and tried to run away. In that case, her father too? Had her father also been a human billboard? Her vision went dark as she shook her husband violently.

"Honey, what's going on? Was it you, that clown? The company's sales department and the acting classes, they were all lies? Huh? Speak! Hurry up and speak!"

Now, I'm in real trouble, thought Roksan.

When he realized that his wife had discovered the whole thing, Roksan sobered up instantly. A bottomless pit of despair had opened before him.

His wife cried and screamed.

"You've been lying to me. And my father has been lying to me, too! The entire world has been lying to me! Liars… Oh, I could just die."

Those words did not surprise Roksan much. Oddly enough, the idea of dying did not seem surprising to him anymore. Who was is that said that? That it is not surprising that people are born and that there is nothing to be surprised about when they die. After all, what difference was there between birth and death? He was thoroughly crushed and was grumbling to himself. Roksan, does a man like you still deserve to live? You who abandoned your mother while boasting that you would become a famous actor, you who stayed in this wretched country?

"I didn't lie. It was just a rehearsal… Everything. It's because it's always been that way. The world is a stage and people are actors. Isn't life itself an acting class? Shit! And this too! Isn't this a stage?"

The wooden floor of his house indeed looked like a stage. A stage where the curtain had just been lifted and where a play was about to begin. There was also a rope strewn across the floor. He only had to grab the rope and the play would begin.

He staggered towards the rope. He realized it was a clothesline that his wife had left there. He knew what he had to do. He grabbed the rope, tied a slipknot.

"Since this is all an acting class, this will be my last class."

He looked at the slipknot. The last class.

He had once read a book called *The Last Class*, where an old teacher holds his last class with students in the French region of Alsace, which was then occupied by Prussia. The children had forgotten their national language. The teacher wrote "Vive la France" on the blackboard and said, "It's over… go on now." With what words should Roksan conclude his last class? His father-in-law's voice suddenly echoed in his head: "I hate those who've turned the world into a stage and people into actors! I hate them, I hate them a hundred, a thousand times."

I hate them too, those who've turned the world into a stage and people into actors! I hate them a hundred, a thousand times.

He wrapped the slipknot around his neck. His wife grabbed him.

"Honey, what are you doing? How can you do this? You think you can leave me alone? I… I'm pregnant."

Roksan stared at his wife, struck by terrible anguish. He knew he could not take his life, not now. But he also couldn't let this new life in his wife's womb become the child of a clown.

"Honey, let's go to home. Let's go to our fatherland," his wife said.

"Go back home?"

"Today I received a letter from your mother. Look."

With his eyes filled with tears, Roksan read his mother's letter.

"My son, come home. Come home, not to your mother, who looked for you and cried in Kyoto and Niigata, but to the motherly embrace of your socialist nation. A few days ago, I had the honor of meeting the fatherly Leader. He greeted the expatriates and listened to my story and said that it must be very hard for you to live in Japan. He promised that someone will find you and bring you home, so that when you come here, he can make you a movie actor. My son, our socialist country embraces all its children without discrimination. Come home. My arms are small, but your country's arms are immense. So, come home quickly."

Roksan buried his face in the letter.

"Mother!"

Outside, the light from the streetlamps dripped over the road, and the cars' headlights passed by at full speed. This highway which looked like a meandering river, was it not a river of joy, a river of emotion?

"Honey!" cried Roksan, turning to his wife. "In this picture, you can see the father embracing his debauched son and bringing him a fattened calf. But it is the fatherly Leader and the Great General who brought me back and made me, Pak Roksan, a movie actor. It is they who nominated me for the main part of a great revolutionary work, they who today grant me the highest honor for an actor. How many mothers and fathers in this world could give me as much as our leaders have given?"

Instead of answering, his wife simply wiped her tears.

"Dad! Mom! Come on!" cried Roksan's daughter, unable to wait any longer. "Are you done thinking about the past?"

Roksan moved away from the window and towards his daughter.

"We just finished," he declared.

"Is that so?" asked his daughter suspiciously. She was about to ask him something when roaring sound of a choir came out of the television and filled the house.

The best, the best
Ah- the best

Then, as if speaking for both Roksan and his wife, the choir sang,

"Our general is the best!"

POWER

CHAPTER 8

LIFE[1]

Paek Namnyong was born on October 19, 1949, in Kwanghwa, Hamhŭng city, South Hamgyŏng Province. Paek grew up reading Korean folktales, and European literature, particularly Romantic-era Russian and French novels which have shaped his writing style. He started his professional life as a lathe operator but wrote short stories in his spare time. After submitting multiple pieces to his local newspaper, he was selected to receive training at Kim Il Sung University through a correspondence course. Upon graduating with a degree in Korean literature, he became a member of the Writers Union in Chagang Province, in the North of the country. While there, he drew inspiration from stories of the local courtroom for his novel *Friend* (*Pŏt*, 1988). A tale of love and divorce – a taboo topic almost unheard of in literature until then – with a mix of social criticism and humanist ethics, the book quickly gained tremendous popular and critical success and cemented Paek's career. *Friend* has since been adapted for television in the DPRK, published in South Korea and translated into English, French and Japanese.

Since the publication of *Friend*, Paek Namnyong has enjoyed an active and successful writing career and has become one of the major figures of North Korea's literary scene. His works often explore questions of duty and ethical dilemmas, such as the judge from *Friend* pondering about how his decision to

---

1 Paek Namnyong
  1985
  Translated by Immanuel Kim.

157

grant or deny a divorce will affect different people, the character Hyeok in the novel *Second Placement* (*Tu pŏntchae paech'ijang*, 1983) hesitating to accept a promotion she fears might be undeserved or the main character of "Life" standing up against nepotism. Paek's focus on his protagonists' sense of duty and ethics contrasts with his descriptions of the moral failings of characters in positions of power: party cadres, managers, or bureaucrats. Indeed, Paek may not be a dissident writer – he is the author of several books on the achievements of Kim Jong Il and a member of the April 15 Literary Production Unit, a group dedicated to writing fictionalized biographies of the Leaders – but he certainly is a critical one, pointing out the banality of corruption, abuses of power and self-serving greed among the higher echelons of DPRK society.

"Life" is an exemplary story of the country's Hidden Hero campaign. Dean Ri is indebted to his doctor for saving his life. The doctor's son has applied to the university where Ri works, but his test scores were below the standard. The Dean is pressured to accept the doctor's son into the university, but he then would have to reject a student who has passed the entrance exam. The Dean finds himself having to choose between adhering to the meritocratic rules of the university system or following his superiors' request to accept the undeserving student and his own sense of gratitude towards the doctor. His final decision is unspectacular but heroic nonetheless, upholding the principles deemed to sustain the nation and its socialist system.

Along the walking path, trees blazed orange as if they were on fire, reflecting the setting sun. The August heat rose from rocks on the path, but there was also a cool breeze coming from upstream. The river shimmered in the sunset, weeping willows bending their branches into the water, and all along the walking path was a line of fat pine trees and rusty benches where hikers could stop to enjoy the scenery.

Dean Ri Sŏkhun took it all in as he strolled, deep in thought.

In the past, early morning hikes, fresh air, and leisurely contemplation had always given him peace of mind. But his walk tonight aroused a deeper and more intimate sensation. Sŏkhun had just spent twenty days fighting for his life in the hospital, followed by several months convalescing at a rehabilitation center, but it had felt like years.

"Dean Ri, long time no see."

Sŏkhun turned around at the sound of the coarse but cheerful voice behind him.

A man in his fifties, wearing a large brimmed straw-hat and holding a broom in one hand and a dustpan in the other, approached Sŏkhun with a wide smile.

It was the caretaker of the small park, responsible for cleaning the paths along the river. Sŏkhun frequently met this caretaker in the mornings. The two men would smoke a cigarette together and talk lightly of small things—the weather, city happenings—but Sŏkhun had never happened to catch the caretaker's name. The caretaker had neither business dealings with the dean nor a particular relationship; he was simply someone the dean met every morning for a chat.

"You haven't changed," said the dean as he peered inside the dustpan full of pieces of paper, apple peels, and cigarette butts. "You should take Sundays off."

"I just came out for an evening stroll but noticed the trash," the caretaker said. "After people go to the movies, they come here. The few people who disregard the social contract and public order leave their trash around, and it ruins everything for everybody else."

The caretaker placed the dustpan down to his side and chuckled at himself as he realized how odd it sounded to say, "social contract and public order." Rather than appear irritated at having to work on his day off, he seemed rather proud, satisfied at the thought of people coming to the place that he worked so hard to keep clean.

He set the broom down next to the dustpan and pulled a pack of cigarettes from his shirt pocket.

"Dean Ri, did you go somewhere in the past few months?"

"I took a step into my own grave and came back," Sŏkhun said, smiling.

"Goodness, that's no joke! You must've been on the brink of death," the caretaker said.

"My small intestine got tangled, so I had to undergo a serious operation."

"How did something like that happen so suddenly?"

"During the Korean War, shrapnel penetrated my intestine, requiring surgery. Then, a few weeks ago, the walls of the intestine closed in and got entangled, causing intestinal obstruction. I lost consciousness for a few days."

"Goodness, I nearly lost a regular visitor to my small park," said the caretaker with a sigh that conveyed both relief and sympathy. Then he said solemnly, "People neglect past injuries because they're easily forgotten. During the war, I myself was injured on my side, and even fifty years later I still get nightly pains."

"You should go to the hospital before it gets worse," Dean Ri suggested.

"Well, not yet. I'm enjoying life too much." The caretaker spied a man squatting in the park some distance away and shouted out, "Excuse me, sir! Why throw the cigarette butt on the ground when the trashcan is right in front of your nose?" The caretaker then approached the man as though he were a policeman apprehending a thief. The embarrassed man fled. Without further comment, the caretaker brushed the cigarette butt into his dustpan. Then, feeling sorry that the dean had witnessed the exchange, he looked up at him and raced back to the walking path.

This was the kind of exchange they often shared: They would meet as though they had a deep relationship, and then part ways without a second thought. The caretaker prioritized cleaning up trash over getting acquainted with a person.

Sŏkhun suppressed the urge to pursue further conversation with the caretaker. Instead, he started walking again along the path. But then, suddenly, he remembered that he wasn't in this place to take a leisurely evening stroll.

No, his wife had earnestly requested that he invite the head doctor of the Gastroenterology Department in the city hospital to their house. Don't forget about the gastroenterologist who saved your life, his wife had urged him. She knew all too well the trouble doctors had gone through to save her dying husband before, on the battlefield. So, she had told him to invite the doctor for dinner. She prepared a grand meal and also put on soft music on the record player. This would be her way of honoring the doctor who saved her husband's life during the war, and also the doctor who saved his life in surgery, and at the rehabilitation center.

Dean Ri went to the hospital to find out where the doctor lived.

The sun set, and the sky darkened to charcoal.

The doctor's apartment was on the third floor, next to the hospital chief's apartment. It was an apartment with small windows. The doctor was not at home.

A little girl, still so small that she barely reached the doorknob, came out and greeted Dean Ri. She told him that her father was angry with her older brother and had left the house.

"Do you know where he went? I have an urgent matter to discuss with him," Sŏkhun told her, patting the child's head.

"Is it a house call?" the child asked, using her father's professional terminology.

"Hmmm, yes. Something like that."

The innocent expression disappeared from the girl's face and was replaced by a very mature look of concern. It was hard to believe the girl was only seven. She must have subconsciously absorbed her father's professional mien, a look she'd surely witnessed many times when he was with the many patients who came to see him at nights, in the rain, and in the snow.

"You will find him way over there," she answered, "Between the two apartments."

"The local bar?"

The girl nodded, fluttering her long eyelashes. Her fathomless dark eyes reflected the dark atmosphere of the house.

"Little girl, don't you worry. Your father will return home happy."

She did not respond.

Sŏkhun caressed her head and then walked back down the stairs.

The bar was in a plaza lined with streetlamps and neon signs. The doctor enjoyed spending his Sunday evenings at this bar. He liked to listen to the small chitchat and laughter. Many patrons stayed till closing time, and travelers killed time before their train arrived. Although the windows were open, there was no ventilation in the bar. There was a musty smell of stale cigarette smoke, alcohol, and greasy fried foods.

When Sŏkhun opened the door, he was met by a large crowd of loud patrons, standing around. He nudged past many people before finally getting to the doctor, who was in his white cap and gown sitting alone in the corner of the bar with his head resting on the table. The doctor looked up at Sŏkhun. Normally, the doctor was well-dressed in ironed clothes, handling his patients with the utmost care and respect. But the man now resting his head on the table did not resemble the doctor Sŏkhun had known.

"Doctor Chŏng," Sŏkhun called out.

The doctor recognized Sŏkhun and cracked a smile. It was apparent that he was troubled about something, but he maintained the smile.

"Dean Ri... It's you," mumbled the doctor.

Sŏkhun pulled up a chair and asked, "Is there something wrong? Why are you here all by yourself?"

"Dean... Ri, I would advise you... not to drink... alcohol. It is...harmful... to your health."

He was slurring his words but seemed serious.

"I quit many years ago. I've come to escort you to my home," Dean Ri said.

The doctor tried to lift his head up by holding on to the sides of the table, but then his head flopped forward again. He moaned and began to mumble some words.

"Intestinal...obstruction...is like my son...a dreadful condition. There is no medication...for such a condition. You eat...and it acts like it digests well... but then boom! It causes so much pain...I've spent...my entire life...fixing this condition...There is nothing more important to me...than my patients."

The doctor pushed a plate of fried duck toward Sŏkhun.

"Doctor Chŏng, let's go to my house."

"Why...is there someone in pain?"

"No. It's been a while since I've seen you! Let's have dinner together."

The doctor rubbed his temples in an effort to sober up.

"Thanks...but," he said, and then after a pause continued, "I don't go to a house...that does not require my service."

"My wife is waiting for us."

"Ah! The woman who was sitting...by your side. For four days in the hospital recovery room! What a committed woman. Tell her," the doctor slurred, "that I'm happy...to see her husband healthy."

Sŏkhun did not know how to respond.

"So, tell me," the doctor asked, "Does it still hurt?"

"No. I'm fine now."

"Avoid alcohol, cigarettes, cold foods...hard foods, spicy foods."

Sŏkhun was touched by how the doctor, despite his current intoxication, still cared for him, insisting on dispensing medical advice.

The doctor tried to get up again by placing his hands on the sides of the table. With his dilated eyes, he looked at Sŏkhun .

"Dean Ri...would you care to listen...to what I have to say?"

"Of course. Please."

"A few days ago...I submitted my medical essay to the commission board and won many awards from the province and other places...I finally became a respectable doctor. Now, why am I bragging about this? Well, you see, I have a son," the doctor said. "This kid failed to pass his college entrance exam...So, I met my nephew...who is an admissions supervisor at a university. I begged my nephew to show me my son's entrance exam. He missed two questions from the cutoff! Just two! It's so embarrassing that a doctor's son can't go to college."

Sŏkhun was at a loss for words.

"I'm telling you...I tried," said the doctor as he clenched his beer glass, which looked as though it would break in his hands.

"I failed as a father. I did all that I could to force him to study...to guarantee success...I would yell at him, beat him over the head, knowing that his thoughts were elsewhere. At one point, he finally sat his ass down and studied. But he couldn't pass the damn exam...Well, it's all in the past now. Dean Ri, what good is it to heal other people's problems when I failed to heal my own son's problem. I have nothing to show for the next generation and our society... What kind of a doctor am I, if I can't meet our nation's expectations? It's so depressing."

Sŏkhun spoke in a soft voice.

"Which university did your son apply to?"

"It's so embarrassing because it was to your school."

Sŏkhun was shocked. He avoided making eye contact with the doctor and stared instead at a corner of the table. The situation became fraught. On the one hand, he wanted to help the desperate doctor and his son. On the other hand, he must follow the code of ethics and fairness to all who applied to his university.

"Doctor, what's your son's name?"

As the dean in charge of admissions, Sŏkhun knew that he had the power to determine the fate of a student. The moment he asked that question, he furrowed his brows, knowing that he had betrayed his ethics.

"Chŏng Ch'ŏruk is his name..." said the doctor, trailing his response. He felt uneasy that he'd told the dean about his son's problem. His drunk face turned even redder.

Even as he was regretting putting himself in this situation, Sŏkhun pulled a notepad from his pocket and wrote down the son's name. The doctor looked at the dean with hopeful expectations.

Sŏkhun had to complete piles of applications that the assistant dean could not finish.

As the dean, Sŏkhun was always busy doing administrative business. A university is very much like a business, but it's the only kind of business that cannot measure the value of knowledge with numbers or production costs. A university is the training ground for students, where they apply their education to build a brighter future for the country.

When Sŏkhun had at last finished reviewing all the applications, he sat across from the admissions supervisor to discuss the matter of admittance. The supervisor, well-respected among faculty and staff at the university, was a burly man in his forties with the thick neck of a wrestler. He'd been nicknamed "anchor" for never allowing personal issues to set him adrift and for always being utterly fair when admitting students.

"Comrade Supervisor, if you're done with reviewing the applications, then let's begin the admissions process tomorrow," Sŏkhun suggested.

"I also want to hear suggestions from the other professors," the supervisor added.

"Very well. Let's try to complete this in the shortest amount of time. How many applicants were there this year?"

"There were 215 applicants, sir."

"Is there any space for more?" Sŏkhun asked with hesitancy.

Last night, his wife had insisted he plan to ask this question. She'd told him sternly, "You have to help the doctor. He rescued you from the brink of death. A true man is loyal to his comrades."

The supervisor looked at Sŏkhun's face closely, searching for something, before finally answering:

"Comrade Dean, this is the official document that was sent from the Commission Board."

"Hmm. I see."

Sŏkhun lit a cigarette and pulled the ashtray closer toward him. He glanced at the supervisor. The supervisor seemed uneasy.

Is he on to me? wondered Sŏkhun .

Despite the fact that he was a respectable dean at the university, Sŏkhun felt that the supervisor was peering into his conscience. His abdominal pain returned. Failure to assist the doctor, he thought, would prolong the time he'd have to deal with his stomach pain.

"Comrade Supervisor, tomorrow give me the names of the others who applied but couldn't make the cut."

"Yes, sir. Ah, do you mean student number 133?"

"133? Who's that?"

"His name…is Chŏng Ch'ŏruk."

The supervisor hesitated before saying the name and then, afterwards, cracked a sheepish smile.

Oh, this must be the doctor's son. So, the supervisor is thinking the same thing as I am. Good, thought Sŏkhun and let out a sigh of relief.

"Don't you think if he works hard for a year, he can be at the same level as others?" Sŏkhun asked, trying to make a case for the doctor's son.

"Yes, of course. It all depends on how hard he studies. Ch'ŏruk is a bright kid like his father. It's his mother who spoiled him and let him do whatever he wanted. It's really her fault that he couldn't pass the entrance exam."

"Fine. Bring Ch'ŏruk to my office and also…um…student 215, the one who just barely made the cut."

"Yes, sir. But, comrade Dean, there may be one more student who we have to consider."

"What?" Sŏkhun asked, furrowing his brow. "Who is it now?"

"It's the daughter of the Vice Chairman of the Province Party Central Committee. She, too, took the entrance exam, but her score came up a bit shy of the cut."

The supervisor rushed his words, his voice wobbly with nerves when he mentioned the Vice Chairman's daughter. People with authority made him feel apprehensive.

"When you were at the rehabilitation center," the supervisor explained, "he called three times." His expression was one of dismay and innocence, as if to say, "What control do I have over such things?"

"You couldn't refuse the Vice Chairman?" Sŏkhun asked, annoyed. "Fine, bring her in, too."

Sŏkhun was distressed. Having already betrayed his own conscience and strayed from the code of ethics to do the doctor a favor, he now found himself in no position to remind the supervisor that there should be no exceptions to the admissions evaluations. How out of character this felt! But it seemed there was no turning back now. The doctor, who had sacrificed himself for others, was now in dire need of someone's help. What was Sŏkhun's reason for wanting to see student 215? It was to replace him with the doctor's son. This, he vowed, would be the first and last time he betrayed his conscience, which gave him a bit of solace.

The next day, Sŏkhun met with admitted students. The third student to enter his office was student 215, who walked in wearing a faded school uniform. He sat down before Sŏkhun . He looked extremely nervous, perhaps because he was thinking of the questions that would be asked of him. The student's thick eyebrows, large eyes, broad nose, and thick lips all looked familiar to Sŏkhun.

He reminds me of someone. Maybe he's the younger brother of one of the university students, Sŏkhun guessed.

Barreling past the niggling question of why the student's face rung some bell in his memory, he proceeded with a barrage of questions.

The student's name was O Kyŏngnam, and he'd graduated from Kangan High School. The way Kyŏngnam was sitting with his hands folded on his lap suggested that he was a country bumpkin rather than a city boy.

Sŏkhun stared at the student regrettably, knowing that the only reason Kyŏngnam was in his office was to strip him from his rightful place in the university. This made it difficult for Sŏkhun to ask him the routine questions. Kyŏngnam had been plucked arbitrarily from the lot of students who had been admitted and was now in the position of losing his spot. Regret gripped Sŏkhun.

The more he wanted to help the doctor, the more he was straying from his conscience. It was a delicate balance between saving the life of someone who had saved his own life and upholding his ethics. He felt like he was walking on the blade of a knife. Nevertheless, the ship has already left the port. Much like the law of physics, the momentum of his actions has already begun. There was no turning back.

Sŏkhun began quietly, "I see here that you earned a low score on your entrance exam."

A sudden expression of anxiety and regret shrouded Kyŏngnam's face.

"Your math score is particularly low," Sŏkhun continued.

"I made two errors in calculating the differentials," Kyŏngnam replied softly.

"Do you understand the concept of differentials?"

"Yes...that is...I believe it is calculating the principal part of the change in a function y=f(x) with respect to changes in the independent variable. In physics, the derivative of the displacement of a moving body with respect to time is the velocity of the body, and the derivative of velocity with respect to time is acceleration. Therefore, mathematicians argue that a flying arrow appears to be still in space."

"You seem to know it well, but you solved these problems incorrectly."

"Please, allow me to solve those questions again," Kyŏngnam asserted.

"University is very different from high school; we do not give second chances. Not everyone gets accepted. You cannot turn back the clock here. We evaluate you based on merit only."

Kyŏngnam could not respond. He bit his lips and lowered his head. All of his self-confidence had left him.

Sŏkhun realized that he was being overly harsh. Although Kyŏngnam's score was the lowest among the students who made the cut, he had still made the cut. Why, then, was Sŏkhun being so curt with him? Was it to encourage Kyŏngnam to do a better job on the exam next year when he reapplied to the university? Was it tough love? Even if that were the case, Sŏkhun could have offered reassuring words rather than impetuous criticisms.

Sŏkhun proceeded to ask the student a few questions, about politics. Kyŏngnam responded with assurance, nailing each question on the head.

Sŏkhun intended to ask Kyŏngnam about philosophy next, but Kyŏngnam incorporated philosophy into his answers to the questions about politics. He began with the notion of dialectical materialism and went through each of the historic changes that had occurred. He didn't simply know the concepts but a deep understanding of the principles of each historic phase.

"Who taught you philosophy?" Sŏkhun asked. "I'm sure they didn't teach you this at school."

"From my father."

"I see. Then, why did you apply to the Engineering Department and not the Social Sciences?"

"My father taught me that in order to appreciate applied science, one needs to understand how one lives in this world, that everything is connected and that in order to evaluate the movement and changes in human history one will have to understand the principles of philosophy."

"At which science research facility does your father work?"

"He works for the Province Administration."

"What does he do?"

"He is a street cleaner."

Sŏkhun was shocked, so shocked that he could only stare at the student. Those eyes, the nose, the lips...

He must be the caretaker's son! Sŏkhun realized.

He felt as if he had been lashed by a whip. Slowly, he stood and walked to the window. The wind brushed along the zelkova trees. Someone in a raincoat, hunched, was walking across the university lawn. That person reminded him of the caretaker.

The caretaker! At this very minute he must be out on the street picking up other people's trash or tending to the flowers in the small park for others to enjoy. Every morning for so many years, the street cleaner had been cleaning up other people's trash— cigarette butts, orange peels, pieces of paper—while the city was still asleep. Whether in the pouring rain or a snowstorm, the care-taker cleaned the streets, valued his job. Even if it had snowed all night long, he swept the path so that no one had the bottom of their trousers wet with snow. No one would ever know how the streets and the park remained so clean.

Sŏkhun continued staring out the window, while Kyŏngnam remained in his seat with his hands folded in his lap.

"You may leave now."

Sŏkhun tried his best to make his voice sound soft, but his troubled expression was difficult to hide.

As soon as Kyŏngnam left, the supervisor entered. He sensed tension in the air and proceeded cautiously.

"Shall I call in Chŏng Ch'ŏruk next?"

"No. Tell him to go see someone else. I just want to be alone," Sŏkhun said.

The supervisor was perplexed.

Sŏkhun glared at the supervisor for a moment and turned back to the window. He felt like he was suffocating. His true colors, he realized, were seeping through the seams of his conscience. He was enraged at himself for even putting himself through this moral test.

It was pouring outside, and the wind blew away everything in its path. The small zelkova trees were swaying wildly because they were not tied to stakes and were taking a beating. Sŏkhun knew that stakes would support the trees, and that after a few years the trees would be able to support themselves. Had the gardeners forgotten about posting the stakes? Had they just tossed the seeds, hoping that the seeds would grow into mature trees all by themselves? Sŏkhun looked out his window every day, but this was the first time he'd noticed the trees.

All through the night, the restless river murmured, and small waves broke gently against the riverbank. In the morning, fog covered the landscape.

Sŏkhun took his morning stroll earlier than usual. He hadn't slept well, and his head was heavy. Along the path he walked, mature trees towered over swaths of delicate ground foliage. It was an altogether harmonious landscape, but it seemed to have no effect on Sŏkhun. He was preoccupied with dread at encountering the caretaker this morning. If he could, he wanted to avoid meeting the caretaker, which was why he'd set off on his stroll earlier than usual.

All at once, he remembered something from a fall morning last year.

There'd been a refreshing morning breeze that day too. Sŏkhun had been standing in front of large trees next to the main street, admiring the landscape painted in autumn colors. But something was not right. The main street, the small park, and the park's walking trails were all covered with autumn leaves. *What's happened?* Sŏkhun had wondered. *Why haven't the paths been swept?*

He'd looked around for the caretaker and eventually found him coughing on a bench in the small park.

"You must be cleaning a different section of the park," Sŏkhun said.

"What are you talking about?" asked the caretaker, wiping his mouth.

"I see that you haven't swept the main street."

"Ah, there was so much trash and cigarette butts everywhere that I haven't had a chance to sweep the leaves."

Sŏkhun nodded.

"Comrade Dean, why don't you enjoy this beautiful autumn morning by walking on the fallen leaves? It feels quite nice. People seem to like it on their way to work. It won't be long till all the leaves fall in winter, and then new buds will blossom in the spring. You will have to wait a whole year before you can step on the leaves again. So, enjoy yourself now. Besides, I don't think it will make much difference if I sweep them after everyone has gone to work." With that, the caretaker laughed wholeheartedly.

Sŏkhun was moved and said, "I didn't know you were such a romantic, and yet you're here sweeping the streets. You should have found work in the arts or something."

"Come on, comrade Dean. What I do *is* art. I clean the streets to maintain the aesthetics of the city. This work is just as important."

Underneath the caretaker's humble exterior, there was depth that made him noble.

In his youth, he had spilled blood to protect this nation and now, in his old age, he swept the streets to provide satisfaction and joy to the people. He considered the job his life's calling, which was why he never missed a day of work. He had the stern demeanor of a Supreme Court justice, and a clear conscience that was, free of any wrongdoing. It was with this noble man that Sŏkhun spent his mornings, smoking a cigarette and exchanging small talk.

That was last year. Today was different. Now Sŏkhun was ashamed of measuring himself against such a virtuous man. He was the dean of the university, a respected position in society, but what he'd done was deplorable.

The early fog began to lift. The birds chirped. It was a peaceful morning, but Sŏkhun was filled with anxiety. He hurried through the small park to avoid running into the caretaker, the man who had committed his life to sweeping. His eyes widened. There, behind a cluster of trees, the caretaker sat hunched over on a wet park bench, one hand on his side and the other supporting his head. His broom and dustpan were strewn on the ground.

Unable to escape without offering his usual morning greeting, Sŏkhun approached the caretaker and asked, "Did you sleep well last night?"

The caretaker slowly lifted his head. He wiped the cold sweat from his forehead and forced a smile. Alarmed, Sŏkhun tried to help the caretaker sit up.

"What's the matter? Are you hurt?"

"No, I'm fine now."

The caretaker tried to stand up, but his legs collapsed.

"I had a sudden stomach cramp. It might be the changing of the season getting to me," said the caretaker as he bent down to pick up his broom and dustpan.

Sŏkhun reached out to stop the caretaker from making any sudden moves.

"Why don't you rest today? You don't look well. You should go to the hospital."

"You're the fourth person today that has seen the messy streets. I have to clean this area."

The caretaker went about his usual business. Sŏkhun trotted after him.

"Give me the dustpan. *I* will empty the trashcans."

"Just continue your morning stroll. I'm almost done over here," the caretaker told him.

"It's too much to do by yourself."

Sŏkhun struggled to take the dustpan away from the caretaker, but, in the end, he managed to wrest it away from the man.

The fog lifted, and on the hillside there was a rosy tint that spread across the morning sky.

Sometime in the afternoon, the supervisor brought the applicants' files to Sŏkhun's office.

Sŏkhun began to review each application.

The supervisor said, "I put them in order, according to their scores. But..." He paused for a moment, leaned his large body over Sŏkhun's desk, and continued, "The last two students, you know, are the ones we discussed."

Sŏkhun scrolled down the names with his pen and stopped at student 214.

"Song Sunhŭi?" asked Sŏkhun .

"She's the daughter of the Vice Chairman of the Province Party Central Committee."

"She's the one who fell well below the cutoff, correct?" Sŏkhun asked.

"Well, it was actually only by one point. On my way to work this morning, I saw the Vice Chairman pull up in his private car, and he told me that he was going to come by your office to speak to you in person."

"What's the name of the student who was taken out for the Vice Chairman's daughter?" asked Sŏkhun with a shudder.

The supervisor nervously shuffled through his notes and found the name.

"It's Han Kŭmok, sir."

Sŏkhun stared at the supervisor sternly for a while, and then crossed out 'Song Sunhŭi' and replaced it with 'Han Kŭmok.' The supervisor shifted his gaze away, so as not to look directly at the dean. He stared at the names that had been crossed out. Sŏkhun went down to the next name.

"Chŏng Ch'ŏruk," Sŏkhun muttered. For some reason, he couldn't move his pen.

"He's my uncle's.... I mean, he's the son of the gastroenterologist of the city hospital," added the supervisor.

Sŏkhun placed his hands on his forehead and began to think. Everything flashed before him at once: the face of the doctor as he looked down at him when he was recovering from the hospital, the doctor's white gown, the smell of medicine. And then he saw, as well, the caretaker and his straw hat and his competent son.

Why did I do it? He asked himself then. *Why did I write down the name of the doctor's son at the bar? Was it out of gratitude for him saving my life? Was I that happy to be alive? Or was it to repay him for the surgery? Or because I had to be loyal to him? No. I should have thought about it more carefully before I pulled out that notepad. My position at the university and my gratefulness to the doctor are separate matters. I should have thought about all the other parents who had been assured of their child's acceptance to the university... like the caretaker.*

The fact that he's not my friend and has nothing to do with my line of work makes him no less important. Yes, I see him in the mornings, but there's a chance I will never see him again. I don't even know his name. But that doesn't make his life or his work any less significant than mine, the doctor's, or the Vice Chairman's. He doesn't need to apologize for being a caretaker. I would rather pull out my intestines and suffer in bed for the rest of my life than to see the caretaker's son dropped from the pool of admitted students.

Sŏkhun carefully crossed out the name 'Chŏng Ch'ŏruk' and replaced it with 'O Kyŏngnam.' He looked up at the supervisor, who wore a blank expression.

"Comrade, why do you think we give entrance exams?" asked Sŏkhun .

It seemed like a simple question to the supervisor, who responded quietly:

"Because not every student can come to university."

"That's right. Not everyone can be admitted to the university. Comrade Supervisor, that is why we give exams."

Sŏkhun got up from his seat and paced around his office. The wooden floors squeaked each time he took a step.

"The score on the exam is not just a number. It is a gauge that measures whether students will be able to carry out their service to the country with their knowledge. It judges their intellectual capacity. We cannot admit those who received a low score, no matter how much we want to. During their free ten-year education, they have decided not to study as hard as the other students. Why should the university honor students who studied less and earned low scores?"

There was nothing the supervisor could say to this.

The dean continued: "You and I must reject the idea of accepting students based on their parents' position in society. That's the capitalist way of thinking. The Vice Chairman and the doctor's social status should not make the decision for us. The Vice Chairman and the doctor must be judged according to their capabilities, and their children must be judged according to theirs. Entrance exams gauge the merit of the students who will decide the future of our nation."

The supervisor remained silent.

"We need to accept top students and shepherd them at our university so that they can continue to advance the technological skills for our country. Therefore, we should not be persuaded by anyone's social position and power, nor by anyone's personal loyalties or debts to another. Remember this: I may be the dean and you are maybe the supervisor at this university, but we are normal people like everyone else. When we allow hierarchies and personal favors to dictate our actions, we are committing a crime."

Silence filled the room. Sŏkhun signed his name at the bottom of the list of admitted students and handed the file back to the supervisor.

The supervisor stood there in front of the dean, not knowing what to do. Sŏkhun felt a bit sorry for him. Perhaps the pain that stung his own conscience now also stung the supervisor. Sŏkhun looked at the supervisor with gentle eyes and said, "Comrade supervisor, listen. Why is it, do you think, that people have given you the nickname 'anchor'?"

"Well, I'm not sure," the supervisor said. "They're probably referring to my fair treatment toward others," he finished, with a rueful smile.

"That's a good evaluation of yourself. Respect others. Don't let one iota of your good character deviate from the right path. You may need to measure your character often." And with that Sŏkhun let out a sudden bark of laughter.

"I understand," the supervisor said. A dark shadow still covered his face as he walked toward the door.

Late that evening, Sŏkhun put his bag over his shoulder and left his office.

As he exited the administration building, he noticed someone walking there with his head down. As he approached the man, he was surprised. How could he have failed to recognize the doctor, the very doctor who had saved his life through great devotion and expert care? The doctor looked back at him.

The two men stared at each other in silence. It seemed something was troubling the doctor's mind, but all he did was stare at Sŏkhun .

"Doctor Chŏng, have you waited for me this whole time?" Sŏkhun asked.

"I'm coming from meeting with my nephew—the supervisor."

Neither man said more for a bit. But then, finally, the doctor broke the silence.

"Dean Ri, I think I've put you under a lot of pressure."

He paused for a moment and then proceeded:

"Every day, I hold a stethoscope to my patients to see if their heart is beating correctly. But then I realized that it was my own heart that was not beating correctly. In medical school, we learn the code of ethics. We learn that malpractice or breaking the code of ethics is the death of our profession. Even though I knew this, I asked you to turn a blind eye to *your* code of ethics to admit my son to your university. Can you imagine me holding a sharp scalpel, deciding the fate of a patient's life?"

Sŏkhun did not know how to respond.

"It's getting chilly," the doctor said. "Please try to stay warm. If your body gets too cold, your intestines could flare up again. Ask your wife to pull out some warm blankets."

Sŏkhun looked at the doctor with compassion and gratitude.

CHAPTER 9

SPRING EVENING[1]

Chŏng Ch'angyun graduated from the Chosŏn Writers Union College in 1958 and began his writing career by joining the Usan Creative Unit, a group of professional writers located in Namp'o city. A skillful storyteller, he achieved critical recognition with stories about the Korean War such as the novella *Gunfire* (*P'osŏng*, 1966) and the short story "The Nomad of Tŏkhŭng" (*Tŏkhŭng nagŭne*, 1983) and production novels set in industrial settings. He was later accepted into the Central Writers Union in Pyongyang. Chŏng is renowned for his witty prose and surprise endings, as well as for having never written a story about the North Korean leaders – a rare characteristic for a writer of his standing.

Yet, the absence of cult of personality stories in Chŏng's bibliography does not mean that his writings are apolitical. To the contrary, he did not shy away from using his humor to pursue ideological ends. In the short story "Lonely Island" (*Oeroun sŏm*, 1985) for instance, Chŏng lampoons the greed of capitalist South Koreans. The story starts with the commanding officer of a naval base on a South Korean island leaving for an urgent mission. Shortly after his departure, news reaches the island that the officer has suddenly fallen ill in Seoul and died. The sailors all hurry to ransack the admiral's possessions and sell them while they wait for a new officer to be dispatched. When the new

---

1 Chŏng Ch'angyun
  1985
  Translated by Immanuel Kim.

officer arrives, the sailors go out to greet him only to discover their former officer, who had sent news of his death as a prank.

"Spring Evening" is another example of Chŏng's playful writing and love for surprise endings. A supervisor is exhausted from working and dozes off in the back seat. The driver takes this opportunity to meet his fiancé, who complains to him about his working long hours. The supervisor wakes up and finds the driver with his fiancé. Instead of reprimanding him, he concocts a plan to let the two young lovers spend a night together. The novel ends with the supervisor giving the driver his blessing to spend some time with his fiancé, with a double entendre – translated as "sleep well" – that can suggest both getting a good night's rest and sexual intimacy.

It was late in the evening when Supervisor Hwang left Sanggo district collective farm, feeling accomplished.

Today, his factory had succeeded in test-driving the latest farming machine. Technicians had come earlier to teach the factory workers how to operate the new machine. Once the test-driving was completed, it was time for the supervisor to go home.

On the moon-lit road, the convertible car raced as if it were out of control. It was a warm spring evening. The driver, who had a flat, slender face and stubby nose, usually had a solemn demeanor, but this evening he appeared to be in a joyful mood. He was humming a tune. The supervisor had never seen this kind of elation from the driver.

The driver was always awkward at social gatherings. When other comrades would talk and laugh about things and then glance over at the driver, he'd quickly lower his head and act like he was examining his jacket to see if all the buttons were intact.

That same driver now appeared to have lost all sense of inhibition and was cheerfully humming a tune as he drove the supervisor home. The driver's elation must be due to the success of the new farming machine, the supervisor surmised. And the long distance to home could explain why he was driving so very fast. The supervisor had always admired him for his driving skills, but tonight was exceptional. Despite the uneven gravel road, the driver raced full speed.

Spring's warm breeze brushed across the car and lulled the supervisor to sleep.

The supervisor was a large, husky, middle-aged man. According to the previous driver, who had been insolent and lazy, the supervisor was so large that: "If another man like the supervisor got in the car, the shocks would break."

Although the supervisor was tough in other ways, he could not fight his drowsiness.

In the past few days, he'd not had a good night's sleep, having spent a night in his office preparing paperwork for the department, and then another night on the road preparing to introduce a new pig-iron dissolving method. And last night, he couldn't sleep because of the latest farming machine. Long conference calls, endless meetings, and hosting other supervisors all made it difficult for Supervisor Hwang to sleep well at night. But on a night like this, when everything had worked out well and the bright stars calmed him, there was nothing preventing him from drifting off.

The driver's humming seemed to drift farther and farther away as the supervisor fell deeper and deeper into his sleep.

Over an hour must have passed when he finally woke up and noticed that the car was now strangely still, parked on the side of the road. He saw at once that the driver's seat was empty. Outside, the car, along the road, were a few cozy residential houses.

He assumed that the driver had gone to fetch some water for the car's water tank. He waited for a bit, but the driver didn't show up. Suspicious, he got out of the car, headed towards the houses, and asked the first person he encountered, "Did you happen to see the driver for that vehicle over there?"

"Well, let me see now. A short while ago, he parked the car and ran toward the brook as if he had an emergency."

Clearly, something unexpected had happened.

The supervisor walked around the village and eventually made his way toward the brook. There, he spotted the driver sitting on the bank next to another person, a young woman with thick braided hair. This was quite unexpected.

So that's why he's here.

The driver's behavior was despicable to the supervisor. He wanted to call him out and scold him for having neglected his duty. He was overcome with rage and was about to let out some very harsh words. What made him even more uncomfortable was what he overheard of the driver's anxious, pleading tone. It was the anxious tone of the driver who could not even keep himself honorable in front of the woman.

"Please, calm down. I told you that I had never had any time to come by here," the driver explained.

"Goodness, comrade. How many times have you come by since we got engaged? This will have been your second visit. Even then, it's only for a short while. Last time you got a day off from work and you wrote to me and asked me to wait for you, but you didn't even show up," the young woman argued.

"I told you that I was busy."

"Are you the only one who is busy around here? You think I have nothing to do?" barked the young woman, who showed no signs of calming down.

The supervisor recalled his driver's daily schedule—hundreds of kilometers driving to and fro, going over mountains and crossing over rivers on a daily basis. And the last time he'd gotten a day off from work, something unexpected had come up and he'd had to take the supervisor to a distant location.

"I'm technically still working," the driver reasoned with the woman. "I was only intending on making a quick stop. You see, the supervisor fell asleep. So, I parked the car for him to get some peaceful rest and made my way to you."

The driver was doing his best to allay the young woman's anger, but it was futile.

"Uh huh. And I was really intending on fixing the pig's pen, but I guess that will have to wait," retorted the young woman sarcastically.

There was silence.

The driver was lost for words. He sighed deeply and muttered, "I'll be going now." He stood up. The young woman also stood, blocking his way.

"You really don't get it, do you. Come in for a minute," the young woman implored.

The situation seemed to have changed. The woman was now on the defensive.

"I can't. If the supervisor wakes up and finds me missing, I'll be in trouble."

"He'll understand. He too must have been engaged at some point. Come in, even if it is for a moment. Just come in, please?"

The supervisor quickly turned around. He returned to the road where the car had been parked. He leaned against the car, looked up at the moon in the clear night, and contemplated the situation.

When he finally heard the footsteps of the driver scurrying toward the car, he bolted inside, closed his eyes, and pretended to be sleeping.

The driver tiptoed towards the car. When he saw the supervisor, he assumed he had been asleep all along. He let out a deep sigh of relief and started the engine.

At that moment, the supervisor pretended to wake up. He asked, "Did you stop for something?"

"Yes, I...uh... had to get some water," the driver lied, without being able to look directly at the supervisor.

"You know what? There's a problem," said the supervisor, looking at the driver with an expression of something really wrong.

"What...what seems to be the problem?"

"I'm so tired, I can't sleep in this car. This is Saemgol farm, right? I know the administrative chairman, here, and I think we will have to spend a night at his place," suggested the supervisor.

"Really? I think I know where he lives!"

The driver turned off the engine, jumped out of the car, and led the way. But it was clear that he had no idea where he was going. He entered several random houses and returned chuckling with embarrassment. The driver was afraid that as soon as he found the chairman's house the supervisor would urge him to spend the night there, as well. But just as he was thinking of excuses to avoid this predicament, the supervisor spoke first, "Don't worry, I can find it myself. We can't be late for work tomorrow, so make sure that you *sleep well.*"

"Huh? Oh right. Yes, it only takes about forty-five minutes from here. Don't worry about a thing and get plenty of rest."

The driver thought it was a bit odd for the supervisor to emphasize *sleep well*, but he ran toward the car with uncontrollable elation. After retrieving something from the trunk, he dashed into the village.

CHAPTER 10

THE LIFE EXPECTANCY CHART[1]

Kang Sŏngyu was born on June 22, 1946 in Chaedong, Ŭnsan district, South
P'yŏngan Province. After graduating with a degree from the Department of
Language and Literature at Namp'o Normal University in 1969, he worked as
a middle school teacher for 11 years in a mining town. He made his literary
debut in 1980 with a novella, *Youth (Ch'ŏngch'un)* that earned him an amateur
prize and the possibility to undergo further training at the Kim Hyong Jik
College of Education to become a professional writer. Kang became a prolific
novelist, essayist, and critic, and was eventually nominated to join the prestigious April 15 Literary Unit.

Kang's works usually draw from his experience as an educator to analyze
the lives and problems of North Korea's intellectual class as well as themes
of mentorship, transmission, and pedagogy. His novel *School Ethics (Kyojŏngŭi
ryulli*, 2000 – later adapted into a seven-part television series in 2001), for
instance, juxtaposes two professors with starkly different approaches to teaching and administrative work to raise questions about the nature of academic
labor and teacher-student relations. Other notable works of his, such as *Right
to Love (Sarangŭi kwŏlli*, 1992), an autofiction set in a university and exploring
the multifaceted nature of love, or *A Different Choice (Tallajin sŏnt'aek*, 2008), a
hidden hero story about a selfless doctor and medical school professor, likewise

1 Kang Sŏngyu
  2000
  Translated by Benoit Berthelier.

explore pedagogical themes, with a particular emphasis on the emotional and relational aspects of teaching and learning.

With its satirical depiction of middle-management and its industrial setting, "The Life Expectancy Chart" departs from Kang's usual depictions of selfless intellectuals. The story, however, draws from well established tropes in North Korean literature. One is, of course, the hidden hero stereotype exemplified by the protagonist Myŏng Pudŏk, a worker so fully devoted to solving his factory's shortages that he seems entirely oblivious to both blame and fame. The other is the critique of bureaucratism (*kwallyojuŭi*), symbolized by Myŏng's manager, Ro Anmun, whose continuous requests for data, reports and indicators hinder the factory's productivity. "Bureaucrats" have, since as early as the 1950s, been a common scapegoat for the country's shortcomings – from the inefficiencies of the centralized planning system to low labor productivity and inadequate public infrastructure – allowing writers to voice common discontents without directly criticizing the country's socialist system or its leaders.

That morning something happened in Pongch'ŏn Shoe Factory's technical department that was too peculiar and too serious to ignore.

As soon as the department's manager, Ro Anmun, arrived at the factory, he started looking for one of his employees, Myŏng Pudŏk, but he was nowhere to be seen. His face red with anger, Ro snatched up a notebook on Myŏng's desk and opened it.

That was how the incident started.

The manager had a good reason to snoop into Myŏng's personal notebook. During the last yearly performance evaluation meeting for all department managers, Ro Anmun had been criticized by the company director. According to the director, his performance had been mediocre, and he was not up to the task. The remarks had deeply hurt Ro, who had always prided himself on meeting deadlines early. After giving it a lot of thought, he came to the conclusion that he must not have pushed his staff to keep the proper pace. He would have to clearly show them what type of department manager he was.

He asked all of his staff to recompile and resubmit their individual output statistics for the previous year's monthly and weekly plans. Then, case by case, he studied the data.

Ro Anmun wanted his superiors to understand that he had all it takes to be a department manager.

He had a reputation as someone who could diligently synthesize data and produce well-written reports. Consequently, he had gained the trust of many in the factory.

After looking at his staff's performance data, he consistently tried to push them to work harder.

But an unexpected problem arose.

While most of the other employees had, in one way or another, complied with his instructions, Myŏng Pudŏk, a fairly new recruit in the department, had only half-heartedly acquiesced and still seemed to be slacking off. The day before the incident, he had even complained to people around him:

"Looks like our department manager is going to fail to meet the *inminban's*² goals for the paper saving campaign. He's always asking us to fill out forms about our production numbers and then he makes us rewrite them again and again..." Myŏng Pudŏk sneered.

Ro Anmun shouted, "Look here, comrade Myŏng! You think this is the time to be joking around? Do your work instead of blabbering. You have until tomorrow to submit your data. I want it on my desk in the morning. Absolute deadline, no buts. Understood?"

Ro Anmun had sharpened the blade of his voice and left Myŏng speechless. This might have been the reason why Myŏng had remained at his desk that night, scribbling on some paper long after all the other employees had gone home.

When he left the factory himself, Ro Anmun pretended not to notice Myŏng's presence.

The next morning, Ro stopped by a work site where he had to be. When he finally arrived in his office, he was ready to give Myŏng an earful if he had once again ignored his instructions.

But there was no trace of the data, nor of Myŏng himself.

How is this possible, thought Ro. *I even had to stop by that work site on the way here... Well, I don't have anything special to do now so let's handle this. Maybe he wrote down his data on that notebook that he left on his desk.*

Ro Anmun then opened Myŏng Pudŏk's notebook.

Inside it, all the pages were covered in numbers and figures that Ro did not understand. There were also a few blueprints sketched on pieces of paper as small as the palm of a hand. Myŏng Pudŏk had once bragged that his notebook

---

2 The *inminban*, literally popular groups, are local units grouping the residents of a neighborhood under the direction of a neighborhood chief (*inminbanjang*). The group performs various form of communal labor: pulling weeds, cleaning trash, ensuring governmental health directives are followed.

contained the solution to the factory's shortage in adhesive material, so he might also have kept the data that Ro needed there.

But as Ro kept on searching the pages, there was nothing like the numbers he had asked for.

With a bitter taste in his mouth, he was about to close the notebook when he glanced at some strange characters that caught his attention. He lowered his head and looked closer.

At the top of the page, the words "Life expectancy chart" were scribbled. Below them were a few cryptic sentences: "Production Period: January 2000. Standard Life Expectancy: 100 years. Basic variable: Daily time spent living. Ignore blood type and diet."

What abyss of nonsense had Myŏng fallen into with this gibberish?

Using italics, boldface and footnotes, Myŏng Pudŏk had listed the names and positions of several of the factory's employees, including his department colleagues, the director, the chief engineer, the manager of the materials department, etc. The notebook also mentioned their gender, actual age and the time they potentially had left to live.

Ro Anmun became livid. He was dumbstruck. His face slowly took on a frightful expression. The corners of his lips began trembling.

"Director Han Segŏl: Actual age 54 years, 78 more years to live. Materials department manager: U Kyŏngch'an: Actual age 47 years, 80 more years to live. Technical department manager Ro Anmun: Actual age 49 years, 1 year and 1 month left to live."

Ro Anmun's slightly drooping cheeks became dark like a burnt stone and started shaking.

Just thinking about the fact that Myŏng Pudŏk had written that he only had one year and one month left to live, his sight became blurry and his gut wrenched in unbearable pain.

His heart was boiling like gruel left on an excessively strong fire. He was pacing the room and trying to calm himself when the door opened. Tall like an electric pole and with high cheekbones, the director, Han Segŏl, entered the room, followed by several other department managers.

"Comrade Ro, today we are having a meeting with the other department managers in this room. I had to use my office to store the materials that suddenly arrived last night..."

With a look of satisfaction on his face, Han pulled up a chair and sat on it heavily.

"This is all thanks to the good work of the materials department manager. If he keeps working like that, I don't mind him using my office as a warehouse another hundred times. With comrade Chang Uni, it looks like the year 2000 will also be the beginning of a new era in the domain of production. Hahaha."

The materials department manager and the other department manager were clearly happy and all smiled and shared in the director's jovial mood.

However, Ro Anmun's face remained stiff and tough, like a piece of rubber that has become unusable after being overheated.

He smashed the "life expectancy chart" with his fist and stood up. He shrugged his shoulders and lowered his head slightly.

Han Segŏl asked him a question in cheerful tones:

"Come on now, manager Ro! Why the long face? It looks like you've just chewed a rotten bean. What happened to you?"

Having said this, Han slapped his knee with a hand like a pot lid.

"In all my life, never have I seen…" Ro Anmun muttered with a bitter taste in his mouth.

"What's the matter?" Han Segŏl asked.

While he was still smiling, the director now also looked slightly concerned.

"This belongs to Myŏng Pudŏk," said Ro Anmun as if he were chewing on something.

He pushed the notebook in front of the director.

The department managers, who had been skeptically staring at Ro, now turned their curious eyes to the notebook.

"A life expectancy chart?" the director murmured.

After looking over the page and mumbling for a bit, the director widened his eyes and let out a raucous laugh: "Hahaha!"

"So, is that right? I still have 78 years to live? That means I'll live past 130 years? That's a good one. Haha!"

One after the other, the department managers started chatting among themselves.

The laboratory manager said, "Hey, same thing for the materials department manager. My, my, this thing is full of centenarians! Except comrade Ro? This guy is really something. He gave his own manager only one year to live…"

In the heat of the moment, the manager of the laboratory had said this enthusiastically and without hesitating. He looked at Ro with embarrassment.

The room once again filled with joyful laughter. The director's slender body was undulating as he laughed. He spoke to Ro as if he had meant to comfort him:

"This little jokester was probably just pulling a prank on you. Why are you getting mad about something that he just scribbled for fun? As I see you, you're staunch and built like a mortar. You're definitely living longer than my skinny self. Come on, calm down and let's start the meeting."

Han Segŏl pushed aside the notebook as if nothing had happened.

Ro could not let it go and said, "It's not something that we can just laugh over and let pass. This is nothing less than the most fatal of all insults, damn it!"

The director turned serious and pulled the notebook back towards him.

"Really? Well, if it is so, we'll have to try and quell your outrage. To be honest, I also don't really understand what went through his mind when he did those life expectancy calculations. Let's see. Comrade manager of the laboratory! Please go to the materials department and bring comrade Myŏng Pudŏk. He doesn't even go home these days. He sleeps over there and claims that he'll solve our adhesive issue all by himself. Don't say anything, just tell him I want to see him."

The laboratory manager opened the door and, as soon as he had left, a wind of disarray blew into the room. It must have been the relaxed atmosphere that comes with winter's end.

Ro Anmun could not suppress his indignation, and his face was now almost purple with rage. He lowered his head and sighed.

The room's mood turned awkward with no one knowing whether they should laugh or cry. Han Segŏl tried to change the mood:

"This guy, Myŏng Pudŏk, he's truly something. When he's working, he gets completely into it, but outside of work you never know if he's being serious or if he's joking. A few days ago, his wife told me this story… One day, he was eating breakfast and he found some grains of sand in his rice. His wife felt sorry for not cleaning the rice properly and did not know what to say. But he just went and dropped the rice in a bucket of water without saying anything. The wife asked, 'What are you doing? Why are you putting hot rice in cold water, especially when the weather's freezing?' Her voice was trembling, half-sorry, half-worried, but his answer was priceless: 'If I keep on eating it, I'm going to break a tooth. So, I'm just going to clean it myself, okay?' He was laughing but his wife replied, 'If you want to lash out at me, go ahead.' He looked at her and said, 'Why would I get angry? If I get angry, you're going to get mad and I'm going to lose my appetite. I don't have the time to get angry. I have to eat quickly and get back to the factory.' Then he proceeded to stuff all the rice in his mouth. Hahaha. After that, his wife was careful to never leave any sand in the rice when cleaning it."

"He has a peculiar way of telling people things, but he's truly a brilliant guy. There aren't many like him," complimented one of the managers.

The room erupted in laughter.

At that very moment, the door opened and Myŏng Pudŏk entered with the laboratory manager. He was holding up his hands which were completely covered by a dark substance. He looked irritated.

"Did you call for me? If it's not urgent, I'll be back later... I was just about to synthesize heterogenous substances and write down my observations. I'll be right back," Myŏng Pudŏk said.

He had not even come in but was already ready to leave. His behavior had left everybody speechless. It was impossible to know what sort of things he had struggled with over the night, but his face was covered with all sorts of chemical substances. He looked like one of those clowns in makeup.

The director told him off, "It's always like that with you comrade, eh? You always do what you want. Looks like you're not thinking straight." And with that, he banged the desk with his fist.

Myŏng Pudŏk merely stretched his neck into the room as if he was wondering what was going on and stared at the director.

"Comrade director. Is it because you think I've done something wrong that you're banging on your desk like that?"

"Would anybody in his right mind have acted like you did? What sort of sick joke is this?" the director retorted, pointing to the notebook. "Calculating the life expectancy of other people... Come on! Answer me! What is that chart all about?"

Han Segŏl pushed the "life expectancy chart" in front of Myŏng Pudŏk and knocked his fingers on it.

After taking a couple steps closer, Myŏng Pudŏk lowered his eyes and, with a slight smile, tore off the page from the notebook and stuffed it in his pocket.

"Oh that... it's just something I calculated to pass the time... How did it get to you comrade managers? Weird."

Before Myŏng could finish rambling, Ro Anmun's voice cut through the air like a knife.

"Who do you think you're fooling? Hiding your dirty stinky mind behind jokes? You won't even explain what the chart means? You dirty little..."

Myŏng Pudŏk's eyebrows had hitherto just been gently moving up and down, but as soon as Ro dropped the swearword, they furrowed and raised their tails:

"Comrade department manager. No need to get angry. I just wrote down my opinion. I mean, maybe you really do only have one year left to live. But what I wrote down, I just wrote it down for fun, so forgive me."

Myŏng Pudŏk cracked a smile.

Ro Anmun's face had lost all of its colors. He started swearing at Myŏng again.

"What is it with you and all of these bottom of the barrel ideas? Why don't you ever do the work I tell you to do? Don't think you're getting away with this. You'd better let us know what you were really thinking. Why did you do those stupid calculations? Ah, really I ..."

"Come on now, Comrade Ro, it's not like you to speak so sternly," Han Segŏl said, firmly chastising Ro for being out of line.

Everybody was looking at Myŏng's somber and threatening face, knowing that something terrible was about to happen.

But unexpectedly, he merely rubbed his hands, looked at his watch and offered this odd answer:

"Ah, will you look at that! With all this nonsense we've already lost 20 minutes. Comrade director, I still haven't had breakfast. And they're waiting for me at the work site. I won't draw that kind of chart again so please let me go."

Han Segŏl looked at Myŏng Pudŏk with both pity and admiration. There was an imperceptible smile on his tightly closed lips.

"Are you saying that you don't have anything more to tell us?"

As soon as the director asked him this question, Myŏng Pudŏk quickly glanced at Ro Anmun and smiled:

"Well... all right... It looks like none of you will do your jobs until I've explained everything. In one day, I sweat and do the job that others take three or four days to do. Meanwhile, others spend their time playing around with data and forms and don't spend more than three hours per day doing actual work. It's unbelievable... They stop by one of the work sites, and only say a few words or complain... So, for fun, I tried to calculate the life expectancy of every employee based on how much time in the day they actually spend working. The more one works, the longer one lives. Haha..."

It was as if he was trying to contain his laughter while telling a joke. Blazing embers were burning in his eyes.

"All right, well, back to work everyone." He bowed to greet everyone, turned around and opened the door.

He stopped for a while as if hesitating, then turned around and added:

"It's true that slackers are despicable, but even worse are those that only pretend to work and don't think twice about stealing other people's precious time by coming up with useless tasks. So please get rid of such people."

Myŏng Pudŏk went out and closed the door.

Silence fell over the room, heavy like iron.

A strong winter wind was beating on the window, causing the blinds to whistle and rattle against the windowsill.

Ro Anmun closed his eyes and lowered his head. He looked like a trampled blade of grass.

Han Segŏl went on, "What I was planning on discussing in today's meeting is not very different from what Myŏng Pudŏk just said. For this year 2000, you will have to work hard. You will have to try and compute your output statistics yourself, to figure out what you have brought to the Party and to our people up until now. We should live to become indispensable."

Han Segŏl's energetic voice echoed warmly above the sound of the winter wind.

BIBLIOGRAPHY

An, Tongch'un. *P'yŏngyangŭi ponghwa* [The fire signal of Pyongyang]. Pyongyang: Munhak Yesul Ch'ulp'ansa, 1999.

Anonymous. "Widaehan suryŏngnimkkesŏ chesi hasin ungdaehan kangnyŏngŭl nop'i pattŭlgo hyŏngmyŏngjŏk munhak chakp'um ch'angjakesŏ saeroun angyangŭl irŭk'ija" [Let's uphold the magnificent principles of the Great Leader and enhance the production of revolutionary works] *Chosŏn Munhak*, 11 (1980): 7-12.

Bandi. *The Accusation: Forbidden Stories from Inside North Korea*. New York: Grove Press, 2017.

Berman, Antoine. *The Experience of the Foreign: Culture and Translation in Romantic Germany*. Translated by Stefan Heyvaert. New York: State University of New York Press 1992.

Berthelier, Benoit. "Quantifying Quality: A Computational Approach to Literary Value in North Korea." *Journal of Asian Studies* 81 no.2 (2022): 267-288

Boase-Beier, Jean. "Who needs theory?" In *Translation: Theory and Practice in Dialogue*, edited by A. Fawcett, K. Guadarrama García and R. Hyde Parker, 25-38. London: Continuum, 2010.

Brookes, Peter. *Realist Vision*. New Haven: Yale University Press, 2005.

"Chayŏnjuŭi" [Naturalism]. In *Munhak Taesajŏn* [Great Dictionary of Literature]. Pyongyang: Sahoe kwahak ch'ulp'ansa, 1999.

Corbin, Alain & Georges Vigarello. "Entretien avec Alain Corbin." *Perspective* 1 (2018) : 71-86. https://doi.org/10.4000/perspective.9187

Damrosch, David. *What is world literature?* Princeton: Princeton University Press, 2003.

Djagalov, Rossen. "The Zone of Freedom? Differential Censorship in the Post-Stalin-Era People's Republic of Letters." *The Slavonic and East European Review* 98 no. 4 (2020): 601-631.

Gorky, Maxim. "Soviet Literature." *Marxists Internet Archive* (2004). https://www .marxists.org/archive/gorky-maxim/1934/soviet-literature.htm (Accessed August 15, 2021)

Gorky, Maxim. "Comments on Socialist Realism." In *Documents of Modern Literary Realism*, edited by George Joseph Becker. 486-488. Princeton: Princeton University Press, 2015.

Kang, Chol-hwan and Pierre Rigoulot, *The Aquariums of Pyongyang*. New York: Perseus Press, 2001.

Kim, Jong Il. *Chuch'e munhangnon* [Theory of Juche literature]. Pyongyang: Chosŏn rodongdang ch'ulp'ansa, 1992.

Kim, Immanuel. "The Interview: Life of North Korean Author Paek Namnyong." *Journal of Korean Studies* 21, no. 1 (2016): 245–257.

Kim, Yŏngmin. *Han'guk kŭndae munhak pip'yŏngsa* [History of modern Korean literary criticism]. Seoul: Somyŏng ch'ulp'an, 2012.

Liubimov, Nikolai. "Translation – An Art." In Brian James Baer. "Translation and the Making of Modern Russian Literature." London: Bloomsbury Publishing, 2015.

Meschonnic, Henri. *Poétique et politique du traduire*. Paris: Equivalences, 1994.

Paek, Namnyong. *Kyesŭngja* [The Successor]. Pyongyang: Munhak yesul ch'ulp'ansa, 2002.

Papazian, Elizabeth A. "Literacy or Legibility: The Trace of Subjectivity in Soviet Socialist Realism." In *The Oxford Handbook of Propaganda Studies*, edited by Jonathan Auerbach, Russ Castronovo, 67-90. Oxford University Press, 2014.

Pasco, Allan H.. "Literature as Historical Archive." *New Literary History* 35, no. 3 (2004): 373-94.

Pihl, Marshall R.. "Engineers of the Human Soul: North Korean Literature Today." *Korean Studies* 1 (1977): 63-110.

Putnam, Hilary. *The Threefold Cord*. New York: Columbia University Press, 2002.

Ri, Hoyun. *Hyŏngsangŭi pŏt* [Creative writing helpbook]. Pyongyang: Munhak yesul ch'ulp'ansa, 2012.

Ri, Sinhyŏn. *Kanggye Spirit*. Pyongyang: Munhak yesul ch'ulp'ansa, 2001.

Rorty, Richard. *Philosophy and Social Hope*. London: Penguin Books Limited, 1999.

Rorty, Richard. *Philosophy and the Mirror of Nature*. Princeton: Princeton University Press, 1979.

Rushdie, Salman. "Truth, lies and literature." *The New Yorker,* May 13, 2018.

Ryang, Sonia. "The Denationalized Have No Class: The Banishment of Japan's Korean Minority—A Polemic." *The New Centennial Review* 12, no. 1 (2012): 159-187.

Sin, Hyŏnggi and Oh Sŏngho, *Pukhan Munhaksa* [North Korean Literary History]. Seoul: P'yŏngminsa, 2000.

Shaw, Meredith. "Inside North Korea's literary fiction factory." *The Conversation*, January 26, 2018. https://theconversation.com/inside-north-koreas-literary -fiction-factory-89901 (Accessed August 24, 2021.)

Venuti, Lawrence. *The Translator's Invisibility*. London & New York: Routledge, 1995.

Venuti, Lawrence. "The Translator's Invisibility." *Criticism,* 28, no. 2 (1986): 179-212.

Vials, Chris. *Realism for the Masses: Aesthetics, Popular Front Pluralism, and U.S. Culture, 1935–1947.* Jackson: University Press of Mississippi, 2010.

Witt, Susanna. "Between the Lines : Totalitarianism and Translation in the USSR." In *Contexts, Subtexts and Pretexts: Literary translation in Eastern Europe and Russia*, edited by Brian James Bear, 149-170. Amsterdam, John Benjamins, 2011.

Zhdanov, Andrei. "Soviet Literature. The Richest in Ideas. The Most Advanced Literature." In *Soviet Writers Congress 1934: The Debate on Socialist Realism and Modernism*, edited by H.G. Scott, 15-24. London: Lawrence and Wishart, 1977.

INDEX